Portraits  of the Past

Tales from Grace Chapel Inn®

Portraits of the Past

Rebecca Kelly

Guideposts

NEW YORK, NEW YORK

Portraits of the Past

ISBN-13: 978-0-8249-4762-0

Published by Guideposts
16 East 34th Street
New York, New York 10016
www.guideposts.com

Distributed by Ideals Publications
2636 Elm Hill Pike, Suite 120
Nashville, Tennessee 37214

Library of Congress Cataloging-in-Publication Data
Kelly, Rebecca, 1961–
  Portraits of the past / Rebecca Kelly.
      p. cm.— (Tales from Grace Chapel Inn)
  ISBN 978-0-8249-4762-0
 1. Bed and breakfast accommodations—Fiction. 2. City and town life— Fiction. 3. Sisters—Fiction. 4. Pennsylvania—Fiction. I. Title.

  PS3622.I45P67 2008
  813'.6—dc22

                                                          2008027528

Cover by Lookout Design Group
Interior design by Cindy LaBreacht
Typeset by Nancy Tardi

Printed and bound in the United States of America

10 9 8 7 6 5 4 3 2 1

Acknowledgments

Storytelling is an art that is handed down from one generation to another. I would like to thank my mother, Joan, and my grandmother, Thelma, for all of the wonderful family stories they have told me over the years and for inspiring me to tell my own.

—Rebecca Kelly

Chapter One

Seen from a distance, the little town of Acorn Hill, Pennsylvania, appeared to be the pleasant work of a country artist. The composition of blue skies, green hills and quaint houses could have been created with a series of simple, candid brushstrokes, applied to canvas with an affectionate hand. Indeed, the result might have pleased any artist seeking to convey a cheerfully uncomplicated portrait of life.

Yet there was more to the town than its picturesque appearance revealed at first glance. With further study, one could see the subtler details and unexpected depths: the civic pride of a close community, displayed most prominently by the dignified presence of Town Hall; the sense of permanence and quiet devotion that glowed like the lovely colors in the stained glass windows of Grace Chapel; and the honest, home-style hospitality, reflected in the neatly hand-lettered, daily menus in the front window of the Coffee Shop.

A visitor who happened upon Acorn Hill might well have found his gaze drawn to the place where all of these qualities blended together in the graceful lines of an old Victorian bed-and-breakfast on the outskirts of town. Grace Chapel Inn may not have dominated the landscape, but its gentle presence seemed to watch over it.

The three sisters who owned and operated the inn may have had something to do with that.

Although the long, sunny days of summer were almost over, advance reservations for Grace Chapel Inn's four guest rooms already promised to keep the Howard sisters busy well into the winter months.

"It's all yours," Louise Howard Smith said to her middle sister, who had come to relieve her at the reception desk. "Or would you prefer to balance the accounts payable ledger?"

Alice Howard thought of the long columns of numbers that never added up to the same total for her as they did for her sister. She shook her head, making her short, auburn hair bob. "Only if I deserve cruel and unusual punishment, and you want to spend three days again trying to find where I lost two cents."

"It was four days and two cents." The eldest of the three sisters, Louise, looked every inch the practical and meticulous woman she was. Her elegantly cropped silver hair reflected the no-nonsense side to her personality, the same way that the neatly pressed white blouse, dove-gray sweater and tweed skirt she wore showed her quiet sense of style. "No, you better stay right here. Pennies are not your friends."

Alice chuckled. "That I believe." She glanced at the desk calendar. "This is the week when all three of our long-term guests are checking in, isn't it?"

"Yes, it is. That end-of-summer vacation package that Jane posted on our Web site proved to be quite effective." Louise collected some paperwork that she had been sorting and opened the door to the office. "Call me if you get busy and need help."

Ever since she and her two sisters had converted their childhood home into a business, Alice had discovered that she liked many things about being an innkeeper. Of course, it was hard work at times. Having up to four guest rooms occupied simultaneously; serving a hot, delicious breakfast to the guests each morning; and managing the cleaning, shopping, bookkeeping and property maintenance took dedicated effort and organization from each of the sisters.

Still, being an innkeeper could be fun. Running a bed-and-breakfast allowed Alice to meet people from all over the country. Every new guest brought with him or her a little window to another part of the world. She loved hearing their guests' stories about hometowns and the other places where they had lived or visited.

If asked to choose her favorite part of being an innkeeper, Alice would have picked managing the reception desk. She was an active "people" person, and the front desk was the hub of activity at the inn. Checking in the new guests and being the first to meet them was a special treat, but she did not like saying good-bye to departing guests since many of them became friends during their stay, and it saddened her to see them go.

All in all, running the bed-and-breakfast with her sisters gave her as deep a sense of satisfaction as did her work with the patients at Potterston Hospital.

She tried to arrange her time on her days off so that she could tend to matters related to registration. That allowed Louise time to do the daily bookkeeping and their younger sister Jane a chance to work uninterrupted in the kitchen or the gardens.

Out of habit, Alice checked the daily schedule, which listed guest arrivals and departures along with any deliveries or special tasks that needed attention. There she saw that the Hagen family would be leaving that morning, and their newest guest, a Basil Kirchwey, was due to arrive at any moment.

"Basil Kirchwey, Basil Kirchwey," she murmured under her breath as she prepared his check-in folder.

If a guest mentioned his hometown or point of origin when he made a reservation, Alice or her sisters would note it on the schedule next to the guest's name. Mr. Kirchwey had a blank space next to his, so he must not have mentioned the place from which he was traveling.

"Unusual name, *Basil*." She bent to retrieve some forms from the lower shelf. "I wonder if he's from Europe, perhaps England."

Louise emerged from the office. "Did I leave the invoices from yesterday's mail out here?"

"I believe so. Let me check." As Alice looked for them, she caught a glimpse of herself in a nearby mirror and took note of the casual, practical outfit that she was wearing. "Louise, do you think I look like an 'Alice'?"

Her sister peered over the rims of her reading glasses at her. "You certainly do not look like a 'Brunhilde.' Why do you ask?"

"It doesn't matter—never mind." Footsteps descending the staircase drew her attention, and Alice looked up to see Valerie Hagen carrying a small suitcase and a number of shopping bags.

"Good morning, Valerie." She went around the desk. "Do you need some help with your luggage?"

"No, thank you, Alice. My husband and daughter are bringing down the rest." Valerie set her burdens to one side and took a moment to slip on a soft mauve sweater that matched her corduroy slacks and cotton blouse. "I can't believe how quickly the time has gone. It seems like we arrived here only yesterday."

When the Hagen family had checked in seven days before, the petite, well-groomed Valerie had looked pale and unhappy, and had seemed utterly frazzled.

Valerie's state had been entirely understandable. The Hagens had been stranded when their rental car broke down just outside of town. They had sought accommodations when the rental company informed them that because of standing car reservations, a replacement vehicle wouldn't be available for several days. No other rental car company had cars available, either. Their best offer had been a ride to the inn.

The delay had meant that the Hagens were not able to continue their journey or spend their vacation at a popular

East Coast vacation resort as they had planned. The news had been especially upsetting for Amanda, the Hagens' fifteen-year-old daughter, who had had her heart set on going to the beach.

"Do we *have* to stay here?" the teenager had complained as her parents checked in. "This is like in the middle of nowhere, Mom, and there's going to be nothing to do."

"It's not as if we have a choice," Valerie had snapped at her daughter. "Please remember this is also the first real vacation your father and I have had all year. I don't want to spend it watching you sulk."

Alice understood the Hagens' displeasure at being kept from their destination; it was not as if Acorn Hill could compete with luxurious accommodations and the many other amenities offered by an oceanfront resort. After she settled them in their rooms, she quickly apprised her sisters of their visitors' unhappy situation. With Louise and Jane's help, they decided to do what they could to entertain Valerie and her family until their replacement car arrived.

On their first day in town, the Hagens grudgingly went along with Alice to visit a nearby farm fair, where two of the girls from Alice's ANGELs church youth group were competing in a horse show. As Alice suspected, Amanda had not spent much time around horses, and the youngster instantly fell in love with the beautiful thoroughbreds. She also struck up a friendship with Brian Troy, a handsome high schooler who subsequently came to occupy her thoughts even more than the horses did.

The next day Louise walked into town with the Hagens, where both Amanda and her mother explored the various shops while Richard, a book collector, spent a happy hour browsing through Viola Reed's Nine Lives Bookstore.

Jane took her turn on the third day by inviting Richard to go fishing with her down at the creek, while Amanda went to the movies with Brian. Valerie took advantage of the time alone and spent the afternoon sunning herself in the garden.

By the time their new rental car was delivered, the Hagens were having so much fun "doing nothing" that they decided to spend the rest of their vacation right where they were.

No one would guess the woman standing in front of her now was the same one who had arrived in such a fret, Alice thought. Valerie had color in her cheeks, her eyes sparkled, and she had taken to wearing her pale blonde hair in a pony-tail. Everything about her radiated contentment.

"I wish you could stay a little longer. We're going to miss you." Alice liked to be sure that their guests were pleased with everything before they departed. Contented guests often resulted in repeat or new business for the inn, but more impor-tantly, their memories of Grace Chapel Inn would be happy ones. "Did you find everything here to your satisfaction?"

"Everything about your inn has been charming and so restful. My husband is a changed man."

"It's nice to be able to actually relax while you're on vacation, isn't it?" Alice smiled. "I'm so glad."

"It's easy when you can stay in a lovely home like this, and have such nice people looking after you. And the town . . . I didn't know places like Acorn Hill still existed. Seeing all those wonderful old houses and the little shops is like taking a trip back through time," Valerie sighed. "Now if I could just talk Richard into moving to the country permanently."

"Don't listen to a word she says, Miss Howard," Richard Hagen said as he brought their suitcases downstairs. As Valerie had indicated, the tall, distinguished-looking lawyer had undergone his own transformation, and, like her, hardly resembled his former self. "My wife may *claim* that she loves all this fresh air, but I'll wager she's been secretly pining for her hairdresser and her manicurist all week."

Valerie gave him a mock-severe look. "Now Richard, you know that I haven't complained once in this lovely place."

"That's true, you've been quite contented here." Her husband put down their cases and slid one arm around her waist.

Amanda Hagen joined her parents. A miniature of Valerie, she also had her father's perceptive dark eyes and direct manner. Her face was lighted with a sweet smile.

Alice hardly recognized the sullen, argumentative child who had arrived the week before.

"I want to stop by that book shop on our way out of town," Richard told his wife, and then turned to Alice. "Do you know when it opens, Miss Howard?"

"The Nine Lives Bookstore is open from ten until five." Alice took a moment to add up the charges for the Hagens' stay.

"Well, if you're going to buy books, then I should be able to stop and pick up a treat for myself," Valerie said. "I never got to browse around that bakery in town—what's the name of that one on Hill Street, Alice?"

Alice looked up. "That would be the Good Apple Bakery. I highly recommend Clarissa's chocolate-chip cookies." Through the window she spotted a good-looking boy walking up the drive. "Amanda, I think you have a gentleman caller."

The teenager smothered an excited squeal and rushed out to the front porch, where the flushed boy greeted her and shyly presented her with a single red rose. Alice and the Hagens exchanged smiles as the two youngsters sat down together on the porch swing.

"Darling, somehow I doubt that our daughter will have any objections to spending another vacation in Acorn Hill," Valerie said as she gave her husband a significant look.

Richard was keeping a fatherly eye on Amanda. "Yes, but now I might," he joked.

Louise came out of the office to say good-bye to the Hagens, and once their guests had departed, Alice checked the wall clock. "Mr. Kirchwey should have arrived a half hour ago. I hope he's not lost."

"He may simply be delayed." Louise filed the Hagens' paid invoice. "Shall we see what Jane is cooking up for lunch?"

Chapter ✦ Two

Jane Howard's long, dark ponytail swung back and forth, as she went from chopping salad greens on a board at the counter to checking on something sautéing in a shallow pan on the stove. Every now and then she would stop to read something from a folded magazine next to the chopping block. Louise and Alice entered together.

Alice breathed in the tantalizing aromas coming from the stove. "That smells like chicken, and something else." She went to inspect the pan.

"A little turkey-bacon. I'm making a California Cobb salad." Jane scooped up the diced romaine and chives and dumped them into a large serving bowl.

The strips browning in the pan looked just like regular bacon to Alice. "I've never had bacon made from turkey before."

"Actually, you have, several times. I switched to it last month because it's low-fat and much healthier for us." Jane flashed an unrepentant grin at her. "There's a pitcher of iced tea in the fridge, Louise. Alice, would you slice some of that rye bread I made yesterday?"

Accustomed to working together, the three sisters had everything for their meal prepared a few minutes later. Jane topped the salad with diced chicken, turkey-bacon pieces and crumbled Roquefort cheese, then laced it with her homemade vinaigrette dressing before bringing the big bowl to the table.

"I picked the last of the watercress and the tomatoes from the garden this morning, so it should be pretty tasty." Jane placed the folded magazine next to her plate and took off her apron before she sat down. "I need more tomatoes, though. I just didn't get what I wanted from the garden this year."

"Well, I'm not going to complain." Alice admired the beautiful salad for a moment before reaching to join hands with her sisters. "God, we thank You for this food, for rest and home and all things good. For wind and rain and sun above, and most of all, for those we love. Amen."

"Amen." Louise took a slice of the caraway-seed bread and reached for the butter dish as Jane used a pair of tongs to portion out the salad. "Let's not overdo it with the butter, ladies. We have to watch our cholesterol. We owe it to our hearts and arteries."

Louise abruptly put down the butter dish and regarded Alice, who was biting her lip. "Are you sure we can't send her back to San Francisco?"

"You've had *my* cooking, Louise." She pressed her napkin to her mouth, and then cleared her throat. "What do you think?"

Her older sister sighed. "I suppose we are stuck with her."

Over lunch they discussed their success with salvaging the Hagens' vacation, along with daily tasks that had to be completed. Alice mentioned that Basil Kirchwey had reservations for two weeks.

"That reminds me," Louise said. "What was that business about looking like your name?"

"Nothing important." Alice felt a little embarrassed about it now.

"We will nag you about it until you tell us," Jane warned her. "Just FYI."

"Okay. I was just thinking what a name says about a person." She wrinkled her nose. "*Alice* is kind of plain and ordinary."

"Excuse me," Jane said, pretending to be offended, "but I believe *I* have the name most associated with the word *plain*."

"*Alice* is a pretty, unpretentious name," Louise said, "and something more exotic or complicated would not suit you at all." She glanced sideways. "As for you—"

"I know, don't even think about changing it. Not a problem, I like mine." Jane paused to turn the page of the magazine she was reading. "It could be worse, you know, Alice. I went to school with a kid named Delilah Jones. Every time that poor girl picked up a pair of scissors, the boys would cover their heads with their hands and run away shrieking."

"I won't complain then." Alice looked at the folded magazine by her sister's plate. "What's so interesting in that? A new recipe?"

"Nope. This is a trade magazine I ordered on-line." She flipped over the pages and lifted it to show them the cover of *Innkeeper's Journal*, before folding it back to the article that had caught her interest. "They have all kinds of tips on how to successfully run small bed-and-breakfasts like ours: the best kinds of advertising, how to build client loyalty, and even contacts for wholesale suppliers. This article is about developing innovative, nontraditional marketing concepts. We could really put some of these ideas to work for us."

"Is it something that we truly need?" Alice asked.

Jane had worked in a busy San Francisco restaurant for several years, so she was accustomed to the more competitive nature of business in the big city. Alice, on the other hand, had spent almost all of her life in the little town of Acorn Hill, where most people thought peace and quiet ranked far above increasing profits.

Her younger sister frowned. "I don't know what you mean."

"You already maintain a Web site for the inn, and we've been doing so well on our own. We've had a great summer, and we've got advance reservations right up through Thanksgiving weekend."

Jane shrugged. "It never hurts to think about trying some new ideas. Look at how well our end-of-summer vacation deal worked out." She turned the page. "Oh, neat. Look at this. They did a survey of all the inns around Philadelphia and Pittsburgh. There are statistics and pie charts and everything." She held up the magazine again to show them.

All that Alice saw were some complicated-looking charts and dense rows of numbers with decimal points and fractions. "My, that's . . . fascinating."

"Pie charts are all well and good," Louise said wryly, "but I would be happy just to have a local business directory with a map for our guests."

Alice knew how she felt. "Me, too. It seems like all I do lately is hand out flyers, or tell people where something is, or where they can get it in town."

Jane pursed her lips. "You know, what Acorn Hill really needs is an information center."

"We *are* the town's information center, dear," her eldest sister said, then added, "not counting Aunt Ethel, of course."

Ethel Buckley, who lived in the carriage house behind Grace Chapel Inn, was their late father Daniel's sister and—despite an *occasional* tendency toward interfering—she was a loving presence in their lives. Because their feisty aunt had a penchant for collecting gossip, she always had the jump on the latest local news. Ethel's decision to serve as Director of Committees at Grace Chapel only improved her ability to keep abreast of what was happening around town.

"It says here that a group of innkeepers got together and obtained permission to put materials in visitor booths at all the rest stops along the interstate," Jane said, consulting the article. "Tourists and shoppers traveling through the area can pick up free maps, shopping guides, flyers and coupons, as well as brochures on the different inns and motels."

"The interstate isn't all that close," Alice reminded her.

"That also sounds more like something you'd find in metropolitan areas, where you get a lot of tourist traffic."

"A plan for us doesn't have to be a big-scale advertising project like the one in the magazine. We can adjust it to suit our needs. If we work with the other merchants in town, we could put together some sort of booth or display in town." Jane thought for a moment. "Ideally we'd want to do the same thing with ours. You know, use it to provide visitors with information about our businesses, along with simple maps of the area and listings of local events and attractions. Besides, it's not as if we have hundreds of merchants, so it wouldn't have to be huge or anything."

"It's an interesting idea, Jane, but we don't have room here for even a small booth or table." Louise nodded in the direction of their front reception area. "Having it here wouldn't be very effective anyway. Not every visitor to town comes to the inn."

"You're right, it would be better to have it centrally located. If we only had some kind of common area, like the rest stops these innkeepers in the article used." Jane drummed her fingers on the table before she brightened. "I know, do you think Lloyd would let us set up something like this at Town Hall?"

Lloyd Tynan was a lifelong resident and the current mayor of Acorn Hill. The sisters liked Lloyd, who was a helpful, cheerful man. On occasion, however, he could be quite stubborn and just as vexing as their aunt when she was being contrary.

"I am not sure Lloyd is a proponent of change, and there would probably be some opposition from the local residents," Louise said. "Not everyone is happy about the increase of visitors to our town, you know. This would be like waving a red flag under a few noses."

Jane grimaced. "I don't want to do that." She closed the magazine and rested her chin on her hand. "It was a fun idea, anyway."

Jane looked so glum that Alice reached over and patted her hand. Alice seldom gave as much thought to financial matters as Jane and Louise did. Like her father, Alice tended to rely on the Lord to see them through without giving much thought to practical matters.

But Jane had a point. Their guests regularly asked for information about the area, and while the sisters kept some flyers at the desk, they rarely had exactly what the guests were looking for. That kind of information, for example, would have come in handy when Alice had checked out the Hagens. Instead of having to ask about store hours, they could have picked up the information from something like a visitors booth themselves.

Alice told her sisters what Valerie had said about Acorn Hill being a trip back in time, and added, "I think a lot of people who come here would be interested in learning more about Acorn Hill and our history. If we were to include some things like that, or even make our town's history the theme of the display, it wouldn't seem quite so commercial."

"We certainly have plenty of history to work with," Louise said. "But how would you present it?"

"We could ask the local merchants and residents to donate things associated with Acorn Hill's history." Alice glanced at the ceiling. "We have all those antiques stored up in the attic that we aren't using. Our contribution could be something like Mother's old writing desk or her collection of children's books."

Jane grinned. "Sounds like we've come up with a nontraditional, innovative marketing concept of our own."

"Yoo-hoo, girls!" Ethel Buckley called out from the front of the inn. A few moments later she appeared in the kitchen doorway. "Oh, here you are."

The Howard sisters' aunt was a mildly plump woman with short, dyed red hair and a pleasant face. Today she was wearing one of her "summer outfits," a cotton jersey knit dress covered with a bold sunflower print that matched the oversized, yellow-and-brown silk flowers circling the crown of her floppy straw hat.

"Hello, Auntie. Love the hat." Jane rose to give Ethel a kiss on the cheek. "Do you want some lunch? We've got plenty left over."

"No, that's all right, dear, though I wouldn't mind a glass of something cold if you have it. I just got home from a committee meeting at church and I'm parched." Ethel glanced back over her shoulder. "I came over because some man showed up on my doorstep asking for directions to the inn."

Louise's eyebrows rose. "He couldn't see it from your house?"

"Maybe he forgot to bring his white cane and guide dog," Jane joked as she poured their aunt a glass of iced tea.

"No, he's not blind. He's"—Ethel glanced over her shoulder again, and lowered her voice—"I think he's a little odd. When I came up the drive from church, I found him standing at the end of my porch with his back to me. I had to repeat myself twice before he heard me, and then he nearly knocked over one of my potted plants."

"I bet he was just dazzled by your outfit," Jane teased.

A strange thumping, clanging sound came from the front of the inn, startling all four women.

Louise frowned. "What was that?"

"That would be him. I brought him over and asked him to wait out front." Ethel leaned forward and lowered her voice to a discreet murmur. "Girls, I don't want to tell you how to run your inn, but you might send this gentleman over to that nice motel in Potterston."

"You mean that motel by the hospital?" Jane sounded scandalized. "I've heard that place has hideous orange bedspreads, industrial carpeting, and all the furniture bolted to the walls or the floor."

"There are very good reasons why they do that, dear." As they all heard another thump, her aunt gave her a strained smile.

"Here, Aunt Ethel, sit down. No, that's okay, Louise," Alice said as her older sister began to rise from her place. "You and Jane tell Aunt Ethel about the idea for the Visitors Center. I'll take care of this." She was fairly sure the man was their missing Mr. Kirchwey.

There was no sign of anyone, however, when Alice went out to the reception desk. She frowned as she turned around, looking for him.

Finally she called out. "Hello? Sir?"

"Here. I'm here." Something bumped again. "Ouch!"

A man popped up from behind the desk. Startled by his unexpected appearance, Alice drew back a step.

The man was tall and thin, and wore a black and green checked jacket over a matching green shirt and black trousers. Under his chin was an electric blue bow tie, which contrasted sharply with the green and black. Alice had no idea what his face looked like, as most of it was covered by a black bowler hat that had somehow been pushed down over his eyes.

"Blast it!" The man pushed his hat back, revealing a long thin nose, large, slightly protruding blue eyes, and thick black eyebrows. He reached up and ran his fingers over the crown and brim of the bowler as if checking it for dents.

Alice wondered if she should do the same for his head. "Are you all right, sir?"

"Right as rain." He had a distinctly reedy voice that did not hold even the faintest trace of a British accent. As he spoke his prominent Adam's apple bobbed up and down as if it were attached to a hooked fish somewhere inside him. "Thanks."

Alice waited for him to say more, but he only tucked his bowler under his arm and bent down again. "Did you drop something back there?" she guessed.

"No. I mean, yes. I was just getting this." He straightened and showed her the counter bell in his hand before he placed it on the blotter. "I was leaning over to have a closer look at that picture you have on the wall there"—he indicated an old framed photograph of Acorn Hill behind the counter—"and I accidentally knocked the bell off the desk."

"I see." She produced a tentative smile. "Thank you for picking it up."

"Of course. My fault that it landed there. My elbow's fault, anyway." He gave her a lop-sided smile before he inspected the photo on the wall again. "Great picture. Nineteenth-century, isn't it?" He took out a pen and spiral-bound notebook from the pocket of his black and green checked jacket.

Alice began to speak again, but paused when he swiveled to place the notebook on the desk and quickly wrote something down. Politely she waited until he was finished writing. "The photograph was taken in the twenties, I believe."

"Was it?" He turned to look at the photograph before he wrote something else, then looked up. "Was there something else?"

She didn't know quite how to ask him to move out from behind the desk without sounding rude. "My aunt said that you were looking for our inn."

"Yes, I was." Finally it seemed to dawn on him that he was standing on the wrong side of the desk. "I'm sorry, I'm not paying attention, am I?" He pocketed the pen and notebook as he quickly hurried around to the front.

She suppressed a chuckle as she took her place behind the desk. "So, how may I help you?"

"I have a reservation." He removed his bowler, then nervously turned it between his hands the way he would the steering wheel of a car. "I'll be staying here for a few weeks." His dark eyebrows drew together. "I did remember to make a reservation, didn't I?"

Alice took out the schedule and asked, "May I have your name, sir?"

"Um, Basil Kirchwey." He spelled his name for her.

"It's nice to meet you, Mr. Kirchwey. I'm Alice Howard." She reached across the desk. "Welcome to Grace Chapel Inn."

"Thank you." Basil engulfed her proffered fingers in his much larger, bonier hand.

The blue bow tie drew her gaze like a neon sign. She was almost tempted to ask him if it was a lucky bow tie, but she decided it would be discourteous to call attention to it.

Basil released her hand and glanced past her shoulder, then took out the notebook and wrote something else. "I've really been looking forward to this trip," he murmured, in an absent way.

She could not see exactly what he was writing. "Are you here to visit family, Mr. Kirchwey?"

"No, I'm just vacationing." He pocketed the notebook.

Alice got the distinct impression that her question had made Basil somewhat anxious. "Well, I do hope you enjoy your stay with us."

He sucked in his upper lip and then released it. "Thank you. I'm sure I will."

Alice decided to put him in the Garden Room, which they had decorated in cool, soothing green tones, and which had the most "peaceful" atmosphere of the four guest rooms. "Please let me or one of my sisters know if there is anything you need."

"Right." He placed his bowler back on his head and glanced at his watch. "It's been a pleasure meeting you, Miss Howard." He picked up a small suitcase, turned and started for the door.

"Mr. Kirchwey?"

He stopped and looked back at her.

Alice held out his key. "Wouldn't you like to go up and see your room first?"

Chapter ⚬ Three

Jane had just poured coffee for Louise and refilled Ethel's tea glass when Alice returned from checking in their new guest.

"So what's the verdict?" Jane asked, noting her middle sister's distinctly puzzled expression. "Do we ship him over to the Potterston Motel, or do we risk life, limb and our breakables?"

"I don't know. I don't think he's clumsy, exactly, more like he's very . . . nervous, and on edge. Or a bit stressed out. He seems very nice, though." Alice sat down and gratefully accepted the fragrant cup of tea that Jane offered her. "The odd thing is, I'm almost certain that he didn't hear half the things I said to him."

"He would not be the first businessman in need of some rest and relaxation," Louise said. "Remember how Mr. Hagen was the day he and his family came here? I have seen concert violins that were not strung as tightly as that man."

Jane nodded. "I remember how he kept changing his order that first morning, as if it were a tie that he didn't like. Mr. Hagen will never know how close he came to making his *own* breakfast that day."

"Did you find out what he does for a living?" Ethel wanted to know. "Or where he's from or why he's here?"

Alice shook her head. "I asked while I was showing him up to his room, but all he said was that he was self-employed and on vacation."

"*Hmm.* Very strange." Their aunt tapped her fingers against the tabletop. "I couldn't get a word out of him either."

Jane gave her a shocked look. "You couldn't? Not even by using the famous Ethel Buckley, ultra-hypnotic, tell-me-everything-about-yourself stare?"

Their aunt turned to Alice. "Do you think we could send her back to San Francisco?"

"I have already suggested that," Louise advised her gravely. "Alice says no."

"There's nothing more annoying than a man who won't talk about himself." Ethel eyed Jane. "Besides Miss Smart Mouth here, I mean. This Kirchwey fellow strikes me as the secretive sort, though, the type who plays his cards close to his chest. You know, it could be deliberate . . . oh, what do they call that?" She concentrated. "Misdirection."

"But does a man have to tell you his life story the moment you meet him?" Alice asked.

"If he has nothing to hide, he might," her aunt countered. "Why shouldn't he talk a little about what he does and where he's from? What's the big secret?"

"I don't know." She rested her chin against her hand. "It does make a man seem much more, I don't know . . . intriguing."

Her aunt's fingers resumed their tapping. "It makes me think he's hiding a checkered past."

"Do people still have those?" Jane grinned, delighted. "Do I qualify?"

"Yes, they do. No, you don't," Louise said. "I think you are all letting your imaginations run away with you. Mr. Kirchwey may simply be reserved around strangers."

"Or he could be here to spy." Jane's dark eyes sparkled as she went to get her magazine from the counter.

Alice nearly choked on her tea. "*Spy?*"

"Of course, that's the logical conclusion," Louise said, folding her arms, "since Grace Chapel Inn is a veritable magnet for espionage." She faced her younger sister. "Have you been reading those John le Carré novels again?"

"I didn't mean *that* kind of spying." Jane sat down with her copy of the *Innkeeper's Journal* and flipped to the front. "I meant that he could be here to do some undercover investigating."

Her older sister's fine silver eyebrows rose. "Of what? Acorn Hill's notorious criminal element?"

"No, silly. He could be here to spy on *us*." She flipped through the pages until she found the column. "Here it is. The Innside Reporter goes to bed-and-breakfasts all over Pennsylvania to evaluate, review and rate them. There's a new column every other month." She passed around the magazine so they could see the latest review.

"Is this reporter's name Basil Kirchwey?" Louise asked.

"The Innside Reporter doesn't use his real name. It's all done anonymously." Jane tapped her fingertip to the top of the article. "See these little coffee cups here? They're like hotel and restaurant star ratings, from one to five, with five being for the highest quality."

Ethel squinted at the page. "I only see half a coffee cup there."

"Unfortunately that's all they deserved. Here, let me have it." Jane took the magazine from her aunt and read from the opening paragraph of the article. "'Rarely have I received such poor personal attention as that offered by the indifferent staff of Red Badger Creek Inn. The inn's continental breakfast was self-serve and limited to two main courses, prepackaged cereal or overripe fruit. The staff was conspicuously absent; when I did find someone with whom to lodge various complaints, he was either rude or full of pitiful excuses. I made repeated requests for clean towels, which were never supplied; I had to use the same ones for three days.'"

"Oh my." Alice's eyes rounded. "That *is* bad."

"Wait, it gets worse." She skipped down to the last paragraph. "'The mattress was lumpy and the linens threadbare. The room's thermostat had never been hooked up, but when I tried to open the only window in my room, I found it had been painted shut. But the most annoying aspect of my stay was listening to the owner's dog, which was chained in the backyard and howled incessantly every night. I was relieved to return home so I could get some sleep.'"

"After going through that ordeal, I doubt that I would have given them the half-cup rating," Louise said.

"It's almost like a guide of how *not* to run an inn." Alice looked over at the family cat, who was sprawled on a nearby window and basking in the sun. "Thank heavens for Wendell. At least he doesn't bark."

Hearing his name, the gray and black tabby lifted his head, yawned, and then remembered his priorities and settled back into his nap.

"But why doesn't this reporter fellow write under his real name?" Ethel wanted to know. "Seems a bit dishonest not to."

"He does it so he has a better chance of getting the same treatment as any other guest," Jane said. "Think about it. If the owners of a bed-and-breakfast knew that the Innside Reporter was checking in, they'd probably fall all over themselves to give him the best service in order to get a good rating in the magazine. By keeping his real name secret, the reporter finds out what the service and accommodations are really like."

Alice's expression grew worried. "Do you really think Mr. Kirchwey could be this Innside Reporter?"

"I think we should stop speculating about a man who arrived here fifteen minutes ago. Besides, what are the chances that the Innside Reporter would pick our . . ." Louise set down her coffee cup and frowned a little as she picked up the guest card Alice had brought in with her. "Is this the correct spelling?"

Alice nodded. "He even spelled it out for me."

Her older sister stared at the card. "I believe I have read this name somewhere before."

Jane leaned forward. "Where did you see it, a travel magazine, maybe?"

"I really can't say, except that it looks very familiar." She shrugged. "It will come to me. I rarely forget an unusual name."

"If you've seen his name in print, then I doubt he's the *Innside Reporter*." Jane turned to Ethel. "Now, Auntie, about our community information and historical center, will you talk to the mayor and see what he thinks of the idea?"

"I'd be happy to, dear, although you might want to organize a plan for what you intend to do. Lloyd likes to see things spelled out in black and white, if you know what I mean. Now I'd better head home and start working on my committee reports before the pastor hunts me down." Ethel put on her sunflower-topped hat and patted the crown. "Thank you for the tea, girls. See you later."

"What sort of plan would the mayor need to see?" Alice asked after their aunt had departed.

"Jane, with your talents I think that you could put some things together to show the mayor," Louise said. "You did so well with the interior decorating when we were renovating the inn."

"Maybe if we go with advertising integrated with the antiques. . . ." Their younger sister got a faraway look in her eyes. "Sure, I could see doing something like that."

"I think you'd do a wonderful job," Alice added.

"All right, looks like I'm elected." Jane rose and started clearing the dishes from the table. "What do you think about getting June Carter, Craig Tracy and Sylvia Songer to join in and help us? They're among the friendliest merchants in town. I think they'll be the most proactive, too."

"The three of them are also very creative with their personal business displays." Louise nodded. "Excellent choices."

"We can ask them after church services tomorrow," Alice suggested. "Aunt Ethel and the mayor will be there too."

Jane grinned. "Sounds like a plan to me."

∽

Louise looked forward to Sunday services all week. Her father had served as Grace Chapel's head pastor for more than forty years, and she had many happy memories of listening to his weekly sermons when she was a girl. Attending church services always restored her spiritually too, giving her the chance to reflect on the blessings and challenges of the past week and to find the willingness and strength to accept the challenges ahead.

Her father had believed in the importance of joining with others in prayer and praise to the Lord, she remembered. *When God's people gather together for worship, they unite as a family. They help one another by standing together in the house of God as His children. It makes us powerful, Louise, in ways that nothing else can.*

Louise had always considered herself a strong woman and she had tried to live according to the principles and beliefs that her parents had instilled in her. Yet after she had lost her husband Eliot to cancer, she had truly faced a struggle. She had loved him so deeply that her pain over his loss had been overwhelming, and she had wanted nothing more than to be left alone so that she could grieve. It had been a terrible period.

Over time the pain lessened, but it was replaced by a heavy sense of emptiness and sadness. Indeed, she had never felt as lonely in her life as she had during those three years after Eliot's death. Since returning to her childhood home in Acorn Hill, however, she had found purpose and meaning in her life again. She would never again have the life she shared with Eliot, but she was healing, and building a new one.

She turned her head to look at her youngest sister. She wasn't the only one who had come home wounded.

"'Consider it pure joy, my brothers, whenever you face trials of many kinds, because you know that the testing of your faith develops perseverance,'" Rev. Kenneth Thompson said as he read from James 1:2–4. "'Perseverance must finish its work so that you may be mature and complete, not lacking anything.'"

We will need plenty of perseverance to make this community Visitors Center project a success, Louise thought as she bowed her head for the closing prayer. *I only hope Jane does not become easily discouraged.*

She often worried about their youngest sister, who for most of her adult life had lived far away from Acorn Hill. Jane had always been something of a rebel to begin with and had left Acorn Hill as soon as she could to see something of the world that she had so longed to explore. While she was away, she had met and married Justin Hinton, who, like her, worked as a chef. The marriage had ended in an unhappy divorce. After Daniel Howard's death, Jane had finally returned home, a changed woman. Louise had been startled by how much older and quieter Jane had seemed.

She had also recognized the shadow of pain and loneliness in her youngest sister's eyes. It was almost a reflection of the miserable emptiness she had felt after losing Eliot.

Gradually Jane had adapted to living with her sisters again in her childhood home and, like Louise, had begun the healing process. Although she had come a long way since they had opened the inn, at times Louise knew Jane still grew impatient with the slower, more cautious pace of life in a small town.

Yet telling Jane that things had to be done differently here only made her feel more like an outsider, and she could be very sensitive to criticism. At first Louise had not recognized this, which had resulted in a number of spats with Jane during their first months of living back home together, but now she knew better. She knew where to assign the blame for that too. Prior to their divorce, Jane's ex-husband, Justin, had done everything he could to bolster his own flagging self-confidence by attacking Jane's.

Sometimes I don't know if I am acting like her sister or her mother, Louise thought. Absently, she followed Alice out of the church and was so preoccupied with her thoughts that she nearly walked right past the pastor.

"You're either having very deep reflections about my sermon, Louise," Rev. Thompson said, startling her, "or you're thinking, as I am, that you left the coffeemaker on at home."

The man who had taken Daniel Howard's place as head pastor of Grace Chapel was tall, slim and dark-haired. His austere features made something of an intimidating first impression, until one noticed his quiet, kind eyes or heard the gentleness in his deep voice.

"I'm sorry, Pastor." She held out her hand to shake his. "You gave a lovely sermon today, and I am almost positive I turned off the coffeemaker."

"I'm glad to hear that." He smiled, and the effect seemed to chase away the sterner lines on his face. "How are things at the inn?"

"Busy, but running smoothly, thank you." She saw Jane and Alice gathering with some of the merchants on the church lawn.

His gaze went past her right shoulder. "Hello, Jane. Am I monopolizing your sister?"

"Not at all, Pastor." She threaded her arm through Louise's. "But if you two are through speaking, I would like to snatch her away from you."

On the way to join Alice and the merchants, Louise noticed a few heads turning. "Has anyone said anything negative about our idea so far?"

"Yes, everyone hates it. They think I'm crazy for proposing it. I believe I'm to be run out of town before sunset," Jane said, very matter-of-factly. "Will you miss me when I'm gone? Will you write?"

"Yes, after we have had the party and finished all the champagne." She sighed. "The way my little sister teases me —it's shocking. I never thought that I was so transparent."

"Glass is murkier, Louise. But you're tied with Alice for first place as the world's most lovable big sister." She gave her arm a squeeze. "Remember, I'm tougher than I look."

"And here I had my heart set on that champagne."

Fred, Sylvia, Craig and June were already discussing the project with Alice when Louise and Jane joined them.

"It would be so much more personal than taking out an ad in the paper," Sylvia was saying. Acorn Hill's resident seamstress never seemed to be still; even when she was, her dark eyes darted back and forth, and her expressive hands made quick little gestures. "I have a wonderful vintage dress that I've restored which would serve as a historic display of what women in this area made and wore in the early 1900s." Sylvia, who made her own lovely clothes, was interested in all aspects of dressmaking. "I could set it up on an antique tailor's form and post a card with facts about sewing methods of the past."

"I have some framed photos from the ladies' garden auxiliary shows they used to hold near here at the turn of the century," Craig Tracy said. The owner of Wild Things florist shop, Craig always attended, and sometimes even competed in, regional flower shows. "They're very Victorian. I can make up some live arrangements to complement the photo images, maybe put it all together on a rack of some kind."

"Already plotting to take over Town Hall, I see," Lloyd Tynan said as he joined them. The short, stocky mayor wore a lightweight, pale green suit with a matching striped tie. "Will I still have an office when you're through?"

"We'll only need a little space out in the lobby," Alice hastily assured him. "Everything else we need can be bought or donated by participating merchants, Mayor."

"I don't think it will cost much to put this together." Fred Humbert took out a notepad and pencil. Highly respected for his ability with tools, Fred was usually the first person people consulted on any type of building project. "If you'll tell me what you need, I'll provide the building materials at cost."

"We can assure you that it will be all in good taste, of course," Louise added.

"No need to be concerned about that." June Carter, the owner of the Coffee Shop, had a twinkle in her eye. The friendly, robust woman who prided herself on getting along with everyone gave Lloyd a pat on the shoulder. "You trust us, don't you, Mayor?"

"From what Ethel told me, I think it will be fine. As long as there is nothing outlandish involved," he added, giving Jane a direct look.

"Scratch the performing monkeys and the marching band," Jane told Fred in a stage whisper, making them all laugh.

"Where is Aunt Ethel?" Louise, who had not seen her since they left the church, glanced around.

"She was right over there, talking to one of her committee members." Lloyd turned in that direction, and then frowned. "Who is that fellow?"

Louise followed the direction of his gaze and saw Ethel speaking to a tall, white-haired man carrying a cane. "That would be Mr. Lester Langston, one of our guests from the inn. He checked in last night." Many of their guests attended services at Grace Chapel.

"I'll start setting up the town model first thing tomorrow, before I open the store." Fred scratched the side of his head with the eraser end of his pencil. "Mayor, would you mind meeting me at Town Hall at eight? Mayor?"

Lloyd nodded absently. "Eight, right, I'll be there. Excuse me." He went over to join Ethel.

Louise watched as her aunt took Lloyd's arm and led him over to speak with a couple from the Seniors Social Circle. For a moment she thought the mayor looked upset, and wondered if he truly believed, as he had joked, that they were trying to take over Town Hall. Lloyd was a genial man, but he took his job as mayor very seriously. Jane would really have to watch her step.

I'm being too overprotective, Louise thought as she regarded her youngest sister's animated expression. *Everything will be just fine.*

Chapter Four

Louise had expected Monday breakfast at the inn to be busy since they had two long-term guests checked in and a third expected shortly, yet only Lester Langston showed up for the meal.

"I have to be at the courthouse three days a week," he told Louise as he sat down and set his cane to one side, "so I usually make do with coffee and a bun."

"That will be fine, and if you would prefer something more, we have a variety of fresh fruit and muffins," she suggested as she filled his coffee cup. "Do you work in the legal field, Mr. Langston?"

"Yes, I'm a lawyer." He gave her a very serious look. "Do you know the difference between a bad lawyer and a good one, Mrs. Smith?"

"I have rarely had to consult with one, but I would hope I do."

"A bad lawyer lets a single case drag out for a year." He glanced at the door and lowered his voice. "But a good lawyer can make it last even *longer*."

Louise was still chuckling when she took his order into the kitchen and passed along Lester's joke to Jane as they prepared his meal.

"I've heard all sorts of lawyer jokes, but you rarely meet

a lawyer with a sense of humor," Jane said as she expertly sliced up a cantaloupe and arranged it beside a variety of her fruit and nut mini-muffins. "Did you see Mr. Kirchwey come down yet this morning?"

"No, I haven't seen him at all."

"Me, either. And he didn't show up for breakfast yesterday." The front desk bell rang. "If you'll see who that is, I'll take care of this, Louise."

Louise walked out to find a short, plump brunette in her late twenties standing by the desk. "Good morning, may I help you?"

"Hi, I'm Gwendolyn Murphy." She set down a rectangular metal case and a duffel bag beside a large suitcase. "If this is Grace Chapel Inn, as the sign says, I'm checking in."

"You're in the right place." Louise went behind the desk and retrieved her paperwork, then observed the young woman as she filled it out.

Gwendolyn Murphy wore her curly, dark hair in a neat French braid, but little wisps had escaped to frame her round cheeks and slightly pointed chin. She was a little pale, so that the freckles on her nose and cheeks stood out, but her brown eyes were bright and her gaze very discerning. Her fingernails were trimmed short, Louise noticed, and she wore no rings.

"I'm an artist," Gwen told her as she handed over the completed registration form. "So I'll probably be doing a lot of sitting around and sketching."

"Ah. I must confess, I was wondering about the metal case there." Louise nodded toward her luggage. "Are you a professional artist?"

"Strictly a dedicated amateur," Gwen assured her. She glanced at Louise's hands. "You have the hands of a painter."

Louise laughed. "The only things I paint are rooms, and only then under protest. I am a musician."

"Oh, really? What do you play?"

"The piano. I also teach some children in the area."

"Do you?" Gwen arched her eyebrows.

At that moment Jane emerged from the kitchen. "Is this our latest arrival?" She introduced herself and nodded toward the dining room. "If you're hungry, you're more than welcome to come in and order breakfast. Otherwise I'm just going to end up baking things for tomorrow to tempt you."

"No, thanks. I'd rather get settled in my room." Gwen collected her cases. "Where is it, by the way?"

"I can take you up and show you," Louise said as she handed the new guest her room key.

Gwen gave her a distinctly unfriendly look. "No, just tell me which one it is." Once Louise had directed her to the Sunset Room, she went upstairs without another word.

"A tad grumpy, isn't she?" Jane asked.

"I have no idea why." A door banged upstairs, and Louise frowned. "She seemed very friendly until just a few moments ago."

"Maybe she's tired from the trip here." Her younger sister nudged her. "Quit looking so worried. You know you'll charm her just like you do everyone else."

As Louise went to check on Lester in the dining room, she wondered what had caused Gwen Murphy's abrupt change in mood and behavior. *From the moment that I mentioned teaching music, she acted like a completely different person.*

∽

Lisa Masur, a member of Grace Chapel's ANGELs, an organization founded by Alice for young girls, brought a relative with her to their weekly meeting at church on Wednesday evening.

"This is my cousin, Darla," Lisa said as she introduced her to Alice. "She lives in Potterston, but she's staying with us for a few months while her parents sell their house and transfer jobs." Her brown ponytail swayed as she turned to give her taller cousin a look of distinct hero-worship. "She's fourteen."

"Welcome, Darla." Alice smiled at the red-haired girl. Although her youth group was usually reserved for eleven- to thirteen-year-old girls, she encouraged the children to bring visitors to their meetings. "Which church do you attend in Potterston?"

"My parents don't make me go to church," the girl replied, a sulking note in her voice. "I wouldn't have come to this except my aunt talked me into it."

"It's really fun, Dar," Lisa said. "Plus you'll get to meet all my friends."

Alice was not deterred by the child's attitude. In the past she had worked with a number of children who, for various reasons, did not attend church or youth groups. She always thought of them as lost lambs looking for a shepherd. One of her ministry's goals was to show girls like Darla the path to faith, which would bring them to Christ.

"You never know what something is like until you give it a try." Alice looked around the meeting room and saw that the rest of her girls had arrived. "If everyone will sit down, we'll have our opening prayer."

Lisa led her cousin to one of the desks, and Alice heard Darla mutter, "She makes you *pray*?" as they sat.

This one might be more mule than sheep. As soon as the children were seated, Alice opened her planning book.

One of the important aspects of the ANGELs group was teaching the girls to develop their faith. Alice found the best way to do this was with a weekly theme. She chose themes that were interesting and goal-oriented, which appealed to the girls and helped them to focus on the lesson. Her opening prayer also introduced the theme, which this week was "Stop, Look and Listen."

"Let's pray together now," Alice said. She watched the girls bow their heads—all but Darla, who stared back at her defiantly until she gave in to Lisa's nudging and dropped her chin a notch. "Heavenly Father, we thank you for giving us a world filled with wondrous things. May we always find the time to open our hearts and appreciate Your many blessings on our journey through life. As we come together this evening to share Your Word and Your light, help us see where we can do Your good work, and hear the voices of those in need so that we may answer with Your blessings. Guide us in this and in all things, through Christ our Lord. Amen."

"Amen," the girls echoed.

Instead of restricting the girls to discussions or Bible study, Alice liked to teach using games, crafts and songs. Her newest game, "Truth or Verse," was modeled on the classic game of truth or dare, and gave the girls a chance to learn more about each other, as well as to test their knowledge of the Bible.

When it was her turn, Sissy Matthews decided to choose a truth over a verse, and one of the girls asked her what she loved to do when no one was watching.

Sissy grinned. "Practice my piano lessons."

Some of the girls giggled, but Alice heard someone make a less pleasant sound. Darla, she guessed, from the way the girl was scowling at Sissy.

For the craft segment of the meeting, she showed the girls how to make diaries from recycled paper, and she provided specially formatted pages for them to record their blessings, as well as blank ones for the usual things preteens liked to write about. She wrapped up the evening with a contest of "What Bible Character Am I?" in which she gave the girls the chance to ask her yes-and-no questions until they could correctly identify which Bible character she was pretending to be.

The only girl who did not seem to be having much fun was Darla Masur, who spent most of the time frowning or looking bored. Alice suspected that it was an act put on for her benefit, and perhaps to cover the fact that the girl felt uncomfortable. She had seemed almost angry when she could not guess any of the Bible characters, but Alice suspected that Darla felt inadequate because, unlike the other girls, she obviously had not studied the Bible at all.

After their closing prayer, Alice said good-bye to the girls and thanked Lisa for bringing her cousin. "I'm glad you were able to join us, Darla," she said to the red-haired teen. "I hope you'll come back next week."

"I guess." She eyed Sissy, who was the only girl taller than she in the group. "Not like I have anything better to do." She left with her cousin.

After all the girls had been picked up by their parents, Alice went home and decided to make herself a cup of tea before she went to bed. She found Louise sorting through a stack of old newspapers on the table in the kitchen.

"Are you clipping coupons?" she asked as she filled the kettle and put it on the stove to heat.

"No, just reading some old articles," Louise said, and put down the paper she was holding. "How was your meeting?"

"Great. Do you want to have some tea with me?"

"No, thank you, dear. I'm going to bed in a minute." She sat back in her chair. "Did your craft project go over well?"

"Very. Some of the girls were already writing things in their diaries before the meeting ended," Alice said as she took down one mug. "We also had a new girl tonight. Lisa Masur brought her cousin along with her. She wasn't very enthusiastic—she said that her parents don't take her to church—but with a little time I think I can bring her around. She'd be better off in our older youth group, though, because she's fourteen."

"Masur?" Louise sat up straight. "Not *Darla* Masur?"

"Yes, that's her name. Pretty red-haired girl. Stubborn as a mule." Alice shook her head with reluctant admiration. "Do you know her?"

"I had her for lessons, briefly, a few months ago. Her parents live over in Potterston, but her aunt and uncle live here and recommended me when Darla decided she wanted to play the piano." Louise did not sound too happy about that.

"Did she quit after a few times?" Alice knew that despite Louise's excellent tutoring, some children inevitably lost interest.

"She never attempted to learn anything I tried to teach

her. I was the one who decided to stop the lessons." Her older sister looked as if she might say more, but then only shook her head.

"If you're debating whether to warn me about her less admirable qualities, don't worry. I got a good dose of them tonight, but I still invited her to come to our next meeting." Alice filled her mug and brought it to the table. "If God wanted youth ministry to be easy, He'd make every child as sweet as Sissy Matthews."

"Thank heavens you have the patience for Darla, because I certainly did not." She reached across the table and covered Alice's hand with hers. "Just be careful, my dear. I would hate to see this girl cause problems for you and your group."

"There's no need for concern," Alice said, and smiled. "I believe I'll have ANGELs wings on this little mule in no time." She looked at the stack of newspapers. "Are you done with these? I'll take them out to the recycling bin."

"Yes, thank you." Louise rose and bent over to kiss the top of her head. "Good night, Alice."

"Sleep well."

Alice left her tea to cool, took a flashlight from the utility drawer and carried the bundle of papers out through the door to the garden. Jane, who insisted they recycle whatever they could, kept separate bins for plastic, glass and newspapers at one corner of the house. Alice used the flashlight to illuminate the ground in front of her because she hated the idea of stepping on frogs or the other small creatures that came out at night. A rustling sound made her stop, and her heart caught in her throat when she saw a dark figure standing next to the bins.

"Who's there?" she called out.

Something slammed, a man yelped and some empty plastic jugs fell to the ground. She belatedly remembered the flashlight in her hand and directed its beam at the bins.

"It's me, Basil Kirchwey." Basil stood next to the bins, rubbing one of his hands with the other. As her light reached his face, he squinted and shaded his eyes. "Miss Howard?"

"My goodness, you gave me a fright. Are you hurt?" Alice stepped around the jugs to join him.

"No. Bumped my hand, but it's fine." He flexed it to show her.

Alice lowered the flashlight. "What are you doing out here?"

"I was, um, having a short walk. I knocked into this bin and it nearly fell over." He began picking up the trash that had fallen from the bin. "Let me get this cleaned up."

She put the newspapers aside. "Here, let me help." She had only glimpsed Basil a few times since he had checked in, and when she had, he was either leaving the inn or going up to his room. Although Louise felt certain that he was not the Innside Reporter, Alice was not so sure. "Have you been enjoying your vacation?"

"Yes, my room is very comfortable. Gorgeous furniture. Lots of uh, green." He finished retrieving the jugs and placed them back in the bin.

She was surprised that he had even noticed the décor of his room. "So, what have you been doing since you arrived?"

"You know. This and that. Nothing special." He edged around her. "I shouldn't keep you out here. Sorry again, Miss Howard. Good night."

"Good night, Mr. Kirchwey." Puzzled, she watched him make his way back around to the front of the inn before she opened the newspaper bin, then blinked.

Basil's bowler sat on the top of the unbound stack of newspapers inside the bin.

❧

The mayor had promised to make space available at Town Hall by the following weekend. But because the Howard sisters were busy caring for their three guests during the week, they decided to wait until Friday afternoon to go through the antiques they had stored in the attic.

Jane felt particularly excited about setting up the Visitors Center display, and after reading the *Innkeeper's Journal* from cover to cover, she was bubbling over with new ideas about their own business.

"We could improve some of the little things and expand our marketing efforts," she told her sisters as they went upstairs. "Take the greeting we use when we answer the phones."

Louise looked down at her from the second floor landing. "What on earth is wrong with the way we do that?"

Jane caught up with her. "Don't you think 'Good afternoon, Grace Chapel Inn, Louise Smith speaking' is kind of dull?"

"I think it allows callers to know with whom they are speaking, which is the whole point of a greeting," her older sister informed her dryly. "Otherwise, I would just save my breath and say 'Hello.'"

"How would you change it, Jane?" Alice asked.

Once Jane had thought her middle sister was resistant to new ideas because she had always lived with their father, who had also preferred the familiar to the new. Since opening the inn, however, she had gradually discovered that Alice was not opposed to change; she was just more cautious than Jane was about implementing it.

"I think we should make it more visual and appealing. 'Good morning from the best little bed-and-breakfast in Pennsylvania' or 'It's a beautiful day here at Grace Chapel Inn.'" She moved her hands expressively. "See how those words paint a picture for the caller?"

"Oh, I see." Louise sniffed and continued up the stairs. "You want us to *lie* to them."

"I think we *are* the best bed-and-breakfast in Pennsylvania, so it wouldn't be a lie." Jane stopped on the third floor landing and planted her hands on her hips. "Every day *is* perfectly beautiful here."

"If you don't count that huge storm we had over the summer," Louise said, "the one that tore the roof off Pastor Ley's old house."

"There was also that late frost we had in the spring," Alice put in. "And the time we had that dust storm come in from the east—"

"Okay, okay. So every day isn't perfect or beautiful." Jane lifted her hands in surrender. "You know what I mean. The point is, we take advantage of the contact, and use our greeting to interest callers in our location and to show pride in our business. We need to come up with a greeting that says all that."

Alice sighed. "I think I'd run out of breath before I could say all that."

"It doesn't have to be long," she reassured her. "It simply needs to be a little more, you know, peppy."

"Peppy." Louise eyed her for a moment. "Must I take that magazine away from you?"

"Too late." Jane grinned. "I've already read all of the articles."

"You've probably memorized them." She shook her head as she opened the door to the attic. "Lord, help us."

Ever since the inn had been renovated and the old roof replaced, the attic had served as a storage place for many of the antique furnishings collected over the years by their parents and grandparents, as well as some of the pieces Louise and Jane had brought with them when they moved back to Acorn Hill.

"I remember Fred moving Mother's desk up from the living room when we brought down the larger sofa for the guests, but I did not see exactly where he put it," Louise said as she worked her way through the labyrinth of old furniture.

An old felt hat on a dusty shelf reminded Jane of something Alice had mentioned a few days ago. "By the way, Alice, did you reunite Mr. Kirchwey with his bowler?"

"Not exactly," she said. "I didn't want to disturb him that night, so I left it hanging on the coat rack by the front door. The next morning when I went down, it was gone."

"He's been here almost a week, and I haven't caught so

much as a glimpse of him yet." Jane picked up the hat and idly turned it in her hands. "I wonder what the Invisible Man does all day."

"What I can't figure out is why he was looking through our old newspapers," Alice said. "We put the paper in the parlor every day for the guests to read."

"He may have wanted them for another reason." Jane lowered her voice to a confidential murmur. "He could be gathering intelligence. Or evidence."

"Or maybe he just wanted something to read before he went to bed." Louise regarded them both. "Are we going to stand around and make up stories about Basil Kirchwey's nonexistent secret life all day, or are we going to find Mother's desk?"

"There it is." Alice pointed, and Jane saw the top of Madeleine Howard's diminutive kneehole desk in one corner. "To your left, Louise, just behind that birdcage."

"How neat." Jane went over and peered at the old-fashioned, domed bamboo cage, which hung from a brass-fitted stand. "When did we have a bird?"

"We never had one, but I believe our grandmother kept a pet canary for years." Louise moved the lightweight birdcage to one side. "I remember Mother telling me how it would perch on the side of Grandmother's teacup and sip from it."

"*Euuuww.*" Jane made a horrible face. "Bird germs."

"I wouldn't mind having a sweet little feathered creature to sing to me in my room," Alice said. "I love listening to the birds when I sit in the garden."

"Wendell wouldn't mind either," Jane told her. "But I think the bird would want to vacate the premises immediately. Still, I could probably make this into a bird feeder." She carried it over to set it to one side of the attic door.

Louise tried to shift the trunk that the birdcage had been standing on, but it did not move an inch. She let out an exasperated sound. "Drat this heavy old thing! Jane, come back over here and take the other side, please?"

Alice stepped forward as if to prevent her. "Let us do it, Louise. You might hurt yourself."

"Nonsense." She waved her away. "I'm not so old that I have forgotten how to lift properly."

Before Alice could protest further, a familiar, reedy voice called out, "Miss Howard?"

Alice went to the attic door and looked out, then glanced back over her shoulder. "It's Mr. Kirchwey." She turned and called out, "Up here, Mr. Kirchwey."

"At last, we get to meet the mysterious Basil." Jane waggled her eyebrows at Louise. "Should I ask him why he raided our trash bin the other night? Or should I attempt to delve into the significance of his unusual choice of headwear?"

"You do and I will deport you."

"Sorry to bother you, Miss Howard." The tall, thin man, his black bowler atop his head, appeared in the doorway. He gave the three sisters a decidedly uneasy look. "Oh, you're not alone. Hello."

As Alice performed brief introductions, Jane was hard-pressed not to stare at Basil Kirchwey. He was wearing navy trousers with a blue-and-gray plaid jacket over a white dress shirt. He wore a green bow tie. She also noticed that his trousers were slightly wrinkled, and had what she would swear were grass stains on both knees.

Where has he been kneeling in the grass? Jane wondered.

"Jane." Louise gave her a warning look. "You and I should get back to work."

Jane smiled at Basil before she went to help her older sister with the trunk.

Chapter Five

Like Jane, Alice had noticed the grass stains on Basil's trousers, but she managed to keep from staring. "Is there something you needed, Mr. Kirchwey?"

"Miss Howard, I'm expecting some calls and . . ." He trailed off as he looked over her shoulder. "Is this a bad time?" He stretched up on his toes, trying to see what Louise and Jane were doing.

"We're just moving a desk downstairs." Alice glanced at her sisters, who were now struggling to shift the heavy trunk between them. "If we can get to it, that is."

"Either I'm getting older, or gravity is getting stronger," Jane said, panting a little as she sat back on her heels. "What's in this thing, anyway?" She tried to give it a push, but it didn't budge. "Bricks?"

Alice watched as Louise tested the trunk's weight by trying to rock it, but the trunk was not moving an inch. "I think Mother packed some old books and linens in here."

Her older sister tried to open the lid, but a rusty padlock hung from the front latch. "There are no keys for it, so the only way to open it would be to destroy the latch." Louise straightened and absently pressed a hand to the small of her back.

In her concern for her sister, Alice forgot about Basil and started toward her. "Really, Louise, let Jane and me do this." She nearly jumped out of her shoes when a bony hand touched her shoulder.

"Please, Miss Howard, allow me." Basil took a deep breath and then removed his hat and jacket and carefully set both on a chair just inside the door. "I'll help Jane move that trunk."

Alice looked from Basil to Jane. "Oh no, you don't have to do this, Mr. Kirchwey."

"Men should do heavy work." He tapped his decidedly skinny bicep. "We've got more upper-body strength, you know."

Alice saw Jane begin to say something and then bite her lip.

Basil started toward the trunk, and all she could do was follow. "Well, if you are sure you don't mind," she said, mentally crossing her fingers.

"It'll be a snap," he told her as he rolled up the sleeves of his dress shirt. "All in the arms and the knees." He gave Louise one of his lopsided smiles. "Okay with you, ma'am?"

"I think . . ." Visibly exasperated, Louise exchanged a glance with Alice, and then stepped aside. "Please do be careful, Mr. Kirchwey. We wouldn't want you to hurt yourself . . . or Jane."

He rolled his head and flexed his shoulders before giving her younger sister a slightly stern look. "Don't, um, strain yourself, now."

Jane, who regularly handled huge heavy pots and garden equipment, let her mouth curl with amusement. "I'll do my best."

Alice took Louise's arm. "Let's move out of the way, shall we?" she said, before her older sister became unsettled.

Jane dusted off her hands on the front of her overalls,

then crouched down opposite Basil and curled her hand around the loop of old leather on her side. "Ready when you are."

"On three . . . one, two, *three*." Basil's eyes bulged as they both lifted, and the trunk rose a few inches. His face turned beet-red. "My . . . this . . . really is . . . extremely . . . *heavy* . . ."

"Easy," Jane said, steadying her side. "Try to keep it level. We'll put it over there." She nodded toward a clear spot.

Between them, they lifted the trunk a foot or two off the floor. Alice moved out of their way. Then the red-faced Basil groaned as he struggled backward toward the space Jane had indicated. He began to totter as they drew near, and the trunk tipped forward.

"Watch out!" Alice automatically stepped forward, but Louise tugged her back.

"Put it down!" Jane said as she tried to compensate for the shift in weight.

"I've got it. I've got—" Basil wrenched up on his side, and there was a sudden ripping sound. The trunk dropped suddenly, and he was thrown backward into a collision with the birdcage.

Jane had the presence of mind to get out of the way as the trunk hit the floor. The impact popped the back hinges on the lid, and the weight inside forced the lid open. Books and linens tumbled out.

At the same time, Basil's fall into the birdcage sent it sailing out through the attic door. There was an extended amount of crashing and clattering as the birdcage went bouncing down the staircase.

A small cloud of dust from the spilled contents of the trunk rose and made everyone cough.

Alice made sure Basil was unharmed before she made her way around the mess on the floor to Jane. "My goodness! Are you all right?"

"I'm okay, but I think the trunk and the birdcage are

history." Jane looked over at Basil, who was on the floor and staring in amazement at the torn handle in his fingers. "How about you, Mr. Kirchwey?"

"Blast!" He hoisted himself up and tried to drag a hand through his hair, but then had to untangle the handle piece from it. "I'm fine. I think." He peered out the doorway. "I'm glad that wasn't me."

"Are you quite sure you are all right, Mr. Kirchwey?" Louise, who had also come over, studied him. "You didn't strain your back, I hope?"

"Uh, no. Heavy thing, isn't it?" He gave her a slightly sheepish look. "Sorry."

"As long as you're not hurt, that's all that matters." The sound of footsteps on the stairway made Alice glance toward the attic door, where their two other guests appeared, each carrying a piece of the broken birdcage.

"What on earth is happening?" Gwendolyn Murphy asked. The brunette had a protective smock over her clothes, as well as a smear of bright yellow chalk on one cheek. "And who threw this thing down the stairs?" She held up the birdcage stand, which was broken in two places.

"We just had a moving accident," Jane told her. "Nothing to be concerned about. The only casualty was the birdcage and this old thing." She gave the side of the trunk a little kick.

Lester Langston leaned on his cane as he looked in. He had damp hair and a towel around his neck. "*Hmm.*" He handed Alice a piece of shattered cage. "For a moment I thought someone had fallen down the stairs, and I might have some new business."

Jane smothered a chuckle.

Evidently far from amused, Gwen stared at Basil, who was bending down to examine some of the books from the trunk. Her expression darkened with disapproval as she turned toward Louise. "Do you usually make your guests double as movers?"

Alice saw Louise's mouth tighten. "No, Ms. Murphy, Mr. Kirchwey was kind enough to volunteer."

"Well, if everyone's all right and no one needs legal representation, I'd better finish shaving. Ladies, Mr. Kirchwey." Lester nodded to them and departed.

Gwen did not seem mollified. "That noise made me ruin the sketch I was working on." She swiped her hand at her cheek and glared at the yellow chalk on her hand before wiping it on the front of her smock. "If the trunk was that heavy, why didn't you unpack it first?"

"We would have," Louise said, her voice as tight as her lips, "but the trunk was locked."

"Next time we'll get out the bolt cutters." Jane went over and joined the artist. "Gwen, why don't you come downstairs with me? I need someone to test my latest batch of oatmeal-fig bars, and I've got lemonade to go with them."

"Oh, I suppose so. It's not like I'm going to get any real work done with all this thumping around." The artist indignantly followed Jane out of the attic.

"Good grief." Louise brushed off the front of her skirt. "She makes it sound like we did that on purpose just to annoy her."

Alice had noticed the tension between Louise and Gwen Murphy, which seemed to have been growing from the day the artist had checked in, but she could not fathom the reason behind it. "I'm sure it's just her way of reacting to being frightened by the noise."

Louise shook her head in wonder. "Lend me your eyes someday, Alice. You always see the good in people."

"Not all the time. Occasionally I feel binoculars would come in real handy." Her attention was drawn back to Basil, who was on his knees beside the trunk. "Is something wrong, Mr. Kirchwey?"

"Would you look at these?" Basil was sorting through the

books that had spilled out of the trunk, and the expression on his face was close to utter rapture. "I can't believe it. You've got *The Pretty Village* and a beautiful copy of *Robinson Crusoe*. I've never seen this edition of *The Water Babies*, and there have to be two years of *Parley's Magazine* for children and youth in this bundle."

Alice was more impressed by the change in his voice and expression, from which all of the usual hesitation and nervousness had vanished.

Louise had a similar reaction. "Should we call a press conference?"

Basil's eyebrows drew together for a moment, then he chuckled. "No, but if there were such things as literary pirates, this might be one of their buried treasure chests."

That seemed to mollify her older sister, who was equally fond of old books.

"Do you collect books, Mr. Kirchwey?" Alice asked as she picked up a fragile, delicately embroidered silk pillowcase from the pile of linens that had also fallen out of the trunk.

"I've picked up a few during my research trips," he said absently as he studied another volume, "but none as nice as these. These are in mint condition."

"What is your field of research?" Louise asked as she knelt down beside him. "Are you a historian?"

"Ah, no. My field is . . . a hodgepodge, really." He carefully set the volume he was holding to one side and stood. "Well." He made a show of checking his watch. "Look at the time, I had better go. Sorry again about the accident."

And before Alice or Louise could say another word, Basil hurried out of the attic.

∞

Jane didn't like the way Gwendolyn Murphy had spoken to Louise. In fact, she had nearly snapped at the artist before reminding herself to keep cool and see what she could do to calm down their unhappy guest. It also seemed wise to get her away from Louise, who had looked as upset as Jane felt.

"What were you sketching?" Jane asked as she led the disgruntled Gwen Murphy into the kitchen. Wendell emerged from under the kitchen table, and she bent to give him a quick scratch around the ears. "I can tell it's something yellow."

"A study of three bananas. I stole them from the basket at breakfast this morning. How did you know it was yellow?"

"You've missed a little banana here." She pointed to the spot on her own face that corresponded with the stain that was on Gwen's.

"*Ugh*, I thought I got it all." She swiped at her cheek again. "Do you mind if I wash up over here?" When Jane shook her head, the artist went to the sink. "I suppose you think I made a big fuss about nothing."

Absolutely she did, but she could not say that. "Not really."

"I saw the way your sister looked at me." She accepted the paper towel Jane offered her and dried off her hands. "You two are close, aren't you?"

"Yes, but then, she's a great sister." Jane decided to change the subject before she did lose her temper. "So how long have you been dabbling in the arts?"

"I got interested when I saw an art show in college. I worked one summer earning tuition by drawing sidewalk portraits." She pointed to the ceiling. "How long will this trunk-lifting, birdcage-dropping business be going on? You and your sisters doing some kind of summer cleaning? Or is this some kind of anger management technique?"

"The summer cleaning is finished and anger management is on Thursdays," Jane kept her tone pleasant. "Do you want me to pencil you in for the next class?"

The artist folded her arms. "Do you think I need it?"

"No, but I might."

They looked at each other for a long, silent moment, and then Gwen nodded. "You're no pushover. I like that."

"Thanks." Jane decided Gwen's bark was probably a lot worse than her bite, and felt some of her inner indignation and tension ease. "We're just bringing down our mother's writing desk for a town project. It'll all be over shortly. Okay?"

"I hope so."

"Sit down and relax for a minute." Jane took the pitcher of lemonade from the refrigerator and brought it and a pan of her new oatmeal-fig bars to the table. "Dig in. These are from a health-food recipe I've been experimenting with. I'd offer you fruit, but I don't want to encourage your life of crime."

"It's more fun to steal it. Your sister Louise saw me take them, you know," she said, surprising Jane. "She's got eyes like a cop."

"My sister is a very nice person," Jane insisted, "which you would find out if you got to know her a little better."

"I'll take your word for it." The artist gave the plate a dubious look. "I should warn you, every all-natural snack I've ever tried tasted like chunky cardboard."

"I generally leave out the cardboard when I bake." Jane poured two glasses of the ice-cold lemonade and sat with her. *Maybe if I try to be a little friendlier, she'll lighten up, too.* "Aside from the wrecked sketch this morning, how are you enjoying your vacation?"

"Fine, so far." Gwen nodded and sampled the lemonade. "This is one of the quietest inns I've ever stayed at."

The kitchen door opened and Lester looked around the edge. "Would I be disturbing you ladies if I ask for a glass of water?" He produced a prescription bottle. "I forgot to take my blood pressure medication while I was upstairs."

"You can have water or lemonade," Jane offered. "Can you take your pills with a snack?"

"If it means that I can also have one of those tasty-looking treats on the table, yes indeed," Lester assured her.

Gwen pulled out a chair for the lawyer. "Sit down, Mr. Langston. I was just telling Jane what a nice, quiet place this is. Aside from today's disaster, anyway."

"That was a bit startling." Lester thanked Jane when she brought a glass and plate to him. "Although I think it was rather low on the disaster scale. After all, Mr. Kirchwey didn't come down along with the birdcage."

"Do you like being an innkeeper?" Lester asked.

"That I do." She glanced out the kitchen window at the gardens she had brought back to life. "It's not like anything else I've ever done. The guests are interesting, there's something new to do every day, and—not counting this afternoon, of course—things are pretty quiet and peaceful here. It definitely beats working as a chef in the city."

"You're a pro. That explains the absence of cardboard in your recipe." Gwen helped herself to another bar. "But it has to be a lot of hassle, too, especially with just you and your sisters running the place. When do you get a day off?"

"Innkeepers work seven days a week, I'm afraid. I can take a day off when I need it, but we share the work, and that means Louise and Alice would have so much more to do. I really don't mind staying busy." She shrugged. Wendell stretched and after giving the artist's ankle an inquisitive sniff, flicked his black-tipped tail and strolled off in the direction of the study.

Lester nodded. "The leisurely lifestyle wouldn't suit you. All those manicures and servants and yacht sailing. But if there's an opening, *I'm* always available."

Jane laughed. "I'll keep that in mind."

"But why quit working as a chef? Had to be better money in that." Gwen finished her lemonade. "Don't you miss the excitement of the city, and all the people?"

"Sometimes it's nice to get away from all that," Lester told her, and tapped his medication bottle. "Trust me, I know."

"I do miss it, but not as much as I thought I would." Jane sat back and thought for a moment about what she had left behind in San Francisco. "It's strange. With all the people who came to my restaurant, I never really got to know any of them. There were a few regulars I became acquainted with over the years, but they'd only drop in for a meal and then go. And with things being so busy in the kitchens, I never had the time to sit down and talk to them."

"Or wheedle them out of a bad mood," Lester said, and winked at Gwen.

Jane laughed. "You got me there, but it is part of the job. If a guest is unhappy, we try to fix things."

The lawyer appraised Gwen. "I think if you can get Ms. Murphy here to smile before she leaves, I'd say you've earned your paycheck."

"Oh, I'm feeling better, all right," the artist said, and flashed a very attractive smile. "But what if lemonade and oatmeal-fig bars don't work?"

Jane tilted her head. "There's always the second line of attack. My cherry cheesecake and café au lait."

Lester leaned toward Gwen and lowered his voice. "I think you should have held out longer."

They all laughed.

Chapter Six

"You know, I'm beginning to believe that Aunt Ethel was right," Louise said after Basil's hurried departure from the attic. "The way that man acts *is* very suspicious."

Alice finished retying a bundle of old magazines. "He is jumpy, but it seems to be more from self-consciousness than anything else."

"Or the product of a guilty conscience." She bent down to pick up a heavy mound of brown fabric. "Do you remember that time Charles Matthews tried to sneak that pet frog of his into his piano lesson? That boy practically leapt off the bench himself every time I spoke to him."

"I keep wondering if he is that Innside Reporter Jane told us about," Alice admitted.

"If he is, he will have to make up whatever he writes. He is never here to see what we do around the inn."

"Maybe." Her sister perched on the arm of a cloth-covered loveseat. "He seemed so interested in what we were doing, though, and I can't imagine why. He's done nothing but avoid us otherwise. Unless . . . do you think he wanted to see the upstairs?" Alice looked around. "Goodness, he'll probably write something horrible about our attic."

"This is the cleanest attic in Pennsylvania. Besides, a

little dust . . . never hurt . . ." Louise trailed off as a vague memory of a glossy page flickered in her mind.

"What is it?"

She shook her head, frustrated as the memory faded away. "I still think I have seen that man's name before. In fact, I am almost sure now that it was in one of my old magazines."

"Do you have any travel magazines?"

"No, I have only subscribed to a few about classical music and literature. Judging from Mr. Kirchwey's taste in bow ties, I hardly think he's the artistic type." Louise began unfolding the mound of fabric she had picked up, which turned out to be a large, heavy quilt made of dark wool. "Ugh. I am not going to put this dirty old thing back in there."

Months earlier Alice had found another quilt, one stitched seventy years before by her grandmother as a wedding gift for Madeleine and Daniel Howard. She had fallen in love with the quilt's yellows, greens and purples so much that she had decorated her bedroom and braided an area rug to match the soft pastel colors.

Unlike that lovely heirloom, this quilt was thick, lumpy and covered with moth holes. "Should we try to wash it?" It certainly smelled as dirty as it looked.

"Even if we could get it clean, we would never use it. It's far too heavy. Wool quilts make me itch, too. We may as well throw it away." She gasped when a book suddenly slid out of the folds and fell onto the floor.

"I've got it." Alice bent to pick up the book, which had two dark green cover pieces hand-bound with tied cord over a sheaf of irregularly edged pages.

"Is it another of Mother's old photo albums?" Louise refolded the quilt and set it back on top of the trunk.

Alice opened the front cover. "I don't think so. There's drawing in it."

Louise looked over her sister's shoulder, and her eyes

widened at the illustration on the first page. Someone had carefully made an oval-shaped charcoal drawing of a farmhouse standing atop a grassy hill. The care and detail with which it had been made reflected considerable talent.

She touched the fine paper with reverent fingers. "It might be someone's diary or journal."

"I don't think so." Her younger sister turned the page to reveal more drawings. "Why, it's filled with sketches."

Other than Jane, Louise didn't know of anyone in their family who had such artistic skills. "Do you see a signature anywhere?"

Alice turned the pages, which were filled with detailed drawings of country scenes and portraits of men, women and children. "There are a few names written by the portraits of the kids. *Manfred. Killian. Louisa. August.*" Toward the end of the book was a picture of the head and shoulders of a young woman with long, dark hair and a sad smile. The drawing, larger than the others, took up an entire page. "Here's an Emily." She showed the last portrait to Louise. "Do you recognize her?"

"No, but she looks familiar. Just as 'Basil Kirchwey' sounds familiar. Drat this memory of mine." Frustration made Louise impatient, and the dust and musty smells only added to that. She thought of the pitcher of lemonade Jane had mentioned earlier. "We should take the book downstairs and get something cold to drink."

"Good, you've saved me a trip," Jane said when they entered the kitchen. She had prepared a tray of drinks and snacks to take up to them. "I managed to get all the huff out of Gwen, by the way, and she's back drawing pictures again. What have you got there, Alice?"

"It's a sketchbook. Louise found it with the things that fell out of the trunk." Alice handed it to their younger sister while Louise poured their drinks and refilled Jane's glass. "Look at the portrait of the woman on the very last page."

Jane flipped through the pages, stopping at the large sketch of the sadly smiling lady. "Emily. *Hmm.* Our great-great grandma, maybe?"

"Why do you think that?" Alice wanted to know.

"If she pulled her hair back here and here into a twist," Jane traced lines in the air above the portrait, "she'd look exactly like those pictures of Mother when she was young."

"Of course!" Louise responded. "That is why she looks so familiar. But how did you know?"

"Well, all I've ever seen of Mother were her pictures." Jane's own smile turned a little sad as she studied the sketch. "You two grew up around the real thing."

Their younger sister never knew their mother: Madeleine Berry Howard had died an hour after Jane was born.

"Any time you want to see our mother," Louise said as she placed a gentle hand on Jane's shoulder, "just look in the mirror and smile."

"Or laugh," Alice said. "You have her laugh."

Jane skimmed back through the pages of the sketchbook to the beginning. "*Hmm.* I see some names here, but no signature of the artist. Do we know who drew them?"

Alice shook her head. "Louise and I have never seen the book before. It fell out of an old quilt someone had wrapped around it."

"I would love to use this as part of our Town Hall display," Louise said. "But first we really should identify the artist it once belonged to. The book might even belong to someone other than the Berrys."

∞

Once she had helped Jane finish clearing up after breakfast the next morning, Alice came out of the dining room to find Louise waiting at the bottom of the stairs. She was watching Fred and another man as they carried Madeleine's writing desk down from the attic. The day before, Jane had suggested that they move the lightweight desk downstairs themselves, but Louise vetoed the idea.

"After what happened with the trunk," she had told Jane over dinner, "I'm not taking the chance. I shall call Fred tonight."

"We could get Basil to help." Mischief sparkled in their youngest sister's blue eyes. "Seeing as he has all that experience with lifting."

"I am praying that we can keep Mr. Kirchwey from carrying anything else until he leaves," Louise said. "Mother's desk would only be an invitation to disaster."

Alice had gone up to Basil Kirchwey's room the night before to ask him about the phone calls he had been concerned about prior to the trunk fiasco. But when she reached the Garden Room she spotted the "Do Not Disturb" sign hanging on the doorknob. When she passed his room in the morning, it was still hanging there.

Maybe he did strain something.

"What's the quilt for?" Alice asked Louise as she joined her in the foyer. Louise was holding the old quilt that had been wrapped around the sketchbook.

"I thought I would drape it over the desk before Fred loads it into his truck, to prevent any damage to the wood," her sister told her. "That way, we would get some use out of it before we discard it."

"Couldn't we donate it to the thrift shop over in Potterston?" That was what they often did with unwanted household items.

"I doubt they could find a buyer for something this smelly, ugly, and full of moth holes," Louise said. "Even if someone could clean and mend it, it really is far too heavy to be of any practical use. This was made in days when people didn't have central heating to keep them warm during the winters."

The inn phone rang, and Alice went behind the desk to

answer it. As she picked up the receiver, she saw that Jane had taped a note to the phone: "Try a new greeting!!!"

She took a deep breath before she answered with, "It's a beautiful day here at Grace Chapel Inn."

"How nice for you," a deep, gravelly voice replied. "It's a miserable morning here in New York."

Alice cringed a little. "I'm so sorry to hear that." Whatever other cheerful and peppy words she might have summoned deserted her imagination. "Um, I'm Alice Howard, may I help you?"

"I need to speak to Kirchwey. Is he there?"

This had to be one of the phone calls Basil had been expecting. Alice gnawed at her lip as she glanced at the men, who were only halfway down the stairs. She couldn't see pushing past them to get to Basil's room: Her mother's desk might end up at the bottom of the stairs in pieces. Also, Basil might still have the DND sign on the doorknob, and one of their strictest rules was never to disturb guests who used the DND unless it was an emergency.

"He's not available at the moment, sir," she said diplomatically. "May I take your name and number, and have him return your call?"

"Just tell him to call Johnson in New York, if you would," the man said, and hung up before Alice could ask for a phone number.

She wrote down the message, folded it neatly and placed it in her pocket before rejoining Louise. "That was a call for Mr. Kirchwey. I think he's still upstairs. Or he could have forgotten to take down his DND sign."

"Ask Jane if she saw him," was Louise's advice. "She was the first one up this morning."

"I will when she gets back. Jane's gone over to the farmer's market," she told her older sister. "She said she'd be an hour or so."

Louise smiled. "Knowing how Jane is around fresh produce, I would not expect her until lunchtime."

"Did you read the note she taped on the phone?"

"Yes, and I ignored it. As should you." She nodded toward the reception desk. "I did put that old sketchbook over there by the blotter, in case she wants it."

"I don't want to discourage Jane, but these ideas of hers . . ." Alice glanced back at the phone. "Of course I *like* saying it's a beautiful day, but I'd rather not have to do it over and over."

"It is like saying 'Have a nice day.' After a dozen times, you start losing the sincerity and end up sounding like a machine," Louise said. "But you know how Jane is once she gets a notion in her head."

Alice wrinkled her nose. "It's easier to pry lollipops away from small children."

Louise touched her arm. "I wouldn't worry about how you answer the phone. If you feel like saying something peppy, go ahead, but there's no need to force yourself. There are more important things to do."

"Like tracking down who made that sketchbook . . . and that won't be easy." Alice thought for a moment. "We could show it to some of the older members of the congregation, perhaps. There are a lot of portraits in it. Someone might recognize a relative and remember who drew him or her."

"That's a fine idea," Louise agreed. "We can take it with us to church tomorrow."

As the men neared the bottom of the stairs, sunlight from the front windows made the oak and brass of the desk glow, something Alice had not noticed in the shadowy confines of the attic. "I forgot how beautiful this old desk was."

"I almost hate to donate it for the exhibition, but it's far too small to be of any practical use. I couldn't even fit one ledger and my calculator on top of it." Louise stepped aside as the men carefully lowered the desk to the floor. "We do appreciate you coming over to move this for us, Fred. Thank you again."

"My pleasure, Louise." After he instructed the other man to pull the truck up closer to the front door, Fred crouched to examine the front of the desk. "Fine piece. You don't see this kind of scribe detailing anymore."

"Didn't Mother say she had inherited it?" Alice asked Louise, who nodded.

He pulled down the drop-front panel, which served as the writing surface, and pointed to the little doors and recessed letter holders. "See how the edges and the apron match the outside? That's all hand-carved work." There was a note of approval in his voice; as a man who worked with his hands, Fred appreciated quality craftsmanship.

"Let me get some twine so we can tie down the quilt." Louise set the old quilt on the reception desk before going behind it.

"You know a lot about furniture, Fred," Alice said. "How old do you think this desk is?"

"I'd say turn of the century, but likely Rachel Holzmann down at Acorn Antiques can give you an exact date on it." He tapped one of the small center cupboard doors. "I noticed upstairs that this one appears to be stuck shut."

"I know. My mother was never able to get that door open." Alice peered at it. "It looks like the hinges might be rusted. Just like the lock on that trunk we dropped."

"Metal's the culprit there, Alice. They used untreated brass and tin for fittings and hardware in the old days. Over time they get stiff, just like old folks' joints." He stood and ran an admiring hand over the smooth writing surface on the interior of the drop-front panel. "Sure is pretty, though. Once I get it to town, I can put a little oil on these hinges. See if I can coax that door to open. You don't want to ever remove the original hardware if you can help it."

Alice nodded. She had heard too many horror stories of

people ruining an antique piece by changing the original, and almost always irreplaceable, hardware. Things like refinishing original wood or adding wiring for electrical fixtures, she knew, also destroyed the value of antique furnishings.

Louise returned with the twine, and with Alice and Fred's help swaddled the desk with the quilt and tied it in place.

"Will you need this quilt back, Louise?" Fred asked as he finished knotting the final loop of twine. His helper had returned and stood waiting to help load the desk onto the truck waiting outside. "I can run it back out here once we've got the desk at Town Hall."

"No need for that, Fred. You can throw it away when you are through with it." Louise held the front door open for the men as they carried out the desk. When she turned, she reminded Alice of the earlier phone call.

Alice took the message out of her pocket. "I'd better go upstairs and slip it under Basil's door."

Gwen Murphy came out of the dining room in time to hear Alice's last remark and paused by the desk. "Save yourself the trouble: That Basil fellow isn't here," she told them. "I got up early to do a little sketching in the garden—around six, I think—and I saw him leaving."

Louise seemed miffed by Gwen's comments.

"That's strange." Alice glanced at the message. Obviously he had not been expecting the call from Mr. Johnson, or maybe he had forgotten about it. Of course, Basil did seem a little absent-minded. That would also explain why he hadn't removed the DND sign from his door. "Did he happen to mention where he was going?"

The younger woman shook her head. "I did see him from the garden, though. It looked to me like he was walking into town." She noticed the old sketchbook on the desk. "I see I'm not the only artist in residence." She opened the cover and started paging through it. "Very pretty work. Is it yours?"

Alice went over as Gwen examined the book and recounted the story of how they had found it. "We'd like to know how old it is, so we can accurately date it for the display. Jane guessed it might date back to the end of the 1800s."

Gwen nodded. "Well, I do have some background in art history, and I think it might even be a little older. Also, whoever owned this was quite serious about his work. See this imprint here?" She showed them a faint mark on the inside of the back cover. "Edward Dechaux sold art supplies by trade catalog back in the nineteenth century. His prices could be steep, so anyone ordering from him would most likely be truly dedicated to his work."

"Could it have belonged to a professional artist?" Alice asked.

"Maybe." She tilted her head as she regarded one sketch. "The lines are strong and defined, no hesitancy at all. Also, the artist made contour sketches first, then improved them later."

"What does that mean?" Louise asked.

Alice was startled by her older sister's tone, which was somewhat abrupt.

Gwen lifted her chin. "It *means* whoever drew this was likely doing it from life. The artist stood in front of the subject and looked at it while drawing it."

The tension that seemed to spring up out of nowhere between the two women bewildered Alice. "Do you think it may be valuable, Gwen?" she asked, hoping to distract her.

"You'd have to have it appraised by an art historian, but I think it could be. If it's as old as we've discussed, it's in fantastic condition. The charcoal looks as fresh as if it had been applied yesterday." She flipped through a few more pages. "No evidence of foxing, either."

"What, exactly, is *foxing*?" Louise asked, her voice still hovering just above arctic.

"Yellow and red spots, caused by a kind of mold that

grows on old paper under normal humidity." She glanced at Alice. "You said someone had this wrapped in a quilt? That's probably what preserved it so well. It's a shame there are only a few names written in to use for authenticating the age."

"Maybe someone will recognize the subjects." Alice smiled at the artist. "Thank you for the advice."

"No trouble at all." She shot an odd, brief glance at Louise. "I only wish I could tell you more about it. You know, you might show this to Basil Kirchwey. I heard him talking to Lester the other night, and he seems like he knows a lot about old books."

"We were thinking he might be a writer," Alice said. "Did he mention to you anything about working for a magazine?"

"No." The artist appeared amused. "He hasn't said three words to me. Besides, he doesn't seem like the writer type. And now I'd better get back to work or my still life will grow mold on it." She smiled at her before she continued upstairs to her room.

Chapter Seven

A lice regarded her sister. "Am I imagining things, or did the temperature of the room drop twenty degrees while Gwen was standing here?"

"I don't know what you mean."

"I mean that icebergs are warmer and more cuddly than you were just now," she said.

Louise walked over and closed the sketchbook. "That young woman could use some better manners."

Alice could not understand why Louise had such a cool reaction to the artist. Granted, her older sister was somewhat more reserved with people than she or Jane was, but this was remarkable even for Louise. "She seems quite pleasant."

"Pleasant women do not eavesdrop on other people's conversations, even if they are just about a phone call." Her older sister's temper began to show. "And you saw how she grabbed the sketchbook and started rifling through it, as if it were hers."

Alice blinked. "No, I saw her handle it pretty carefully. That was right before she tried to help us by giving us all that art information."

Louise ran a restless hand through her short silver hair. "You think I'm being unreasonable."

"I think you should remember that she's a guest," Alice reproved, as gently as she could.

"You're right, of course." She sighed.

Alice decided to change the subject to something that perplexed her even more than Louise and Gwen's mutual dislike. "Why do you think Mr. Kirchwey keeps leaving so early? Nothing is open. Even the Coffee Shop doesn't start serving breakfast until seven."

"I have no idea." Louise turned as the front door opened and their aunt came in. "Here is another early riser. Good morning, Aunt Ethel."

"Morning, girls." Ethel was dressed in a cheerful red and white checked gingham dress with a full skirt. She also sported a jaunty new red hat with a large white sisal bow tied around the crown. "I just saw Fred driving back toward town. What was that lumpy thing in the back of his pickup truck?"

"Mother's writing desk," Alice told her. "Fred is going to take it to Town Hall for us."

"Good, you girls don't need to be lugging around furniture." Ethel had definite ideas on what women should and should not do, and heavy lifting belonged in the second category. "I was wondering if I could borrow your hedge trimmer for the day. I want to spruce up the shrubs around the carriage house, and since Lloyd is coming over for lunch I thought I'd put him to work."

"Jane won't be using it," Louise said. "She will be at the market all morning, and then I believe she plans to work in town this afternoon." She studied Ethel's appearance. "Do you intend to garden dressed like that?"

"Goodness no." Their aunt laughed. "The Seniors Social Circle had a meeting this morning. I have to change as soon as I get back home."

"Let me get the keys to the storage shed." Alice went around the desk, and as she did she spotted the sketchbook Louise had put aside. "Aunt Ethel, would you mind looking at something? We found this yesterday when we were working in the attic." She set the sketchbook on top of the reception desk.

Curious, Ethel opened the book and looked through the pages. "Oh my. No, this isn't Madeleine's. It's too old, and she couldn't draw like this."

"Was there anyone you know of in our family who could?" Louise asked.

Ethel's brow furrowed for a moment before she shook her head. "I don't think so. You know your father loved this sort of thing. I think he would have put this out for everyone to see if he had known about it. Where did you find it?"

"It was in an old trunk filled with books and linens— not mother's, either. Maybe our grandmother's or great- grandmother's." Alice glanced up as Lester Langston came downstairs. "Good morning, Mr. Langston."

"Good morning, ladies." Handsomely dressed and carry- ing a briefcase along with his cane, he stopped to give Ethel an admiring glance. "Why, you look as if you just came from a garden party."

"Hello, Lester." Ethel smiled at him. "No party today, I'm afraid. Just a lot of older folks complaining about their arthritis."

The front door opened as Mayor Tynan came in. "Morning, everyone. Alice, if Jane will come by Town Hall this afternoon at three, I can show her where to set up the dis- play," Lloyd said. "Tell her that I've also checked my budget, and the town can cover the cost of the Acorn Hill directory."

Alice beamed. "That's wonderful, Mayor, thank you."

"Is Jane going to do this by herself, or are you or Louise going with her?" Ethel asked. "I can lend a hand after Lloyd and I finish up."

"Fred is working with her," Alice said. "I'm sure she'll let us know when she needs extra hands."

"What sort of display are you putting together?" Lester asked.

Alice briefly explained the Visitors Center project and

how they were hoping to combine merchant advertising with historical information about Acorn Hill, and then added, "It's our first time doing something like this, so there will likely be a lot of trial and error."

Lloyd rubbed his fingers back and forth across his forehead. "Not too much, I hope."

"One of my clients in Charleston did something similar with his chamber of commerce," Lester told her. "During the height of the tourist season, they held an exposition and called it 'Our Town.' They allowed merchants to set up booths outside their businesses, hand out samples and flyers, and hold special events. I was there that week and it was very pleasant. Rather like attending a little fair."

"I doubt we could do anything on that scale, but it is good to know," Louise said. "Perhaps we could schedule some kind of similar event on a smaller scale."

"That's not necessary. We hold all the special events during our Summer Festival each year," Lloyd said. Alice glanced at him and was astonished to see the mayor practically glowering at Lester. "There's no reason for us to turn this into some kind of circus."

"Now, Lloyd, that's not what Lester means." Ethel also gave him a puzzled look.

"No, I only thought I'd pass along what I've seen work," the lawyer said. His eyes twinkled at Ethel. "Of course, there's really only one difference between a lawyer and a clown. The clown doesn't charge by the hour."

Ethel laughed merrily, but the mayor's face reddened, and he looked almost offended.

Alice stepped between the two men and handed the keys she held to the mayor. "A trimmer Aunt Ethel wanted to borrow is in the garden storage shed, Lloyd. Would you mind getting it for her?"

Lloyd nodded and shot an unhappy glance at Ethel before heading toward the side door to the garden.

Lester checked his watch. "I'd better go, too. Have a wonderful day, ladies."

"Now what put that bee in Lloyd's bonnet?" her aunt wanted to know as soon as the men had departed.

Alice felt uneasy. There was something very wrong with the way the mayor had reacted to Lester's suggestion, almost as if he was angry with him. *Maybe they're like Louise and Gwen Murphy. Mutual dislike at first sight.* "I think he only wants to make sure this project doesn't get out of control."

"He could have a tension headache," was Louise's guess. "You saw the way he was rubbing his head. Lord knows whenever I have one I feel like snapping everyone's head off."

"I suppose." Disapproval made Ethel's mouth crimp. "Still, he could have been nicer to Lester. I've never heard Lloyd speak so rudely to someone."

Neither had Alice, so she had no insight to offer. "Perhaps you should leave the garden work for another day, Aunt Ethel."

"I don't like putting off chores, but . . . oh, I know what it is. Lloyd's been talking about losing a few pounds. I bet he skipped breakfast again." Ethel smiled with relief. "I'll fix him a special lunch—that should unruffle his feathers." She went off in the direction of the garden.

"Another problem solved just in time." Alice leaned back against the desk. "I think I need some pepping up now."

The phone rang, and Louise picked up the receiver. "Grace Chapel Inn, Louise Smith speaking," she said, and gave Alice a little wink before she added, "How may I help you on this lovely day?"

∞

After her visit to the farmer's market, Jane could have happily spent the entire day in the kitchen. She had splurged on tomatoes, fresh sweet corn on the cob, the first of the ripe fall pumpkins and new, red baby potatoes, all of which she had unloaded onto the counter and now examined with a keen sense of anticipation.

"I'm going to make you into spiced pumpkin bread," she told the pumpkins, "and you little guys into hot German potato salad"—she rolled one of the potatoes into the others— "and you into corn chowder, if I can keep Louise away from it" —she patted the neat stack of green-husked ears—"but you, you wonderful gorgeous things"—she ran her fingers over the red satiny curves of the tomatoes—"are destined for greatness."

"Jane?" Alice came into the kitchen. "I thought I heard you." Her gaze went to the bounty on the counter. "Wow! Was there a sale on tomatoes?"

"I made a killer deal. Aren't they great?" She would have hugged the pile, but she did not want to squish them. "Do you know what I'm going to make with these?"

Alice tugged at her bottom lip with the edge of her teeth. "Um, lots of BLTs and tomato soup?"

"Ah, my poor, deprived big sister, you have to expand your culinary horizons. These beauties aren't only fated to be sandwiched and creamed. They'll be stewed and stuffed, baked and crushed, pureed and juiced. They'll go into relishes and sauces and soups that you've only dreamed of."

"Good thing we all like tomatoes."

"Like them? By the time I'm through, you'll be deeply, passionately in love with them." She began washing the vegetables and bagging them for storage.

Alice came to help her and filled a storage bag with just-washed tomatoes. "So what's first on the menu?"

"*Hmm.*" Jane had to think about it. "I've never made my toe-curling, knock-your-socks-off spinach penne with marinara sauce for you and Louise, have I?"

"Since my toes are uncurled and my socks are still on, I'll have to say no."

"Well, it just so happens that this"—she waggled a tomato—"is the main ingredient for the sauce. The man who sold them to me picked them from his vines this very morning.

Smell." She held it up to Alice's nose. "Now imagine a pot of these simmering gently with garlic and onion and spices, until the aroma wraps around you like a warm blanket, and your mouth starts to water—"

"Stop, you're making me hungry."

"Hey, I'm allowed to, I'm the cook." With Alice's help, Jane finished wrapping up the vegetables and stowed them in the refrigerator crisper. "You'll have to go with me next time. It's such a great time of year to be at the market. There was this little old lady selling pumpkins out of the back of her grandson's pickup truck. She told me how they used to parch ears of corn by hanging them up by the husks in a drying shed, and then—"

"Wait!" Alice held up her hands. "You can tell me all about it on the way to church."

"We're going to church? On a Saturday?"

"Pastor Thompson called. He has something he thought we might like to borrow for our Visitors Center project, and Lloyd wanted to meet us at Town Hall to show us the space we can use." Alice retrieved her purse from where she kept it under the counter. "Fred took Mother's desk to town this morning, and he's also setting up his model. Craig, Sylvia and June probably have their contributions ready too."

"Gotcha." Jane took her straw-brimmed hat down from the wall hook. "Only promise me one thing, Alice."

"What's that?"

"You'll keep Louise away from my corn," she said, alluding to a memorable and utterly bland batch of corn chowder that their eldest sister had taken pride in making.

"Only if you start making that marinara sauce tonight."

∽

The afternoon was cool and clear as Alice and Jane walked over to Grace Chapel.

"The leaves will be starting to turn soon," Alice predicted, seeing a few scattered spots of yellow among the elm and oak trees near the church. "We'll have to get the heavy sweaters and coats out of storage."

"I have to get the gardens ready for cooler weather, too." Jane's brow wrinkled. "I hope we don't have an early frost. I'd really like a little Indian summer this year."

"One summer wasn't enough for you?" Alice teased.

"Nope, I'm greedy." She lifted her face to the sun and closed her eyes briefly. "There's no such thing as too much sunshine."

The sisters found Rev. Thompson working inside the little church. Since taking the position as the new head pastor, Kenneth had revitalized and inspired the community by renewing various ministries and missions. Like Daniel Howard, he also provided the congregation with the strength and comfort of steady spiritual guidance.

Alice had had some initial reservations about the new head pastor, whose natural reserve and quiet ways had contrasted sharply with her father's congenial warmth. Like everyone else, she had since discovered that he was a gifted, dedicated minister and a truly good man. "Good afternoon, Pastor."

"Hello Alice, Jane." Rev. Thompson, who had been plying a sanding block along the edge of a wooden pew, dusted off his hands. "It's nice to see you."

Alice noticed other sanded areas along the back of the pew, then glanced at the front and found that the entire length had been sanded down. "My goodness, Pastor, did you do all this work today?"

"No, but I have been trying to get a little done each weekend." He nodded toward the opposite pew, which gleamed with a beautiful new polish. "The wood is old but very sturdy, and only needs to be restored. It saves us the expense of replacements, and I enjoy the work."

"I bet these didn't look this good when they were brand-new." Jane went over to admire the finished pew. "I think you could moonlight in furniture restoration, Kenneth."

Fred had mentioned replacing some of the old pews at the last church board meeting, Alice recalled. "It's very good of you to do the work yourself, Pastor."

He smiled. "Wood is like people: It just needs a little extra attention now and then."

"We heard that you have something to lend us for our Visitors Center," Jane said as she rejoined them. "Is it animal, vegetable or mineral?"

He chuckled. "I believe it qualifies as vegetable."

"Good, because minerals are heavy and animals are hard to sneak past Mayor Tynan."

"It's in our book closet."

Rev. Thompson led them to a storage closet where books had been kept for years. The sisters were surprised to see the tidy appearance of the church's book collection, which was usually in a state of semi-disarray. Before Alice could comment, the pastor provided the explanation.

"I found these while I was rearranging our little library here." He took down a neat stack of slim, green, cloth-bound books and set them on a table. "They were pushed behind some reference books and so dusty I imagine that they sat back there unnoticed for years."

Alice picked up the top book, and smiled at the embossed gilt cover, which showed a young girl in an old-fashioned frock sitting under an old oak tree. "*The Little Shepherdess and the Lop-Eared Puppy* by M. E. Roberts," she read from the printing on the spine.

"I loved to read the Little Shepherdess books when I was a kid," Jane said. "There's a scene in that one when this mean old man tells her that her puppy fell down his well and drowned. She goes back later and finds the puppy in the bucket, though, and pulls him out to safety. It made me cry my eyes out."

"There are eleven more of them, all by the same author." The pastor rested his hand on the stack. "I believe they were a gift to the church."

"Why is that?" Alice asked.

"They're first editions, and they're all signed." He showed her the title page of the book she held, where "Yours in Christ, M. E. Roberts" was written in an elegant hand.

Jane appraised the stack. "Who would give away an entire set of autographed M. E. Roberts first editions?" she asked. "And how can I become his or her best friend?"

"I wish I could tell you who donated them, Jane," he told her, "but they don't appear in any of our records. I do think it's better to have them on display as opposed to locking them up in a cabinet, which is really all I can do with them."

"Sure, but we don't want to set these out where anyone can just pick them up and walk off with them, either," Jane said. "We'll probably have some other valuable pieces, too."

Alice hadn't considered that. "Fred might have locking cases we can use for the more valuable donations. Pastor, would you mind holding the books until we can make the proper arrangements for them?"

Rev. Thompson nodded. "I'll keep them in my office at the rectory until you're ready for them."

"We found an old sketchbook up in our attic, and we don't know who that belongs to. It's our week for mysterious books." Jane glanced at Alice, who was grimacing. "And for my sister to make strange faces, apparently. What's the matter, Alice?"

She made a frustrated gesture. "I meant to bring that sketchbook with us, so we could show it to some people while we were in town."

"We could walk back home and get it," Jane suggested.

Alice replaced the book on the stack. "No, I don't want to keep the mayor waiting, and Louise has a new student coming at three. We'll bring it next time."

Chapter ☙ Eight

Since the phone was quiet and all of the guests appeared to be out for the day, Louise headed to the parlor to prepare for her afternoon student. Today would be this child's first lesson, and she wanted to have everything ready. Preparing ahead gave her the time she needed to concentrate on making her student feel at ease with her and with the piano.

Louise enjoyed new students because, having no experience and therefore no self-doubt, they were easy to influence in a positive manner. The youngest often went at playing the same way they did everything else—with boundless energy—and nothing but sheer exhaustion seemed to dim their enthusiasm.

Some of her enthusiasm evaporated when she walked into the parlor and discovered Gwen Murphy curled up on the window seat. The artist was reading a paperback novel and had her bare feet propped against the wall. The sight of her red-painted toenails made Louise's spine straighten. "Hello, Ms. Murphy."

The younger woman glanced up briefly. "Hi."

Louise checked her watch. She still had two hours before her student arrived. Perhaps by then Gwen would have left the parlor. She went to the piano, stepping over Gwen's discarded shoes on the way, and took her teaching folder out of the storage compartment inside the bench seat.

"You're not going to play now, are you?" The artist asked in her blunt way, nodding toward the piano. "I can't read with a lot of noise."

Noise? Louise's music had been called many things, but never that. "No, I'm not," she said, gritting her teeth slightly, "but I should tell you that I will be giving a music lesson to a new student at three. Sometimes the first lessons can be rather . . . loud." *There, that should get rid of her.*

The brunette's dark eyebrows arched. "You mean the kid is going to bang on the keys?"

"Yes."

"Then why didn't you just say so, Teach? That's fine." Gwen went back to reading.

Thank you so much for giving me your permission, Louise thought. Although she usually got along well with their guests, there was something about the young woman's manner that grated on her nerves. It was almost as if Gwen said things deliberately to provoke someone. Like calling her "Teach." The word alone was impertinent enough, but the way she said it was truly insulting.

Still, Louise knew she couldn't expect all their guests to be easygoing and charming like Lester Langston, or practically nonexistent, like Basil Kirchwey. She also had a professional obligation to treat Gwen just as she treated every other guest at the inn.

It would be easier if she would try to be a little more pleasant now and then. As she took out the whole-note chart and finger-exercise sheet for her student, she noticed Gwen was paying more attention to her than to her novel. "I can do this later if I am disturbing you."

"No, now you've got me curious about how you go about teaching little kids to play that monster." Gwen set aside her book.

"It is a rather large instrument, but I wouldn't call it a monster." Louise remembered her first lesson and how the rows of ivory and black keys had appeared endless under her small hands. Yet the music that her teacher had created with those keys had fascinated her so much that she swiftly forgot her fears and immersed herself in learning. "I begin by teaching them how to read notes and music while we work on whole- and half-note scales."

"Seems like a lot to expect from a kid." Gwen sounded skeptical.

"Children often do very well learning to play music at a young age." She placed the sheet music on the lid stand. "They are more open to the experience."

"Not all of them." The artist gave the piano a clear look of dislike.

Jane had done the same thing after their tutor despaired of ever getting her to learn her scales. What no one realized at the time was that Jane was tone-deaf. *Gwen must have had lessons when she was young. Likely she drove her music tutor mad.* "I find that it is best to keep things as simple and enjoyable as possible. If a child feels doubtful about music or about his or her ability to play, I focus more on making the lessons fun."

"I had lessons, but my piano teacher never made them fun," Gwen said, confirming Louise's suspicions. "She used to shout at me and poke at my wrists with a pointer whenever I hit the wrong keys."

"I am so sorry to hear that. That was very wrong of her." Louise felt her antipathy toward the artist fade into sympathy. "Were your parents aware of this?"

"No. She always put on a nice act whenever they were in the room, then the minute they left me alone with her, she'd start snapping and poking me. I tried to tell my mother, but she thought I was exaggerating." Gwen shrugged and picked up her book. "It doesn't matter. It was a long time ago."

Jane had shown the same indifference after the tutor gave up trying to teach her; however, Louise had sensed the hurt she was hiding behind it and had tried teaching Jane herself.

In fact, her youngest sister had been her first—and most difficult—student.

"'Be completely humble and gentle,'" her father had quoted from Ephesians 4:2 (NIV) when Louise had complained about Jane's lack of musical ability and mutinous attitude. "'Be patient, bearing with one another in love.' I know you can reach her, Louise. Don't give up."

She had persisted, and in time Jane actually learned to play a song on the piano. Her little sister had been so proud of her accomplishment that she played the song over and over for anyone who would listen.

Maybe I should apply the same philosophy in dealing with Gwen Murphy, Louise thought. "Creative people need sensitive teachers, I think. I wish you could meet some of my more advanced students. They are such imaginative musicians, and they are progressing so well."

"Mrs. Smith?" A lanky, fair-haired girl appeared in the parlor doorway.

"Here is one of mine now. Hello, Sissy. Come in." Louise smiled at her most promising student. She introduced her to Gwen, and then asked, "What brings you here today? We don't have a lesson scheduled."

"No, ma'am. We were out shopping, and I asked my mom to stop by so I could tell you something." She glanced at the piano, then laced her hands together and looked at the floor. "It's about the school recital."

Louise had arranged for Sissy and two of her other students to play in a recital during Open House Week at their school. "Did you change your mind about what you would like to play?"

"No, ma'am." She looked over her shoulder as her brother Charles called her name from the front of the inn. "Sorry, my mom has groceries in the car."

The girl's distressed expression concerned her. "What is it, dear?"

"It's just that I can't play in the recital." Sissy's cheeks flushed. "Charles had a bad cold and I think he gave it to me. I've been feeling really sick. I told my teacher at school, and she said she'd call you."

"The recital is still a few weeks away. I am sure that you will feel better by then."

"No. I'll be too sick to practice." Charles called Sissy's name again, louder this time. Tears shimmered in the girl's eyes, and her voice shook as she said, "I'm sorry, I have to go. Please pick someone else for the recital, Mrs. Smith." With that she hurried out of the room.

"That's your *best* student?" Gwen Murphy picked up her book, slipped on her shoes, and sauntered out of the room. Just before she left she added, "Maybe you should think again about exactly how you're teaching her."

∞

Mayor Tynan was waiting for Alice and Jane when they arrived at Town Hall. So was Fred Humbert, who was working with his helper to build a stand for his town model.

"I'm going to give you this front space in the lobby here," Lloyd told them as they walked over to where Fred was working.

"You mean we don't get to take over your office?" Jane folded her arms. "I was hoping to call meetings and stamp things and whirl around a few times in that big leather swivel chair of yours."

"Not unless you want to take over doing my budget reports, too." The mayor gestured to the area he had reserved for them. "You should have enough room for everything, and my receptionist will be close by"—he pointed to her desk, which was only a few feet away—"in case anyone needs help."

"That will be handy, although if we have a lot of traffic we might take turns manning the display," Alice said.

"I also found this." He picked up a large white sign with "INFORMATION" professionally printed in red. "We always put this in the front window during Summer Festival, but I think we should keep it there permanently now."

Alice nodded. "We can identify Town Hall for visitors by telling them to look for the INFORMATION sign."

"It's terrific." Jane paced around where the two men were working and examined the wall. "Will it be all right to hang some pictures at the back here? Craig mentioned he had some."

"You can hang whatever you like, as long as it's framed," Lloyd said. "I don't like the idea of tacking up any posters. The last thing we need is some cheap circus atmosphere. Town Hall represents Acorn Hill, and I won't have it made to look ridiculous."

"We'll keep it very dignified, Mayor." Alice noticed the edge in his voice as he made his last comment, and she recalled what Lester Langston had suggested. Evidently the mayor had disliked Lester more than she realized. *But why? Lester is such a nice man, and I love the way he always jokes about being a lawyer. Maybe Lloyd doesn't like his jokes.*

"Oh, Lloyd, you know that you can trust us," Jane said.

Alice spotted her mother's desk, which Fred had moved safely to one side, but the quilt they had wrapped around it was gone. "Did someone throw out that old quilt?" She thought she would show it to Jane before it was discarded.

Lloyd gazed around. "I haven't seen it myself." He raised his voice to be heard over the pounding of the hammers. "Fred, did you put that old brown quilt somewhere?"

Fred came over and joined them. "Vera took it when she dropped by. She acted like she'd found a mink coat."

"More like a gorilla coat, but that's all right," Alice quickly assured him. "I was only going to show Jane how heavy it was."

"Ms. Songer stopped in earlier and said she has her display ready over at her shop," Fred told them. "I think Mr. Tracy and Ms. Carter may too."

Jane checked the wall clock. "We still have plenty of time, Alice, let's go and see Sylvia."

∞

The sisters walked over to Sylvia's Buttons, and Jane paused to look in the front window, where the seamstress had draped lengths of summer-weight fabric in an arrangement that resembled a cascading rainbow. A glittery assortment of gold and yellow buttons spilled out from a tarnished old urn, which was being guarded by a whimsical stuffed leprechaun.

"Look at this, Alice." Jane pressed her nose against the glass. "Doesn't it make you feel like putting on a pinafore and grabbing a little terrier and singing 'Over the Rainbow'?" She started to sing the opening lines, as always, off-key.

"Oh no!" Alice took her arm and guided her to the front door of the shop. "You are not in Kansas anymore, Dorothy."

"Are you just saying that to keep me from singing?" Jane asked, doing her best to look hurt.

Her older sister patted her shoulder. "Sweetheart, I will *pay* you to keep you from singing."

Inside the shop the smell of sizing and new fabric blended with the sounds of a busy sewing machine in the back. "I'll be with you in a moment," the seamstress called out.

A few moments later, Sylvia came out of the back holding an unfolded paper pattern and a folded length of knit jersey. "Alice, Jane, I was hoping you'd stop by. Wait until you see what I've done."

She set the fabric and pattern on her wide cutting table and led them over to a corner, where a dressmaker's form stood covered with a white sheet.

"It came out so well I almost don't want to part with it," she confided.

Jane grinned. "We'll twist your arm and make threats, if necessary."

"You may have to." Sylvia removed the sheet.

An antique calico dress with long sleeves and a full skirt hung on the dressmaker's form. The dark blue floral print of fabric looked crisp and dainty against the contrasting, heavy, black wire of the form. One sleeve had been folded across the bodice and pinned in place to show off the narrow row of white lace bordering the cuff.

"Wow," Jane said. "I feel like putting that on and buying me a little house on the prairie."

"Whoever made it may very well have been a contemporary of Laura Ingalls Wilder," Sylvia told her. "The dress is at least a hundred years old and was completely sewn by hand. The lace was tatted with a hand-held shuttle, and the button holes were whip-stitched by hand." As Alice and Jane admired the dress, Sylvia added, "One of the women in town gave me the form, which belonged to her grandmother. She told me she didn't sew, so she had no use for it." Sylvia made that sound like a small crime.

"This looks like something a farmer's wife might wear to church," Alice said, gently touching the sleeve. "Where on earth did you find it, Sylvia?"

"Believe it or not, at a rummage sale. I don't think it was worn much: The fabric looks like new, but the pattern of the calico is quite old."

"It might have been the woman's best dress for special occasions," Jane said, "like weddings and such."

"That was my thought, too. Originally I bought it so I could take it apart and copy the pattern. Once I got it home and saw the fine quality of the stitching and how well preserved it was, I didn't have the heart to start ripping open the seams." She removed a small typed card from a side pocket in the dress. "I put a few notes about the history of dressmaking on this, which I'll tie to the top of the form, above the collar."

"What about your business flyers?"

"I have them right over here." Sylvia went over to her counter and brought back a neat stack of colorful folded brochures, which she slipped into the end of the pinned sleeve. "How does that look?"

"Great." Jane glanced over her shoulder as the shop's door opened, and Craig Tracy came in. "Hey, Craig."

"Ladies." He smiled at them. "Lloyd told me you were over here with Sylvia, and I thought I'd borrow you to have a look at my display." He glanced at the dressmaker's form. "Is that yours?"

Sylvia nodded. "What do you think?"

The florist's brow wrinkled for a moment. "It's a lovely display, Sylvia. Much more appealing than mine."

"Surely not," the seamstress said. "You've got such a flair with plants, Craig."

He swept an arm toward the door. "If you would step over to my shop for a minute, you ladies can decide that for yourselves."

Sylvia decided to go with them, and the three women followed Craig back to his florist shop, Wild Things. Just as fabrics, clothing and sewing notions crowded Sylvia's Buttons, so plants and flowers dominated the interior of Craig's business. He led them through the labyrinth of houseplants, flower arrangements and decorative gardenware to his workroom in the back.

"This is my humble offering," he said, gesturing toward a three-tiered, white wicker planter, which was fashioned to look like a narrow bookcase with open airy sides. He had placed framed photos at the very back of each shelf, which also contained a number of different gardening items ingeniously displayed: a tin watering can stuffed with seed packs; a rack of small, colorful flowers; and a basket with small bunches of dried herbs tied with ribbon. The items were coordinated with the subjects in the photographs.

"Are you planning to charge people for the things on the shelves?" Alice asked, faintly troubled.

"No, nothing is for sale, but my seed packs will be offered as free samples. I thought putting some out might entice people to come and see the shop," Craig explained. "They double as my advertising." He took down a seed pack and showed them the back, which had a floral sticker printed with the shop's name, address, phone number and hours of business.

"What a great idea, Craig." Jane crouched down to take a bunch of herbs from the basket and sniffed them. "Cilantro and rosemary. I'm in heaven."

"Take one." He winked at her. "Consider it a bribe for a good spot."

"Advertising on free samples. What a clever approach," Sylvia said, but her expression had changed and she seemed a little distracted. "Well, I should get back to my place. I've got a wedding in three weeks and tons of sewing to do. Alice, I have one or two more things to do to finish my display, so I'll call you when it's ready. Bye Jane, Craig." With that she hurried out of the shop.

"I thought she told Fred that her display was ready." Jane frowned. "It looked ready to me, too."

"Apparently not." Alice gave the florist a big smile. "Thanks for doing this, Craig. It will be a lovely addition."

Chapter ⚘ Nine

The sisters left Wild Things and decided that they had enough time to stop in to see June Carter at the Coffee Shop before heading back to the inn.

"I love the smell of fresh-baked pie," Jane said as they entered the cozy shop. She sniffed the air.

June came out from behind the counter to greet them. "Do you want a booth, ladies?"

"No, we're just stopping in to see if you've got something for our Visitors Center." Jane nodded in the direction of Town Hall. "We're starting to set up."

"It's right back here in the kitchen." The diner's owner held up the counter's drop leaf and took them back to where her waitress and cook were working. "Those pies should be ready to come out in another five minutes, Hope," she told the waitress.

"If I stay here long, I'm going to ruin my dinner," Jane confided to her sister in a stage whisper.

"Absolutely not," Alice whispered back, just as loud. "I want that spinach pasta and marinara sauce you promised."

Hope finished loading the dishwasher and wiped her hands on a towel. "What's this about pasta? Are you making Italian tonight, Jane?"

"Not just Italian," Jane said, shaking her finger. "My special recipe spinach penne with marinara sauce."

"That sounds *wonderful.*" Hope looked at her employer. "Could we add some pasta dishes to the menu?"

"We could, but the customers will never get any—or any service—because you and I would be back here gobbling it up." June gave Jane a stern look. "You, stop tempting my staff and wrecking my diet."

Jane put on an innocent look.

"You're incorrigible." The store's owner chuckled as she opened a cabinet. "I've had this ever since I bought the Coffee Shop. The previous owner originally used Hall pottery when this place first opened. Hall made some of the first colored restaurantware ever produced. Of course, over the years a lot of it got broken and chipped, and he replaced it with cheaper dishes. This is all that's left of it now." She took down a single-serving, lemon-yellow teapot and matching cup and saucer. "There's a bit of crackling, and the saucer's been broken and glued back together, so it's not worth much."

"Still, it's a piece of our history." Alice decided that she liked its sturdy, serviceable lines.

"Hope helped me make these." June smiled at her waitress as she took down a handful of kettle-shaped coupons that offered discounts on beverages and various meals.

"Great idea. Your luncheon specials are always terrific." Jane gave the blackberry pies that Hope was taking out of the oven a look of regret. "As are your desserts."

"By the way, Vera Humbert was in earlier and mentioned that she needed to speak with you girls," June said. "She said she'd try to catch you after church on Sunday."

Jane checked her watch. "Actually, we have just enough time to run over and see her now."

"She's not home," June said. "She told me that she had a quilters guild meeting over in Potterston this afternoon." She shook her head. "Though what she thinks she and her group can do with that moth-eaten old quilt, I'll never know."

"Quilt?" Alice echoed.

"Yes, a big, ugly, brown wool thing. Smelled like it hadn't

been washed since Truman was in office." June shook her head. "When she lugged it over here, I thought she might want me to put it in our Dumpster. But when I asked her if I could throw it out for her, she looked as if she might faint."

As they were short on time, the two sisters hurried June's donation over to Town Hall and then walked back to the inn.

"Vera must have had a good reason to take that quilt," Louise said after Alice and Jane had related what June had told them. "She does collect and make quilts. Maybe she needed it for some reason."

"That's what I'd like to know," Alice said. "What on earth could she do with it?"

"She could have some pet moths she wants to feed." There was the sound of a timer buzzing from the kitchen, and Jane smiled. "Time to make some sauce."

Alice stayed at the desk and went over the day's paperwork with Louise until a new piano student arrived a few minutes later. The little girl was six years old and had gorgeous black curls and brown eyes.

"I'm a bunny rabbit today," Alice heard her tell Louise after introductions were made. She went down on all fours and began hopping around her mother's feet. "See?"

Alice squelched a laugh.

"Yes, I do." Her older sister's smile seemed slightly strained. "But today do you think could you be a little girl?"

"No," the child said cheerfully, and hopped away toward the parlor.

"Yesterday she was a dog, and the day before that she was a giraffe," Alice heard her obviously tired mother confide to Louise as they followed the child. "I'm hoping that she'll eventually turn back into a little girl."

∽

While she was straightening up the desk, Alice noticed two more messages written in her older sister's neat handwriting. Both were for Basil Kirchwey from a Mr. Johnson in New York.

Neither had phone numbers, so she assumed that the gentleman had been equally terse with Louise.

"I wonder if he's back." She did not want to interrupt Louise, who obviously had her hands full, so she went upstairs to check Basil's room and deliver the messages.

The "Do Not Disturb" sign had been removed from his doorknob, so she knocked on his door. No one answered.

If the man called three times in one day, his message must be important, Alice reasoned. The problem was that Basil's early goings and late returns were making it nearly impossible to deliver his messages.

Alice decided to use her master key and let herself into the room, where she could leave the slips on his nightstand. She disliked invading a guest's room without notice or permission, but he had not put up the DND sign, and at least this way he would finally get his messages.

"Mr. Kirchwey?" she called out as she opened the door a few inches. When there was still no response, she walked in.

It pleased her to see that Basil had kept his room as tidy as it had been on the day he checked in. She placed the message slips on the night table by his bed, and then hesitated. Basil had left one of his notebooks open on the coverlet. The exposed page was covered with writing—lists of some kind.

Alice was terribly tempted to pick up the notebook and read what he had written. *I might find out if he's the Innside Reporter, and what he thinks of our inn.*

The notebook was lying out, right in the open. Basil would never know she had looked at it. If she kept what she read to herself, no one else would ever have to know. Besides, if Basil was the Innside Reporter, he was staying with them under false pretenses. Surely she and her sisters had the right to know what he was going to say about their business. If he wrote a bad review, it could seriously affect the future of Grace Chapel Inn.

If he didn't want anyone to read it, he shouldn't have left it out like this. Alice began to reach for the notebook, and then stopped. *I can't do this. It isn't right.*

Just a month earlier during an ANGELs group meeting, one of the girls had accused her younger sister of taking her favorite top and getting it stained. The two had squabbled fiercely about it until Alice had called a halt and coaxed the younger sister to admit what she had done and the older to forgive her.

At the time Alice had decided that facing the many temptations to sin would make an excellent subject for their Bible discussion, and she had read to the girls from 1 Corinthians 10:13 (NIV).

Now the same passage seemed to ring in her ears: "No temptation has seized you except what is common to man. And God is faithful; he will not let you be tempted beyond what you can bear. But when you are tempted, he will also provide a way out so that you can stand up under it."

Slowly she lowered her hand, and closed her eyes. "Is this memory Your way of providing a way out, Lord?" she murmured under her breath. "Because it's a really good one." She gave the notebook one last regretful glance before she turned to leave the room.

Outside in the hallway stood Gwen Murphy, who was watching her with interest. "Checking up on Basil?"

"I was just leaving him some phone messages," Alice said, and felt her face heat. "I can't seem to catch him on his way in or out."

"I see." She continued to watch as Alice locked the door. "Any calls for me?"

"No, I'm sorry. Were you expecting some?"

The artist shook her head, smiled and went on to her room. Before she went inside, she took a moment to hang her own "Do Not Disturb" sign on the knob.

Feeling more than a little embarrassed, Alice headed downstairs. As she descended, she could hear the faint sounds of someone's pounding on the piano. *Thank goodness we had that room soundproofed. How does Louise stand it?* She saw her aunt waiting by the front reception desk. "Aunt Ethel, have you been waiting long?"

"No, dear, I just arrived. Jane invited me for dinner, something about some Italian food she's making." She took off her red hat and fluffed her hair. "I'm going into Potterston tomorrow to do some shopping, so if you need anything make me a list. I also need to talk to you girls about Lloyd's birthday and what's got him in such a snit lately." The discordant sounds coming from the parlor made her shake her head. "New student?"

"Yes, and it's her first lesson," Alice said as she went with her aunt into the kitchen. "We just saw the mayor in town earlier, and he seemed fine. Is something wrong?"

"Nothing wrong in here." Jane came over with her hand cupped under a wooden spoon filled with a crimson sauce. "Taste test time."

Alice sampled the offering, which more than lived up to its name. "Oh my. On a scale of one to ten, I give that a forty."

"Never fails." She brought another spoon for their aunt to taste. "You two set the table while Aunt Ethel tells me why she's got that little line between her eyebrows."

"It's the darnedest thing," their aunt said as she helped Alice take down and put out the dishes. "When I had Lloyd over to help me trim the hedges, I was hoping to find out what he'd like for his birthday next month. But he hardly said two words to me the entire time. He acted like I wasn't even there."

"He must have had a headache, like we thought," Alice suggested. "No one talks much when they're not feeling well, Aunt."

"That's not the thing, dear. When we sat down to lunch, he turned back into his old self again."

"Aspirin does work wonders," Jane joked. "I hear you can buy it almost anywhere too."

"I suppose that could be it." Ethel folded dinner napkins into neat triangles and slipped one under the edge of each plate. "I wish I knew what's gotten into him. He's been moody like this all week, but he won't tell me why. He says he doesn't want anything special for his birthday, either."

"He seemed okay when we saw him at Town Hall, and I'm sure he will love whatever you pick out for his birthday gift." Jane turned around from the stove. "Don't overanalyze this, Auntie."

"If it were another man I'd agree with you, Jane." She sat down and leaned back in the kitchen chair. "But this is Lloyd, and he and I have always understood each other just fine." She frowned as she straightened a fork. "Or I thought we did."

"It could be that he needs some space and time to himself." Alice sat next to her and covered her hand with hers. "Men do, sometimes."

"I thought that, too. When I told him I'd be busy working in the garden today and suggested he might like to go fishing, he insisted on helping me. Wouldn't hear of doing anything else. Then he comes over and hardly says a word to me." She shook her head. "What man picks hedge-trimming over fishing, I ask you?"

"Got me." Jane brought the teapot over to the table. "Here, Auntie, have a cup. It's chamomile, it'll relax your nerves. You, too, Alice, you look a little frazzled."

Ethel studied Alice's face. "You are a little pink in the face, dear. You really shouldn't rush down the stairs like that. What were you doing up there?"

"I went to put some phone messages in Mr. Kirchwey's room, and he had left one of his notebooks open on his bed." Still feeling a little ashamed of what she had almost done, Alice looked down into the amber depths of her tea. "There was a bunch of writing in it."

"Well?" Ethel prompted. "What did it say?"

"I didn't read it." The guilt she had felt at being tempted, however, faded under the satisfaction of knowing she had resisted. "I couldn't."

"I would have, in a snap," Ethel said, sounding very virtuous at the same time. "Who knows what that man is up to? I'm telling you, girls, he acts very shifty. I should get him on the side the next time I see him and have a heart-to-heart talk with him."

"I'd like to be a fly on the wall when you do that," Jane said, sounding amused.

"That's all right, Aunt," Alice quickly assured her. "I'm planning to talk with him first thing in the morning."

Ethel raised her eyebrows. "From what I hear, you'll have to get up at the crack of dawn to catch him. Good luck with that."

"Fiddlesticks!" Jane said as she checked in one of the cabinets. "I'm out of celery seed, and I need it for my hot German potato salad tomorrow."

"I can pick up some for you while I'm browsing in Potterston tomorrow," their aunt told her, "if you can wait until after lunch."

"Do you need a ride, Aunt?" Alice asked.

"That's all right, dear. I saw Lester in town this afternoon and he offered to take me. He is going to visit with one of his clients, and I can certainly use a man's advice on what sort of gift to get for Lloyd." She looked at the door as Louise came in. "Music lesson finished?"

"Yes, thank the Lord above." She accepted the cup of chamomile tea that Alice offered to her and sat down, moving slowly as if in pain.

Alice felt terrible for Louise, who was particularly sensitive to discordant sounds. Just being in the same room with someone making noise like that must have been pure torture for her, never mind trying to teach a young child how to turn the noise into music. And yet she kept teaching, child after child, week after week. *I should say something to make her feel better.*

"How did it go?" she asked, and then wanted to kick herself. *Help me out here, Lord, or at least keep me from sticking my foot in my mouth.*

"Mrs. Schuler's little girl is very excited about her new piano lessons," Louise said dully. "I will be seeing her twice a month."

Alice tried to think of something positive to say about that. "That's . . . nice."

"Not really. She is a bunny rabbit."

Ethel's jaw sagged. "She's what?"

"She is *pretending* to be a bunny rabbit, I should say," Louise said. "She told me that everyone knows that bunny rabbits must play the piano with their paws. The same way they use them to hop."

"At least she didn't try to play with her ears," Alice said, wincing.

Louise stirred a spoonful of sugar into her tea. "I think if I had let her, she *would* have played with her paws. I mean, feet."

Jane made a strangled sound.

"It is not funny." Louise looked at Alice, who was trying very hard to keep her shoulders from shaking, and at her aunt, who was trying to bury her face in her napkin. The lines of strain around her mouth disappeared. "All right, it is. I know you must have heard her."

"Oh, we heard her," Jane said, barely containing her mirth. "If it weren't for the soundproofing, so would the people in New York . . . and New Hampshire."

"And Canada," Ethel added.

That was the final straw. They all erupted into laughter, which carried on uproariously together until Louise had to hold her sides and tears ran down Jane's cheeks.

Thank You, Lord, Alice prayed silently as she wiped her own eyes. *We needed that.*

Chapter Ten

A few days after the infamous bunny-rabbit lesson, Louise decided to call Sissy Matthews and talk to her about the recital.

As she dialed the number, she tried to think what could have made the girl want to drop out of the program. Sissy's last lesson had been extremely productive, as she had learned two new, moderately difficult pieces with seeming ease. That was the same day Louise had told her about the recital and asked her if she would like to perform. Sissy had seemed very enthusiastic about it at the time, and had even discussed what she might play.

What had changed between then and now?

Mrs. Matthews answered the phone. "Hello, Louise, how are you?"

"I am just fine, Carol." Louise did not know if Sissy had confided in her mother, so she chose her words carefully. "Sissy stopped in last Saturday and said she was feeling sick. I thought I would call and check on her."

"This is about the school recital, right?" Carol asked. "Every time I've mentioned it to her, she goes pale and says she can't do it. I can't imagine what's gotten into her."

It was worse than Louise had imagined. *It could be stage*

fright. Several of her students had experienced a minor phobic reaction to performing in front of an audience.

"No, she only says she doesn't feel well. If it were Charles doing this, I'd guess he was faking it to get out of something. But my Sissy isn't that way." The girl's mother sighed. "She hasn't been having any problems with her lessons, has she?"

"No, she has been progressing marvelously. Would it be all right if I speak with her about it?"

"Sure, hold on and I'll get her."

After a short silence Sissy's voice came over the line. "Hi, Mrs. Smith." She sounded particularly woebegone.

"Hello, Sissy." She kept her own voice even and cheerful. "I called to see if you are feeling any better."

"No. I've been coughing a lot," she produced what sounded like a counterfeit cough, "and I think I have a fever."

"That's a shame. I was hoping you would feel well enough to play at the recital." Whatever was bothering the child was more important than a recital, however. "I do hope you feel better."

"Thank you, Mrs. Smith."

"Take good care of yourself, and I will see you at your next lesson."

"I . . ." there was silence for a moment before Sissy said all in a rush, "I can't come to my lesson. I'm too sick for that, too. I have to go now. Thank you for calling." There was a click as she hung up the phone.

If the girl was suffering from stage fright, there was no reason for her to avoid lessons. That meant it was something else, perhaps something even more disturbing. Was Sissy giving up on music altogether?

Louise went to the kitchen, where Jane was arranging a variety of roses, chrysanthemums and asters in three vases. It was one of their special, personal touches to put fresh flowers in their guest rooms.

"Hey, there, big sister. I did some extra cutting on our bushes, so we've got blooms to spare." She gathered up a handful and presented them like a bouquet. "Here. Something to chase your blues away."

"They are running for the border now." Louise took the flowers and breathed in their delicate perfume, which made her feel a little better. She had noticed Alice's habit of bringing flowers to place in front of their parents' headstone in the little graveyard not far from Grace Chapel Inn. "I think I'll go for a walk. Do you mind if I take some of these for Mother and Father?"

"Not at all." Jane studied her face. "Want me to go with you?"

"I would rather be by myself, if that's all right with you. I need to think through some things." These things included her feelings about Sissy Matthews and what Gwen Murphy had said to her, which kept repeating in her mind: *Maybe you should think again about exactly how you're teaching her.*

"Okay, but you're missing out on some fantastic companionship and lively conversation." Jane took back the flowers and wrapped them for her. "If you still have that unhappy-Louise face when you come back, I'm going to make you eat cheesecake."

"Thank you for the warning."

Louise took her time walking to the graveyard. The weather had begun to make the transition from summer to autumn temperatures, and the air had a crisp quality that made everything seem fresher and sharper.

As Alice had predicted, the leaves were starting to turn, and subtle oranges and yellows appeared on almost every tree. It was easy to see changes in nature, but far more difficult to recognize the same in people, especially children.

I never saw that Sissy was having any problems, Louise thought. *How could I have missed something like this?*

The possibility that her student might have been hiding this from her for some time troubled her deeply. Perhaps the pressure of performing to Louise's standards and expectations was what had frightened the girl. She did expect quite a lot out of Sissy, not only because she had more natural musical talent than any of her other students, but because she had always shown such dedication to her lessons.

Sissy Matthews had also reminded Louise of herself in so many ways that it had always been a pleasure to teach her, and she had thought that she was instilling in the child the same love of classical music that she had learned from her own tutors.

But what if I have pushed her too hard? She remembered the brimming tears in the girl's eyes, and the panic in her voice. *What if I am the one responsible for all this?* It would break Louise's heart if that were the case. She had never, *ever* intended to upset Sissy.

A figure moving around the headstones snapped her attention back to the present. The tall thin man was kneeling in the grass in front of a headstone, and as she drew closer Louise was surprised to see it was Basil Kirchwey. He had his back to her, so as she approached she politely cleared her throat.

He jumped up and around like a man expecting to be mugged. "Mrs. . . . um . . . I . . ."

Evidently he could not remember her name. "It is Mrs. Smith," she said, "but please call me Louise."

"All right, Louise." He tucked the notebook he had been writing in under his arm. "What brings you here?"

"I came to visit my family." She nodded toward one corner, where they had buried her parents side by side under the shade of an old oak tree.

His gaze dropped to the flowers she carried. "Oh. I'm so sorry."

"Thank you." She tried to imagine why he would be kneeling in front of a headstone, one that did not bear the name *Kirchwey*. "What brings *you* here?"

"I, uh, was just looking. At the, uh, carvings. Beautiful old things." He swung his hand toward the headstone before which he had been kneeling, which was extremely plain and had no carvings on it. "You can see how, um"—he groped for his next words—"how well *chiseled* the letters are."

Louise nodded slowly. "Yes, they are." She let her gaze drift to his notebook, in which he had written a list of names.

At the sound of approaching footsteps he turned his head. "I should be going. Excuse me." He tipped his bowler to her and hurried off.

Basil nodded to Rev. Thompson as he left the graveyard. By the time the pastor reached Louise, the strange man was hurrying in the direction of town.

"Good morning, Louise." He gazed down at the road before turning his attention to her. "I saw you from the church steps and thought I'd walk over. How are you?"

"Fine, Pastor, although I can't speak for our guest." She nodded toward Basil as he hastened on his way. "He seems to be a nervous fellow." She smiled and showed Rev. Thompson the bouquets that she carried. "But I'm not here to criticize the living."

"Let me walk with you." He accompanied her to her parents' graves. "Would some words of prayer be welcome?"

"Very much so." She joined hands with him and bowed her head.

"Heavenly Father," the pastor said, "Your wisdom and patience are an eternal lighthouse in the darkness. When the injustices in the mortal world wound us, help us to find healing through prayer and good works. Let no ordeal, no matter how difficult, wither our souls and remove our trust. When plagued by sorrow and doubt, remind us of what our mothers and fathers endured with the strength of their faith and love. Grant us the ability always to find the same in ourselves, through Christ our Lord. Amen."

"Amen," Louise said, and smiled at the pastor's concerned expression. "I really am fine, you know. But I would love to discover how pastors always seem to know what people are thinking and feeling."

"God knows. Pastors only make educated guesses." He smiled and gently squeezed her hand. "And knowing you as I do, I will also assume that you came here for some quiet time to work things out on your own."

She nodded.

"Then I'll be heading back to the church, leaving a reminder that I'm available if you need to talk. Always remember that."

"Thank you, Pastor, I will." Her father had also combined the same, thoughtful concern with respect for his eldest daughter's need for privacy. *Oh, Father, I wish you two could have met. You would have become such good friends.* She glanced back at the road, but Basil had disappeared. "One question before you go, Pastor. Do you know what that man was doing here?"

He frowned. "I can't say, but this is the third time this week I've seen him here in the graveyard."

"There are no Kirchweys here, but maybe he is researching family genealogy on his mother's side." As she passed the headstone Basil had been examining, the name of the deceased on the one next to it caught her eye. "*Killian Sinclair.* Do you know if *Killian* is a common given name?"

"I don't think so," he said. "I've only heard it once or twice."

She stooped to examine the stone. "'Killian Sinclair, born October 23, 1842, died July 2, 1863. Beloved Son, Husband and Father.' He was only twenty-one when he died, what a terrible shame." She stood. "There's a portrait of a young boy in the sketchbook we found in the attic. The name Killian was written beneath it."

"Perhaps it was him," the pastor suggested. "That would date your sketchbook to the middle of the nineteenth century."

Louise looked at the surrounding headstones, which were among the oldest in the graveyard. "Here is a Manfred Lewis, and an August Taylor. There were portraits of boys in the sketchbook with those same first names, and they also died on July 2, 1863." She peered at other stones and felt a terrible sense of dread. "Pastor, all of these men here died on the same day. How is that possible?"

"They were probably soldiers killed during the Civil War. The date would indicate the Battle of Gettysburg."

"Oh, of course." She pressed a hand to her heart. "I should have thought of that." She looked at the stones again. "We lost so many to that terrible war."

∽

Rev. Thompson glanced toward Grace Chapel. "If you come over to the church when you have time, I can check the old parish registry to be sure."

The excitement caused by her graveyard discoveries made Louise want to go with the pastor rather than be alone with her thoughts. "That would be helpful. As a matter of fact, I'll go with you now."

On their way to the church, Louise mentioned Basil Kirchwey's odd comings and goings at all hours. "Jane suspects he could be a reporter and that he is here to write a critique about our service." She gave the pastor a rueful look. "I'm afraid that I just do not see Grace Chapel Inn's being of interest to a regional magazine. We're too small, for one thing."

"Well, if he is, he's sure to appreciate the many fine qualities of your inn." He opened the door to the church. "Have you asked him?"

"No, it seems so . . . confrontational, particularly if he is trying to conceal his identity." Uncomfortable with the thought, she moved her shoulders. "I dislike being suspicious of our guests. That is no way to run an inn."

The pastor glanced sideways at her. "How do you think you'll feel if Mr. Kirchwey does turn out to be this undercover reporter?"

She considered that. "I am going to feel foolish for not finding out."

"The Bible says, 'Do to others as you would have them do to you.' Luke wasn't talking just about our neighbors, either. God wants us to treat strangers as we would be treated." Rev. Thompson opened the door to the vesting room, where filing cabinets full of records were kept. "Whenever I'm in doubt regarding how to handle someone, that's the logic I apply."

"A one-size-fits-all verse," Louise said wryly.

"If only we could get everyone to use it, the world would be a happier place." He went to the oldest cabinet and took out a huge leather-bound registry. "All the birth, marriage and death records we have from the nineteenth century are in here." He carried the heavy book over to a table and opened it. "Luckily the population of Acorn Hill has remained fairly small over the years, or this might be like looking for a needle in a haystack."

"Are there records about the war losses?"

"I believe there are. Henry Ley was telling me that the first pastor, who came to this area just before the war, held mass memorial services." He turned the front pages and stopped at a long list of names. "The majority of the men from Acorn Hill went to fight for the Union, though there were a few who decided to fight for the Confederacy. Most didn't return home." He turned another page. "Here are the names for the service the pastor conducted in the summer of 1863."

Louise looked at the page, and noticed one line. "Lost at the battle of Gettysburg, July 1 to July 3." She traced her finger down the list until she came to the same names that she had seen on the headstones. "*Manfred Lewis. Killian Sinclair. August Taylor.* They are all right here."

"They probably served in the same unit. Most military units of that era were made up of men from the same region or state." He checked the bottom of the page. "These men were all enlisted infantry—foot soldiers. They experienced the heaviest casualties."

She tried to think how she could prove that the Killian in the sketch was the same Killian Sinclair who had died serving his country so long ago. "Would there be any photographs of these men anywhere?"

"Unless their families preserved them, probably not." He considered the list. "Photographs were expensive, and photographers few and far between. The only times someone had their picture taken were at birth, when they got married, or when they put on their uniform. And occasionally, when they died."

"Our sketchbook may contain the only portraits of these men in existence, all drawn when they were boys." Louise sat back in the chair. "But who drew them?"

"Whoever did, it would seem that the book is quite historically valuable." Rev. Thompson closed the registry. "The sketches would also be of great sentimental value to their descendants. Many of these men were married, and left widows and children behind."

"Like Killian Sinclair. A 'beloved son, husband and father,'" she said, remembering the words on the headstone.

He nodded. "I believe there is a Sinclair family in town, isn't there?"

"Yes, they are members of the Methodist church." Louise tapped her finger against her lips. "I wonder if Killian is their ancestor."

"You could show the sketchbook to them and some of the local families with the same names. One of them might know something about the artist." He took the registry back to the cabinet. "You're welcome to look through the church's records any time, too."

"I do appreciate it, Pastor." A magazine on the table caught her eye, and she picked it up. It was a scholarly review of classic movies, but something about the cover jogged her memory, although she couldn't say why. "Pastor, have you ever seen Mr. Kirchwey's name before? Perhaps in a magazine you've read?"

"No, I'm afraid I haven't."

"I could swear I have read that name somewhere else." She rubbed her temple. "Something to do with history, perhaps."

Rev. Thompson gave her a sympathetic glance. "I wish I could help, but the only historical reading I do is generally of the book-length variety."

"I will have to sort through my magazines when I get back to the inn," she decided. "Maybe that's one mystery I can solve on my own."

Chapter Eleven

Wendell jumped on Alice's bed during the night, waking her out of a sound sleep. As she sat up, he leapt over her, went to the foot of her bed and curled up on her quilt.

"Was I snoring too loudly or something?" Alice asked, rubbing her eyes.

The tabby huffed out a breath and then closed his eyes.

Her alarm clock read a few minutes past midnight. Alice sensed that she would not be able to go back to sleep right away, so she got up and pulled on her robe. She would go downstairs quietly and make herself a cup of hot cocoa. Louise insisted that it was not good to drink cocoa in the middle of the night, but it always helped Alice go back to sleep.

On her way downstairs she heard Basil Kirchwey's voice and looked over the railing. He was standing at the reception desk and speaking into a cell phone. For a moment she considered returning to her room in order not to disturb him, until his voice drifted up to her.

"I finished reading through all the back issues of their local paper, the *Acorn Nutshell*, today, with no luck. But I still have another week, Tom. Yes, it's enough time. I know, I know, I should have started earlier, but I ran into some other problems. Well, for starters, I didn't get your messages.

Another thing, this place is run by three women who never stop asking me questions."

Her grip on the rail tightened. She could tolerate someone criticizing her, but he was maligning her sisters. After she had spent all this time defending him to her aunt, and her sisters, too, it was impossible not to take it personally.

Alice marched downstairs.

"I have to go. I'll call you tomorrow. Night, Tom." Basil ended his call by the time she reached the reception desk. He went to stuff the phone into his jacket pocket, missed, and dropped it. "Miss Howard." He bent down to retrieve the phone. "I didn't realize you were up. It's so late."

She did not intend to be fooled by his hesitant, aw-shucks routine this time, not after hearing the way he had spoken on the phone. "We don't turn into pumpkins after midnight, Mr. Kirchwey." She stalked past him into the kitchen.

Basil peeked in through the door. "Um, are you upset about something?"

"Yes, I am, and you can drop the act."

"Act?"

"I heard you on the phone, and before that in the attic. You didn't seem to have any problem speaking coherently or intelligently then, so why continue to put on this nervous routine for me now?"

His eyes bulged. "But—"

"It's annoying and it's rude. Furthermore, it's unkind." She took milk from the refrigerator and poured it into a pan. "I don't know what you think of me and my sisters—no, I think I do—but we've been very nice to you. We've shown you the same courtesies that we show everyone else. When you've actually *been* here, that is."

"You have," he agreed. "It's just, um—"

"Now don't you 'just um' me." If he was the Innside Reporter, then she was going to give him a real exclusive.

"Running a bed-and-breakfast is hard work, seven days a week, twelve months a year. Have you ever run an inn your-self, Basil?"

He shook his head.

"Then you have no idea how much work we *three women* do to run this place. Before you even think about passing judgment on us, maybe you should check into the other side of the bed-and-breakfast business. The hard work side of it. The getting up at 6:00 AM to cook side of it. The laundry and the cleaning and the accounting side of it." She took a wooden spoon and stirred the heating milk. "I bet you'd get a whole new view on things." She scowled. "If you could even keep up with us."

Basil did not say anything. He was staring at the floor.

Alice took a steadying breath. "Now, I'm having some cocoa. I need some cocoa because I'm not going to get back to sleep without it. I know how much you hate questions, but I only have one more to ask. Would you like some?" He shook his head. "Fine. Then, unless you need me to do something for you, I'd like some private time now. If you're going back out for a walk, I would ask that you not rummage through our garbage bins again. Oh, and those phone messages that you told your friend that you never received? I left them in your room, on your night table. *Four days ago*."

"Thank you." Basil fled.

Alice told herself she had every right to feel annoyed with the man, but when she brought her cocoa to the table and sat down a few minutes later, she buried her face in her hands. "That wasn't very smart, Lord, was it?" she prayed aloud. "I'll apologize to him in the morning."

"That's not necessary," Basil said quietly as he slipped back into the kitchen. "I think I owe you a few apologies, though, Miss Howard. I needed a moment so I stepped out-side," he looked over his shoulder, "to think, not to go through the garbage."

"Please call me Alice." She sighed. "I was the one who lost my temper and I said some very unkind things. I had no right to listen in on your phone conversation and I do sincerely apologize, Mr. Kirchwey."

"Basil." He gave her a lopsided smile. "You're right, I didn't realize how much work you and your sisters do. Or I guess I didn't appreciate it. Anyway . . . Alice . . . I'm sorry for my thoughtless remarks."

She forced a smile. "Change your mind on the cocoa?"

He shook his head. "I think I'll turn in. Good night."

〰

Fred had set up a locking display case for the more valuable items on loan for the Visitors Center, so on her next trip to town, after calling ahead, Jane stopped at the rectory to pick up the Little Shepherdess books.

Rev. Thompson answered the door. "Come in, Jane. Please have a seat. I'll get your books right away."

During her father's term as pastor of Grace Chapel, the rectory had been used solely for storage. The church board had cleaned it out and renovated it to serve as a home for the new pastor, but Rev. Thompson had given it to his associate pastor, Henry Ley, and his wife Patsy when they had lost their home. He moved into a small, comfortable bachelor apartment above the Holzmanns' antique shop and used the rectory only when he needed to visit his office there.

Rev. Thompson returned carrying the stack of green-bound books. "Here are your treasures, Jane."

"We're showing the mayor how the Visitors Center will look," she told him, "so I thought I'd put them in the rare-and-valuable case."

"May I carry them over for you? I've been curious to see what you've been doing."

Jane nodded. "I never turn down someone's offer to carry things for me." *Unless it's from Basil Kirchwey.*

When they arrived at Town Hall, Fred was sweeping up sawdust near his display. Jane directed the pastor to the case, which Fred had set up behind his town model. Next to it was Madeleine's desk, which Jane had decorated with some old stationery, a quill pen, a bottled inkstand and an old brass letter holder for the inn's brochures. June, who had told Jane that she and Clarissa Cottrell, the owner of the Good Apple Bakery, would be combining their displays, had temporarily set up the old restaurantware on a folding table. However, Sylvia and Craig's contributions were still missing.

"What's your verdict, Ken?" she asked when he closed the case.

He inspected the work they had accomplished. "I think you and Fred have done a superb job."

"There's a bit more to do on mine," Fred told him. "Vera wants to make a drape for the bottom of the display stand, and I thought I'd put a Plexiglas cover over the model, to keep little fingers from invading."

"That seems wise." The pastor gestured to the still-empty areas. "How are you planning to use the rest of the space?"

Fred took a folded piece of paper from his pocket and opened it. "I've marked off how much space we have to use in sections"—he showed him the floor plan that he had drawn—"and Jane and I reckon we'll have to rotate some of the spots."

"That way all the merchants get a chance to participate, if they want." Jane saw the two empty spaces he had marked for Sylvia's Buttons and Wild Things, and wished the merchants had finished their projects. Still, she didn't want to delay getting Lloyd's approval any longer. "Okay, I think we should show what we have to the mayor and get the go-ahead."

Lloyd's secretary notified him via intercom that they were waiting for him, and he came out a few moments later. After he shook hands with Rev. Thompson, he turned to Jane. "Ready for inspection?"

She swung her hand toward the displays. "Ready as we're going to be."

Lloyd first walked around Fred's model, which was the centerpiece, while Fred told him about the cover and base drape still to be installed. "Good, good." The mayor bent down and peered at the base. "I'd cover that part of the electrical cord that's showing, just in case a little one crawls under the drape."

He moved on to the locking display case, the glass of which he suggested should be cleaned on the inside to remove a few smudges, and then to June's coffee table, which he decided should be moved to one side away from the other displays to prevent someone's knocking into it.

When the mayor got to Madeleine's desk, he plucked the quill pen from the stand. "I know this is authentic, but it's also got a very sharp point." He showed Jane the quill tip. "This should be filed down or locked in the case. Is the ink in the bottle real, too?"

"Yes."

"That has to go." He removed that and handed it to her along with the quill. "If someone opens or drops it, we'll never get it out of the carpet. Empty it or fill it with colored water."

"Is there anything else we should do?"

The mayor took a long look around. "That's all for now. You can start moving in the rest. Just remember to make safety a priority." His secretary called to him, and he excused himself to take a call in his office.

"Not what you'd call unconditional, lavish praise," Jane muttered.

"At least you got the go-ahead," Fred pointed out. "That's what matters."

"That's true." She looked down at the quill and ink bottle, which she thought had suited the desk so well. "What do you do at a writing desk, other than write letters?"

"I read books and letters at mine," the pastor said.

"Ah, that would work," she said, eyeing the desk. "I need to talk to Viola, maybe we can do the same thing June and the baker are doing and combine our displays." She smiled at him. "Thanks, Ken."

"You're welcome. I'd better get back to the office now," he said. "Keep up the good work."

Jane glanced through one of the windows and saw a black bowler pass by. "Excuse me, Fred. I just saw someone I need to . . . speak to."

She stepped outside and saw Basil Kirchwey headed in the direction of the Nine Lives Bookstore. Since she wanted to check with Viola about donating some books, she decided that gave her an excuse to follow him.

From behind, Basil looked almost drab in his dark brown jacket and matching trousers. Yet when he turned the corner, Jane caught a glimpse of his vivid purple bow tie. The combination was definitely striking for someone who avoided attention as much as Basil did.

She caught up to him in front of Viola's shop. Since the door was closed and no cats were lolling about the front porch, she automatically knew Viola had closed for the day. Basil, who did not, knocked on the door and peered inside.

"I'm afraid the shop is closed, Mr. Kirchwey," she said as she reached his side.

Basil jumped and turned his head to look at her, but he was standing too close and bumped his nose against the door. "Ouch! Blast it!" He covered it with his hand, dropping the paper he carried.

"Oh, dear." Jane bent to pick it up and saw that it was a fax and that the printing was too light for her to make out with a casual glance. She handed it back to him. "Are you okay?"

"Yes." His eyes were watering, and as he took his hand away, she saw the end of his nose had turned red. "I'll just head over to the library."

"Here." She took out a tissue from the pack she carried in her purse and gave it to him. "I really didn't mean to startle you like that, Mr. Kirchwey. It's not broken, is it?"

"Call me Basil." He dabbed at his eyes and gingerly felt his nose. "I don't think . . . it's not broken."

Jane felt terrible for being the cause of the accident. "Listen, why don't you come over to the Coffee Shop with me?"

The rest of his face reddened to match his nose. "That's not necessary."

"Please, it would make me feel better. I'll even buy you a slice of June's famous blackberry pie."

He looked uneasy. "I should really get over to the library . . . but, okay."

Jane did not try to chat with him as they walked back to the Coffee Shop; he seemed nervous enough as it was, and she still felt guilty for making him hurt his nose. Only when they were settled in a booth with the two cups of decaf that Jane had thought it appropriate to order did she try to strike up some friendly conversation.

"We haven't seen much of you at the inn." She added some half-and-half to her cup from the little pitcher on the table. "Have you been out visiting family?"

"Ah, no." He tore open a packet of sugar and spilled a little on the table. "I don't have any family here."

"I see." It seemed reasonable to Jane to assume that he was not in Acorn Hill to do genealogy research. "Our library is terrific, by the way. They keep most of the current bestsellers on hand. What do you like to read?"

"Nonfiction, mostly." He hesitated. "I didn't think a small town would have such a good reference section. Surprised me, the first time I went over there. It's made my research a lot easier."

"Are you writing something yourself?"

His eyes widened. "How did you guess?"

"I think it's the hat," she told him, smiling. "All great writers seem to wear very chic hats."

"Ah." He glanced sheepishly at his bowler. "I don't think I'd call it chic, exactly. Its appeal is sentimental."

That tempted her to ask why, but she was afraid of seeming too nosy. "So, what are you writing? A book?"

"I don't write books." He gulped his coffee.

He seemed more on edge now than ever. *He has to be the Innside Reporter,* Jane thought. *Why else would he act so uncomfortable?* "You know, I just started reading some magazines about the inn-keeping business. I'm learning an awful lot from them. Have you ever written any magazine articles?"

"Uh, a few." He glanced out the window the same way a prisoner might look through the bars of his cell.

She was only making things worse. "Sorry, I don't mean to give you the third degree. I was just interested in finding out more about you."

He gave her a panicked look. "Why?"

"Jane, I thought I saw you." Sylvia Songer came over to their table and smiled at Basil. "I don't mean to interrupt."

"I have to be going." Basil practically leapt out of the booth. "Thank you for the coffee, Jane." He jammed his bowler on his head. "Ladies."

"Wait, Basil, I wanted . . ." Before Jane could finish her sentence Basil fled the diner. "I think I'd like that man if he wasn't so frustrating to talk to."

Sylvia gave her a look of sympathy. "Aren't they all?"

Chapter Twelve

That night Louise gathered all of the magazines she had in her room and placed them in a neat stack on her bed. The best way to look for something was in a logical and methodical way, and she was determined to hunt down the magazine in which she had seen Basil Kirchwey's name.

She started with her old collection of *Fine Arts of Philadelphia*, a magazine she and Eliot had subscribed to for years, which mainly covered artists' shows, gallery openings and the many concerts that they had attended together. Her husband had always jokingly referred to it as their "to-do list."

Oh my darling, she thought as she spotted a listing for a chamber music concert that he had circled, *we had such a wonderful life together.*

There was a soft tap at her door.

Louise took a moment to pull on her robe before she went to answer it. "Just a moment."

It was Alice, still wearing her white nurse's uniform. "There's a message for you on the answering machine. Vera Humbert asked if you would call her tomorrow."

"I will, thank you, dear. Are you just getting home from work?"

Alice tugged at the wrinkled shirt of her uniform. "Yes, and after the shift I've had, I'm headed directly for a hot shower and bed. Good night."

A few minutes later, there was another knock, but this time when Louise answered it, she found Gwen Murphy standing just outside her door. "Ms. Murphy?"

"Hey." The artist was wearing a pair of sweat pants and an oversized sweatshirt. "I'm having problems with the bathroom."

It was late, and Louise was tempted to tell her to use the shared bathroom, and that she would call Fred in the morning. But she was slightly old-fashioned and preferred separate facilities for guests of different genders, unless they were married to each other. "Let me slip on some shoes."

The sink in Gwen's bathroom was filled with dirty water.

"I was washing my face when it started to back up," the artist told her.

"I see that." Louise rolled up the sleeves of her robe and plunged one hand in to check whether the drain stopper was in the open position, which it was.

She pulled her hand out and dried it on a hand towel. "It seems to be blocked. I'll have to get some tools."

Instead of staying in the bathroom, Gwen trailed after her. "You do plumbing work? I never would have guessed that."

"Alice and Jane have a little more experience, but I try to keep my hand in as well." She opened the supplies cabinet and took out a small box of tools and a plastic bucket. "Do you know what clogged the drain?"

"No."

As a last resort, she added a coil of heavy wire to the bucket and walked back to the bathroom. To unclog the drain, she had to use a wrench to remove part of the pipe underneath and clear whatever was blocking it. She sat on the floor and positioned the bucket to catch the water that would empty from the sink when she removed the pipe. Then she began working the connections loose with the wrench.

Gwen stood in the doorway, watching.

It was messy, unpleasant work, but Louise finally detached the pipe and cleared a heavy wad of shredded tissue and hair from it. After the sink emptied into the pail, she reconnected the pipe and tested the drain.

"There." She gathered up everything and carried it out into the hallway. "It should work fine now, but let me or my sisters know if it clogs again."

"Right." Gwen stepped into the bathroom and shut the door in Louise's face.

She restrained a sudden and unwelcome urge to kick the door with her foot. "You are very welcome."

Louise carried the bucket downstairs to empty the dirty water while straining out the blockage material. In brighter light, she could see that the curly mass of hair was the exact same shade of brown as Gwen Murphy's. But it was not so much the color as the amount that concerned Louise.

She seemed to be faced with one of two outlandish possibilities: Either a very large handful of the artist's hair had fallen out in the past day, or Gwen Murphy had taken a wad of hair from her brush and stopped up the sink with it.

～

After hearing about Jane's encounter with Basil Kirchwey in town, and about how he had admitted to writing for magazines, Alice agreed with her sister that there was little doubt that Basil Kirchwey was the Innside Reporter. Later, she decided to set her alarm to get up a little earlier than usual, in hopes of catching him before he went out.

I'll invite him to have breakfast with us and let him know the cat is out of the bag. That way he won't feel like he has to sneak around here anymore.

When her alarm went off the next morning, Alice dressed quickly and went down to set up her guardpost in the kitchen, where she propped the door open so she could see out into the front room while she prepared coffee for her sisters and tea for herself.

The first person down the stairs was Jane.

"What's all this?" her younger sister asked, smothering a yawn as she wandered in and sat down. "Are you trying to take over my kitchen?"

"No, I wanted to see Basil before he goes out for the day. I thought we would invite him to have breakfast with us."

"Should we let him know that we're on to him?" Jane said. "You know, drop some hints?"

"Yes, indeed. I think if we let him know that we know he's the Innside Reporter, he won't be so worried about us finding out." She collected her teacup and saucer. "I'll be out at the front desk if you need me."

"You mean you're not going to make me breakfast, too?" Jane poured herself a cup of the fresh coffee.

"Next time." She went to the door and nearly dropped her tea as she heard someone coming downstairs. "That's him."

"How can you tell?"

"I recognize his footsteps." She hurried out.

By the time she got to the desk, Basil was at the bottom of the stairs and placing his black bowler on his head. He had on his blue and gray jacket, but this time his bow tie was in a shade that could only be described as screaming yellow.

This is it. Alice set down her tea on the desk and produced a friendly smile. *Whatever you do, don't be obvious about it.* "Good morning, Basil."

He dropped the notebook that he was carrying. "Oh, hello, Alice. You're up early." He bent to retrieve it, which made his bowler fall off and roll toward Alice. "Blasted hat!"

"I've got it." She picked up his hat and moved toward the kitchen. "I noticed that you've been here for more than a week now and still haven't tried our fabulous breakfast menu. You remember that breakfast is included during your stay with us, don't you?"

"Yes, but I've been leaving so early—"

"Yes, we've noticed, and while my sisters and I don't begin serving the guests until eight, we thought we'd ask you to join us for our family meal. I also thought it would be a nice way for me to apologize for the way I spoke to you the other night." She pushed open the kitchen door. "Please, come in."

Basil eyed his hat, which she still held. "You're sure it's not too much trouble?" He waved toward the front door. "I can pick up something in town later."

"No trouble at all," she assured him, and kept smiling as he walked into the kitchen. "Jane, Basil is going to join us for breakfast."

"That's great, I've just started the crepes." Jane turned from the stove. "Coffee, coming right up."

He went to sit at the family table, and seemed quite bewildered by all the attention. "I didn't wake anyone, did I?"

"We're very early risers." Alice put his bowler on a shelf and brought him his coffee. "Besides, we haven't had any time to talk with you since you checked in. Well, other than . . ." she trailed off discreetly.

"I have been rather busy," he admitted.

"I'm sorry to hear that. By the way, did you find the messages from Mr. Johnson in New York?" she asked. "I really did leave them on your night table."

"Yes, I did. I had accidentally set something on top of them, which is why I didn't see them before. Thank you."

"You never told us where you were from, Basil. Are you a New Yorker?" Jane asked.

"No, I'm from Baltimore. I only work in New York." He sampled his coffee. "This is great."

"Wait until you try my crepes," Jane told him. "You may

never go back to New York. But then, you magazine writers can work from anywhere, can't you?"

"Basically." He hunched his shoulders.

Alice sensed he was getting uneasy again. "It must be fascinating work: traveling and writing about different places. Do you enjoy your work?"

He flushed. "I try to."

"Jane has been reading some new magazines, haven't you, Jane?" She glanced at her younger sister.

"Travel and trade. I especially like one of the regional travel magazines." She gave Basil a wink. "Lots of terrific articles in that one."

"Yes, I enjoyed reading that one myself." Alice gave Basil an encouraging smile. "Travel writers have such interesting jobs."

"So do you like writing for magazines, Basil?" Jane asked as she expertly flipped two golden-brown crepes onto his plate.

"It's a living." He shifted his weight.

Alice nodded. "I've never traveled a great deal, so I always like hearing about other places. Other inns, for example, and what it's like for people who stay in them."

Basil's gaze shifted between her face and Jane's. "Really? You do?"

"Oh, sure." Jane put the pan back on the stove. "A little constructive criticism never hurts. You can learn a lot from what people think of you."

"It is fortunate you feel that way, Jane, because Mr. Kirchwey is quite the critic," Louise said as she came into the kitchen with a magazine tucked under her arm.

Jane and Alice exchanged an amused look.

"A critic for, say, the *Innkeeper's Journal*?" Alice asked.

At the same time Jane asked, "The Innside Reporter kind of critic?"

"The what?" Basil asked. "The who?"

"No, I am afraid his field is quite different." Louise walked to the table and put the magazine down in front of them. "As it happens, Mr. Kirchwey is a literary critic. He writes book reviews."

All three sisters stared at him; Alice with shock, Jane with startled amusement, and Louise with a decided air of triumph.

Jane broke the silence with "Wow, a literary critic! Are you famous?"

"A little," Basil said.

"Please, don't be so modest," Louise said. "Mr. Kirchwey has been published in the Written Word, the Lyricist, and a number of other classic literary magazines." She folded her arms and stared down at Basil. "He is also quite well-known among certain academic circles, and he has taught or lectured at a number of universities."

"That qualifies as famous in my book," Jane said.

"Yes, well." Basil made an uneasy gesture. "I really don't want anyone to know I'm here, if that's okay. The work I'm doing is a little sensitive, and I was hoping to keep it quiet."

"I can't imagine why." Louise picked up the magazine, flipped it open and showed Alice a lengthy article with the boldface byline that plainly read "By Basil Kirchwey." "You certainly made a large splash with this piece which you wrote about C. S. Lewis and his 'semi-clandestine marriage of convenience' to Joy Gresham."

"Whoa!" Jane had brought another serving of crepes to the table, and now she stood and regarded Basil with genuine awe. "*You* were the one who wrote that piece about C. S. Lewis' supposedly marrying that woman so she wouldn't be deported?"

"Yes. And he did marry her."

Jane glanced at Louise. "Well, if you say so."

"I am afraid that Mr. Kirchwey is misguided," Louise told her. "His work was well-intentioned but flawed. Of course, opinion pieces sometimes are."

"I based my theories on the facts," Basil insisted. "I did prove that Lewis married Gresham solely to give her British citizenship."

"Did you? If you check the next issue of this magazine, Mr. Kirchwey, you can read my letter to the editor regarding the decidedly fragile foundations of your theories."

His eyes widened. "L.H.S.—that was you?" When she nodded, he groaned. "Of all the inns in Pennsylvania—"

"You had to check into ours," Jane finished his sentence for him, and laughed. "Don't worry, Basil. Louise may have some strong opinions, but you'll probably never find another person to talk to who knows more about C. S. Lewis."

"Why would you hide the fact that you're a literary critic?" Alice could not understand it.

He grimaced. "Some researchers and experts became a little upset with me after I wrote the Lewis article."

"Which I will be delighted to debate with you later," Louise promised. "At length."

Basil gave her a wary look. "Yes, well. Anyway, my theories caused a lot of debate, and then the press got involved. I found myself in the center of a literary firestorm, and ever since then I've kept a low profile."

"If you three let my breakfast crepes get cold," Jane said as she set a dish of fruit on the table, "I'll be madder than Louise was when she read that article. Let's have a prayer and then you can eat while you talk." She sat down and joined hands with the others. "Alice, will you say grace?"

They bowed their heads.

"'The Lord is faithful to all his promises and loving toward all he has made,'" she said, quoting from Psalm 145:13–16 (NIV), "'The Lord upholds all those who fall and lifts up all who are bowed down. The eyes of all look to you, and you give them their food at the proper time. You open your hand and satisfy the desires of every living thing.'

Thank You, Father, for these and all your many blessings. Amen."

"Amen."

Jane's crepes were so thin that they could be cut with a fork. Chives and spices speckled the finely diced hot egg-and-ham filling, which gave off a particularly savory aroma.

Basil cautiously sampled the filling, and then closed his eyes for a moment. "Oh, these are delicious. What are they called?"

"Crepes Benedict. Pour a little of this on top." Jane passed him the small pitcher of creamy hollandaise sauce.

"You should be a chef."

"I was." Jane grinned. "So, if it's not top secret, what is an important literary critic like you doing here in Acorn Hill? Besides dodging overly curious innkeepers, I mean."

He returned her smile. "I came here to research the life of M. E. Roberts."

"The man who wrote the Little Shepherdess books?" Jane said.

"That's the author, yes."

Alice took some orange sections from the fruit platter and then offered it to Basil. "Did M. E. Roberts once live near here?"

"No, but in some letters to his attorney he mentioned having friends in a small Pennsylvania town." He helped himself to some grapefruit sections. "A private collector who bought the letters at auction allowed me to read them. They've never been made public."

"Why do you believe Acorn Hill is the town he was referring to?" Louise asked.

"There are several references he made to landmarks that I've been able to identify. If I can prove Acorn Hill is the town Roberts visited, it will help substantiate a theory of mine."

Basil's nervousness gradually disappeared as the sisters asked him about the famous author, who he told them had published only twelve much-loved children's books before he mysteriously stopped writing completely in 1899.

"The odd thing about Roberts was that he was a notorious recluse who refused to make public appearances of any kind." As Jane refilled his coffee cup, Basil smiled his thanks. "There are no known photographs of him and even his editors at Old Cross Publishers never met the man. His heirs' interests were handled by a trust set up by a lawyer, as was every aspect of his career. That lawyer, by the way, died without revealing a single bit of information about Roberts."

"Why was he such a hermit?" Jane asked.

"No one knows. Some historians believe he may have been disfigured. Others think he had some form of social phobia." He made a face.

"Naturally it was much easier in those days to maintain a very private life," Louise pointed out. "No one was required to have things like a social security number or a driver's license."

"Unfortunately that's why it's so difficult to research Roberts." Basil pointed out. "I haven't found any evidence that corroborates my theory or that proves that he visited people here in Acorn Hill, so it may all be a very big dead end."

"What sort of evidence do you need?" Alice asked, thinking of the set of Little Shepherdess books that Rev. Thompson had found at the church.

"Names. Roberts said he used some of his friends' names for characters, and they were quite unusual. Rather like Charles Dickens' characters."

"I'll say." Jane grinned. "It's been forty years since I read those books, and I can still remember the general store lady, Mrs. Clapstorm, and that mean old Mr. Derfman."

"Exactly." He nodded. "I was hoping to match up names

like those used in the books with Acorn Hill residents of the era." He turned to Louise. "That's why I was checking headstones at the graveyard."

"Goodness, you should have said so," Louise gave him an incredulous look. "One of us could have told you that there are no Clapstorms or Derfmans."

"I should have." He ducked his head. "It's just, well, people make me nervous. Especially people I don't know. I never know what to say, and the more nervous I become, the clumsier I get."

"You writers need to get out more," Jane advised him softly.

He nodded. "I've always been a little shy. I think that's why I took an interest in writing about books. You don't have to be a team player to read, and it's easier for me to write ten articles than talk to one person."

"I'm dying to know something," Jane said. "Why did you decide to wear that particular bow tie today?"

"I didn't. I had my brother put my ties in the pockets of my jackets."

"Why would you do that?"

"I'm color-blind," he admitted. "I can remember which jackets go with which trousers by looking at the patterns, but I have too many ties to keep track of which is which. I always have someone sort them for me before a trip or other special occasion." Doubt filled his expression and he looked down at himself. "Why, is something wrong with this one?"

"Well . . ." Jane hesitated, then plunged on. "It's basically the same color yellow the military uses on 'Danger, Radiation' signs."

"I think this is my brother George's idea of a practical joke," Basil said. "Have my other ties been as mismatched?"

"Not if you're color-blind," Louise told him.

He laughed. "No wonder everyone's been staring at me."

Alice felt guilty. "We should have said something."

"How could you have known? Even if you had, I probably would have been too nervous or distracted to listen." He gave Louise a hopeful glance. "I've noticed that you ladies have a wonderful way of making people feel comfortable. I hope finding out who I am doesn't change that."

"You're quite welcome here, Basil," she told him, "and, now that we know that you're not writing about our inn, I believe we will all feel more comfortable around you."

"Excuse me." Jane left the kitchen and returned with the old sketchbook a few moments later. "Since you know a lot about nineteenth-century books and people, and you've almost finished your research, would you be willing to help us with this?" She handed it to him. "We found it in that trunk we dropped up in the attic, and we're trying to identify the artist."

He glanced briefly at a couple of sketches. "I'm afraid itinerant art isn't my area of expertise," he said somewhat listlessly. Then, realizing that he was not being helpful, he added, "But if you'd like, I could provide you with some sources to research."

Chapter Thirteen

After the sisters had finished serving breakfast to the rest of their guests, Basil suggested that they first examine the other objects that had been stored with the sketchbook in the trunk.

"Everything stored in it could have belonged to the same person," he told the sisters. "There might be clues among the other items."

"You three will have to do your research without me. I promised Fred I'd be by this morning to see how things are progressing at Town Hall," Jane said. "I may also have to chase down Sylvia and Craig and find out what the holdup is on their displays."

"While you're in town, dear, would you stop by and see Vera Humbert?" Louise asked as she absently scooped Wendell from the top of the reception desk and placed him on the floor. "She left a message that she has some information about that old quilt."

"Will do." Jane bent to give the indignant feline a pat on the head, whispering, "The trick is to wait until she's out of the room."

Gwen Murphy came downstairs carrying her sketch pad and a plastic bag. "Hello." She turned to Louise. "Do you have a glass bowl of some kind that I can borrow?" She held up the bag. "I'd like to put this fruit in something."

"I believe so. Just a moment." Louise went into the kitchen and returned with one of the decorative carnival glass bowls they used for the dining room. "Will this do?"

"Yeah, that's great." She took the bowl and dumped the fruit in it, then walked out through the front door.

"You're welcome," Louise said dryly.

Alice put the phone on the answering machine before going up to the attic with Louise and Basil. "I'm glad we didn't tell Fred to throw out the old trunk."

"I think it might be a blanket or mule chest instead of a trunk," Basil said as she turned on the light. "They were quite popular during the nineteenth century, since people back then didn't have much closet space."

Alice went over to the trunk, which was set back in the space Madeleine's desk had occupied. "Why did they call them mule chests?"

"Because they are just as hard to move, I imagine," Louise said.

"Actually, it's because people added drawers to the bottom of their blanket chests. They would store the slippers or 'mules' in the drawers, hence the name." Basil knelt down to carefully open the broken lid. "Our ancestors had a real problem storing their blankets and household linens. Besides lacking closet space, they often used attics as extra rooms instead of for storage, and cellars were far too damp to preserve fabrics and paper goods."

The trunk had no drawers at the bottom and, other than the broken hinges on the lid, was still in one piece.

"I recall reading that young women would store linens and things they made in wedding or hope chests," Louise commented to Basil. "When they married, they would bring them along as a dowry."

"That's right," said Basil as he leaned forward and

sniffed. "These interior panels are cedar. That would protect the contents from damp, mold and insects. Since there are mostly linens in this trunk, I'd guess that it belonged to the lady of the house, and the sketchbook to her husband or son."

"The Berry family built this house in the 1890s, so they probably brought the trunk with them from another home." Louise's eyebrows rose. "Why would the sketchbook belong to the husband or son, and not to the lady of the house?"

"Unfortunately women of that period usually weren't afforded the same quality education as men," he told her. "Their art was generally limited to needlework and the occasional watercolor, both of which were taught to them by their mothers or governesses."

"Gwen said that whoever composed those sketches had some formal art education," Alice put in.

Basil began unloading the books. "I'll check these for names and bookplates. Alice, would you and Louise check the linens? It might be helpful to look for monograms or initials."

Alice handed a stack of embroidered work over to her older sister and sat down on a covered armchair to sort through her own pile of linens. "I hope we find something with a B or perhaps an H." At Basil's mystified glance she added, "Our family names are Berry and Howard."

"I doubt our father had anything that dated back that far from his family." Louise refolded an unmarked coverlet. "It probably didn't belong to one of our Berry relatives, either. They came to this region to farm, not to draw."

"Do you know what the Berrys did before they built this house?" Basil asked her.

"According to what we have been told, the first Berry family established a big farm just east of here, where they raised stock animals and some crops," Louise said. "Their sons and grandsons went into business, and eventually the farm was sold. They did try to hold on to some of the land, but the last of it had to be sold during the Depression."

"Maybe Vera will be able to date that old quilt for us," Alice said. "If she does, that might give us an idea of how old the sketchbook is."

⌾

Since it was still rather early to be calling on Vera Humbert, Jane decided to stop at Town Hall first.

"Jane." Lloyd Tynan emerged from the hall leading to his office and walked up to her as she walked in. "I'd like to speak with you in my office."

He looked so serious that Jane became alarmed. "Is everything all right?"

"Yes." He gestured toward the hall. "Please, it's important."

She followed him back to the office, and was further surprised when he closed the door. "Lloyd, you're starting to scare me."

He had the grace to flush. "I don't mean to, Jane, it's just I've been thinking about this all morning, and it has me very unsettled."

"Okay." She sat down. "I did remove the ink and the quill, you know."

"That's not it." He seemed hesitant to tell her.

She understood how he felt. Lloyd was more comfortable joking around than confiding in others. "You brought me back here, might as well get it out."

He nodded slowly. "All right. It's that Langston fellow who's staying at your inn. Ethel doesn't know what she's doing, getting mixed up with him."

Aunt Ethel, mixed up with Lester? He couldn't possibly mean in a romantic way. "I don't understand what you mean," she said, very carefully.

"You've seen the way he is around her. Always complimenting her and hovering around her." He scowled and curled his hand into a fist. "I'm telling you, Jane, he's up to no good. I think that he's after all the money Bob left her."

Her jaw dropped. "What? Oh, I think you're way off track here, Lloyd."

"She went with him to Potterston the other day, and spent the whole day over there with him. I know that for a fact because Ethel didn't come home until well after dark." Lloyd began pacing back and forth in front of the window. "I asked her about it, right up front and out in the open, like I always do, but she wouldn't say a word. Said for me not to worry about it and that it was her business. Now what does that tell you?"

She wondered if she should tell him about the birthday present, then decided against it. If Ethel meant it to be a surprise, telling Lloyd would spoil it.

"Aunt Ethel only went to do some shopping," Jane assured him. "She picked up some spices for me while she was there. As far as I know, Lester was simply going in that direction and offered her a ride. Even you have to admit that doesn't constitute an attempt to get at her money, Lloyd."

"It's not the first time he's taken her around. I've seen her in his car a couple of other times." He stopped and gave her a miserable look. "Jane, I can't stand by and watch this man take advantage of her. Ethel has the right to make her own decisions, of course . . . but it's breaking my heart."

"You're breaking mine here." Touched by his concern for her aunt, Jane rose and went to give him a hug. "I think you really need to talk to Aunt Ethel about this again. Tell her everything the way you just told me."

"And have her accuse me of sticking my nose into her personal business?" The prospect made him shudder. "You know how she prides herself on her independence, Jane. She'll never forgive me for doing that." His intercom buzzed, and he gave it an impatient look before he answered it. His receptionist informed him that Craig Tracy was waiting to see Jane. "Tell him she'll be out in just a minute."

She gave him a long sober look. "Lloyd, I can't claim to

have had all that much success in the relationship department, but I really do think you should talk to my aunt. It's no
good keeping things from the person you care about."

"I'll only make her angry if I do." He sighed, and then
gave her an unhappy look. "Promise me you won't say anything to her about this."

"Of course." She gave him another quick hug and gave
his tie a mischievous tug as she added, "You know I'm counting on your being my uncle someday."

That pleased him. "You never know, dear girl."

Lloyd went out to the lobby with her, where Craig Tracy
was waiting with his white wicker planter. "I finally have this
done," the florist said. "Where should I put it?"

Jane noticed that Craig had changed a few things. There
were more seed packets and herb bunches than she recalled,
as well as some silk ivy cleverly hung around the rack as if it
were growing that way. Before she could comment, however,
Sylvia Songer came in with her draped dressmaker's form.

"Good morning, everyone." The seamstress pushed the
form over to the display area. "I hope I'm not too late with
this. I stayed up until the wee hours getting it done."

"You're fine, Sylvia, but I was getting a little worried."
Jane showed her where to place the form, while Fred helped
the florist move his planter into his space.

Sylvia set the form in position. "I can't wait to see your
reaction," she confided to Jane. "Brace yourself, now." She
removed the draping cloth with a theatrical flourish.

Jane went over to look at the dress she had displayed. The
simple blue calico dress was gone, and in its place was a
fancier, more elaborate garment. "Very pretty."

Sylvia preened a little. "Thank you, Jane. I have to say, it
makes much more visual impact than that farm wife's dress."
She smiled at Lloyd and Craig.

The fancy gown was made of what appeared to be vivid
amethyst silk, which was gathered around the hem with little

white bows. Sylvia had drawn up one edge of the skirt, attaching it with a loop to one sleeve, exposing multiple layers of snowy white petticoats edged with frothy lace. The seamstress had also added other unique touches, such as a strand of pearls around the neck of the form and new brochures for her shop fashioned to resemble dance cards.

"The pearls are faux, of course," she told Jane, "but the silk is real."

Craig came over to inspect the dress. "That's incredibly lovely, Sylvia." He walked around it. "What a good idea with the flyers, too. But is it really what you'd consider . . . historical?"

"I made this for a costume ball I attended a few years ago. The pattern is the exact same one used for debutantes' gowns at the turn of the century," she told him. "Silk from that time period would be dry-rotted by now anyway, I'm afraid."

"Well, it's beautiful." He paused to study Sylvia's display, then his own, before turning to Jane. "I didn't realize that my rack has a couple of uneven legs. I don't want it tipping over, so I'm going to unload the shelves and switch it for another one I have back at my shop."

"Maybe Fred could do something to stabilize it," she said. *And maybe Craig is jealous of Sylvia's work.*

"No, I'd rather be safe than sorry. The last thing I want to do is have it fall over on top of some poor visitor." Craig nodded to Sylvia before he went over to the rack and began unloading the photos and samples.

"Excuse me for a minute, Sylvia." Jane went to join him. "May I ask you something?"

Craig put down the basket he was holding. "Of course."

"Is the rack really unstable, or are you just trying to outdo Sylvia?"

The florist's gaze shifted toward the silk gown. "I don't know what you mean."

She tried again. "This isn't a Christmas lighting competition. It doesn't matter who has the most elaborate display.

This Visitors Center is about our businesses and our history. It's to show people something about our town."

"I don't see why I can't make mine a little . . . bigger," Craig said.

"You can, but then Sylvia may want to make hers a little bigger. Then you'll want to add more, and then she will, and before you know it, things will get out of hand. Both of you are so talented that I know you can make displays that would be perfect for any department store window in any big city."

He frowned. "And why would that be a problem?"

"Well, frankly, we don't have the room. And things like that are beautiful and impressive, but they're also very . . . *anonymous*." She nodded at the window toward the street outside. "Acorn Hill is about peacefulness and family and our personal slice of history. History our ancestors wrote for us. History that we're writing, right now, for future generations." She sighed. "I wish I could explain it better."

"I think you did just fine," the florist told her and gave the rack a little test shake. "Well, what do you know, it's sturdier than I thought."

"I'm going to change mine back, too." Sylvia said from behind them. She gave Craig a slightly guilty look. "I was a little jealous of yours. You always know how to arrange things to get people's attention."

"And I didn't want mine to disappear into the woodwork next to yours." The florist sighed as he bent to retrieve some herb bundles that had fallen from his display. "Your eye for color is extraordinary."

"Here." Sylvia went to him. "Let me help you with that."

As Jane watched the two working together, she smiled. Although they did not realize it, Sylvia and Craig were demonstrating another facet of life in Acorn Hill. *People in small towns might have their differences*, Jane thought, *but they also know how to set them aside to get things done.*

Chapter ⚑ Fourteen

I have found birds and flowers and what looks like a little pig, but I can't find a single monogram on these old things," Louise said, refolding the linens she had checked. "How are you doing with yours, Alice?"

"The same. Beautiful handiwork—the French knots on this pillowcase edging are gorgeous—but no letters or initials anywhere." Alice looked over at Basil, who had finished checking the books and was now carefully replacing them in the trunk. "Did you have any luck, Basil?"

"I'm afraid not." He looked around and frowned. "We should look closely at the quilt you found with the sketch-book, Louise. Did you say someone in town had it?"

"Yes, Vera Humbert does. Do you think there might be some connection?" When he nodded, she groaned. "To think I told Fred to throw it away!"

"Now, now, Vera rescued it. That's all that matters," Alice said. "I'll go and call the Humberts and ask Vera to give it to Jane when she sees her." The bell downstairs at the front desk rang, and she dusted off her hands. "Let me go and see who that is."

"No, I will, Alice," Louise said. "Sissy Matthews was scheduled for a piano lesson today, and I am . . . hoping this might be her."

When Louise got downstairs, she found Lester Langston and Gwen Murphy instead of her prize student. Both were standing in front of the reception desk, and from the sound of their voices, they were having a rather heated argument.

"It's not my fault," the artist was telling him. "You should pay more attention where you leave that cane of yours."

"I told you I would be right back," Lester responded sharply. "Maybe next time you should look where you're walking."

"Excuse me," Louise said, going around to put the desk between her and them. "Did one of you ring for assistance?"

"Yeah, I did. I was just out on the porch, trying to get some work done while the light is good." Gwen flung a hand at Lester. "Then he left his cane next to my table so I could trip over it. I knocked over the fruit I was painting and broke that glass bowl that I borrowed from you."

"I didn't leave my cane there in order to trip you," Lester insisted. "I was only stepping inside for a moment to get the newspaper I'd left in the foyer."

"I wouldn't have tripped over it if you'd taken the thing with you."

"Ms. Murphy, Mr. Langston, please, calm down." When both of them began to speak at the same time, Louise held up her hands. "I understand you are both upset, but shouting at each other—or me—will not solve anything." She waited until they both subsided into unhappy silence before continuing. "Now, let me see if I understand the situation correctly. You left your cane on the porch, Mr. Langston, and you tripped over it, Ms. Murphy?"

"That's right," Gwen said.

"Yes," Lester agreed.

"Neither of you is hurt?" When they shook their heads, she relaxed a little more. "This sounds as if it was accidental instead of something"—she focused on Gwen—"intentional."

"Of course it was," Lester said, quite emphatically. "That's what I've been trying to tell her."

"It's his fault that it happened." The artist would not look at Louise. "I'm not paying for the broken bowl."

"I didn't ask you to, Ms. Murphy. I'll have this cleaned up in a moment. Excuse me." Louise quickly got a broom and dustpan.

"He should pay for it," Gwen said as she followed Louise out to the porch.

"Since the bowl belonged to the inn, and breaking it was an accident, I am not holding anyone responsible." *But you expected me to,* Louise thought, seeing confusion briefly flicker over the younger woman's face. *The same way that you expected me to refuse to fix your sink. What is going on here?*

"That's not necessary, Mrs. Smith." Her offer seemed to make Lester feel ashamed of his outburst. "I did forget to move my cane, so I should be the one to replace the bowl."

The artist's expression softened a few degrees. "You didn't break it. I did."

"Accidents will happen." Politely waving off Lester's attempt to man the dustpan, Louise swept up the glass shards. "Please, don't trouble yourselves about it any further."

"I am sorry about the accident, Ms. Murphy." Lester held out his hand to Gwen. "Next time, I'll take my cane with me."

She gave him a surprisingly warm smile and shook his hand. "I'll try to watch my step a little better next time."

He turned to Louise. "Do you know the only time lawyers get injured, Mrs. Smith?"

She played along. "No, when would that be?"

"When the ambulance backs up." Lester laughed at his own joke as he headed back upstairs.

Louise shook her head and went to discard the broken glass. When she returned to the foyer, the artist was waiting by the desk.

"You're quite the peacemaker, aren't you?" Gwen said. "I wouldn't have guessed that about you."

"My sister Alice is the peacemaker." Calmly she met the younger woman's challenging gaze with her own. "I am more the type who keeps accounts balanced."

Gwen's eyes narrowed. "So am I."

She wants me to accuse her of setting up the accident with Lester Langston and of deliberately clogging the drain in her bathroom. Louise didn't know how she knew that, but she did. "Was there something else you needed?"

"No." Gwen leaned against the desk. "Did you have something else you wanted to ask me?"

She was trying to goad her into a confrontation. Over the years Louise had learned to curb her naturally quick temper, but suddenly it surged up inside her with more anger than she had felt since Eliot's death.

Grace Chapel Inn was a business, but it was also Louise's home. It would only take a few words to send this spiteful young woman packing. Under the circumstances, it might also be the wisest thing to do. Gwen Murphy might not draw the line at clogged drains and semicomical accidents. She might do something that could result in real property damage or even an injury to someone else.

"God wants us to treat strangers as we would be treated," Rev. Thompson's quiet advice echoed in her mind, along with a verse from Ephesians 4:31-32 (NIV): "Get rid of all bitterness, rage and anger, brawling and slander, along with every form of malice. Be kind and compassionate to one another, forgiving each other, just as in Christ God forgave you."

The words gave her the strength to release her anger and let it dwindle away. *I have no idea why you are trying so hard to provoke me, but the only Christian way to fight back is not to fight at all.* After a long pause for her reflection,

Louise answered, "Yes, I do. May I see what you have been sketching?"

Gwen's stunned reaction would have been comical, if it had not confirmed Louise's suspicions. Still, she quickly recovered and shrugged. "If you want. I left my sketch pad out on the porch."

Louise followed the artist out to where she had been working, and studied the work in progress, which depicted a group of potted houseplants that Gwen had set up on one of the little porch tables. She was working in oil pastels, which were much smoother and blended more subtly than the chalk type, and her realist technique was precise to such a fine degree that the finished portion resembled a photograph more than a drawing.

Whatever her faults, the young woman obviously had considerable talent.

"I don't like abstract or conceptual art," Gwen said, "so I'll never be a Pollock or a Van Gogh."

"Your color choices and theme remind me of William Harnett's work," Louise said, studying the composition. "Have you ever seen *A Man's Table Reversed*? It is on exhibit at the Brandywine River Museum, less than an hour from here."

"I've seen photos of it." Gwen came to stand beside her. "I wish I could capture the depths of shadows and define surfaces the way he did."

"The man's pipe in Harnett's painting looks so real that you almost expect it to smell of tobacco smoke." Louise heard the phone ringing. "I better get that. You do impressive work, Ms. Murphy. I hope you will allow me to see more of it."

She turned her back on the gaping artist and only permitted herself a smile when she was inside. *I think I definitely won that round.*

The caller turned out to be Carol Matthews.

"Hi, Louise." Sissy's mother sounded very unhappy. "I know we were supposed to be there thirty minutes ago, but Sissy isn't feeling well again. She went to lie down in her room."

"I am so sorry to hear that, Carol. I'll be glad to reschedule her lesson for another day."

"No, Louise, this is the third time she's ducked out of taking them." Sissy's mother heaved a sigh. "I don't know what's the matter with her—maybe she's just tired of music."

Or of me, Louise thought, her heart twisting. "Is there anything that I can do?"

"I spoke to my husband, and he agreed that we shouldn't take up any more of your time or force Sissy to do something she doesn't want." Carol's voice turned sad. "I'm sorry, Louise, but we'll have to put an end to her piano lessons for now."

∞

After Sylvia and Craig had finished restoring their displays to their original condition and had left to return to their shops, June came over to tell Jane about the cooperative display she and Clarissa Cottrell, the owner of the Good Apple Bakery, had planned to set up.

"What a terrific combination," Jane said once she had heard the details. "The visitors will love it."

"We thought as much." June looked over her shoulder and smiled. "Hello there, Mayor. I haven't seen you for lunch in a few days. Are you brown-bagging it this week?"

"No time, June." Lloyd went over to inspect Sylvia's display. "I thought she had a ball gown of some sort on this earlier."

"She changed her mind, Lloyd."

"Well, see to it that she doesn't change it again." He put his hand around the neck of the form and rocked it, making the farm wife dress's skirts sway. "Fred, we'll need to secure this somehow."

Fred ambled over and lifted the hem to study the base of the form. "I could anchor it with some sandbags. Anything else I'd have to drive into the flooring."

The mayor's secretary came in from an errand and came to a full halt. "Oh my goodness."

Jane followed her gaze. Fred looking under the skirts and the mayor holding the form by the neck made something of a startling sight. "They're just, um, inspecting things."

"Yes, I see that," the secretary said faintly before she continued to her desk.

"Now if the Lord has a real sense of humor," June said, stifling a laugh, "Ethel and Vera will walk in. Or Carlene Moss. Can't you just see this picture on the front page of the *Acorn Nutshell?*"

Jane looked up at the ceiling. "Please, Lord, don't get funny right now."

The Lord must have taken her seriously, for the next person who walked in was no laughing matter.

Florence Simpson completely ignored Lloyd and Fred, and made her way toward Jane. A member of the church board and a woman regarded by some to be the town's most self-righteous busybody, Florence had been the cause of a number of problems for the Howard sisters, starting from the moment they had decided to renovate their childhood home into an inn.

She didn't look as if she had come to wish Jane luck with her project this time, either. Happily, Lloyd and Fred finished inspecting Sylvia's display and walked back to the storage room across from Lloyd's office.

If only, Jane thought as Florence came to a halt in front of her, *I could hide myself in there with them.* "Hi, Florence. Long time, no see."

"Jane. I heard something that I couldn't believe was true." Her small, piercing gray eyes moved over the displays before returning to blaze with outrage.

Outside the sky began to darken, and thunder clapped in the distance.

"Whatever was it?" asked Jane.

"Am I to understand that you have a set of first-edition Little Shepherdess books here? A full set of all twelve, signed by the author, and given to you by Pastor Thompson for this . . . this . . ." Florence's gold bracelets jingled as she made a dismissive gesture toward the displays.

"Community Visitors Center," Jane supplied the term for her. "Yes, we do."

Florence's mouth turned down at the corners. "I thought so. I voted against hiring that Thompson man, you know, and now it turns out that I was right. He's just as controlling and conniving as I suspected."

"Excuse me." Jane clamped down on her temper before she went on. "How does giving some books for a community project equal controlling and conniving?"

The older woman's nostrils flared. "He had no authority to make that kind of donation."

"He didn't donate them. He's lending them to us," she pointed out. "Donations we keep, borrowed stuff we have to give back. Big difference."

Florence ignored that. "Do you even know how much those books are worth?" she demanded, making her extra chin quiver.

"A lot." Jane barely restrained her foot from tapping the carpet.

"I called a friend of mine in Newark who handles auctions and had her check her computer. Those books are worth *ten thousand dollars*." Florence spoke the last three words with the same reverence other people used to say "God in heaven."

If it was true—and Jane had no doubt that it was—then keeping such valuable books safe presented an immediate problem. But that was Rev. Thompson's problem, and her problem, not Florence Simpson's. "Well, thank you for the price check, Florence. I'll let the pastor know, and he and I will decide what to do from here."

Lightning flashed outside, and thunder boomed again, much closer this time.

Something unpleasant glittered in the other woman's small eyes. "We'll just see what the church board has to say about that." Ruffles flared out as Florence whirled around and stomped out of Town Hall.

∽

Lloyd had several other changes that he wanted to discuss with Fred and Jane concerning the displays, so June left before the rain started. The mayor's secretary finished her work for the day and also departed, in something of a rush.

Poor woman, Jane thought as she saw her go. *It's not every day you catch your boss throttling a mannequin. Or watch me conduct a hissing match with Florence Simpson.*

While the mayor went on at length about what he wanted done, Jane began to feel slightly irritated again. Most of what Lloyd wanted had little to do with safety and everything to do with his personal preferences. Some of it seemed petty and a waste of time. The run-in with Florence only magnified the irritation factor.

Jane was tempted to pull the mayor off to the side and ask him about his requirements, but Lloyd finally reached the end of the "minor adjustments" he wanted and decided to go home himself. Since they were still waiting for Craig to return, he gave Fred the keys to lock up.

"Is your aunt home tonight?" the mayor asked Jane on his way out.

"She usually is." Maybe his concern for Ethel was what

was making him so prickly about everything else, Jane thought. "You should call her, ask her out for dinner. Take her to a movie. Just talk to her, Lloyd."

He started to say something before he gave her a sheepish nod and departed.

Jane glanced at her mother's writing desk, which needed to be cleaned and polished. "I'd better bring what I need tomorrow to redo the inn's display." She went over to lower the lid and see how much space she had to work with. "Fred, were you able to fix that little cupboard door?"

"I coated the hinges with a little oil and let them sit, but I haven't tried to open it yet." Fred wiped off his hands on a rag before he carefully tugged on the door pull.

There was a high-pitched squeak before the little door popped out. Fred worked the hinges back and forth for a moment, and then he went still.

"Take a gander at this here, Jane." He pointed inside the little space.

Jane bent over and saw the edges of some yellowed envelopes, and reached in to take them out. "They look like old letters."

She removed a bundle, which was neatly tied together with an old ribbon. The top letter had a rose-colored three-cent stamp with a profile of George Washington on it, which prompted her to check the postmark. It was very faded, but she could just make out the year.

"Good Lord." She blinked. "Fred, these were mailed back in 1861."

Chapter Fifteen

Alice sensed something was wrong with Louise from the moment she returned to the attic and said she would not be able to continue to help them search. Her older sister looked pale and almost shaky, but she claimed she was only tired and needed to take a rest.

"We've gone through the rest of what was in the trunk anyway and didn't find anything," Alice assured her. "You go have a lie down and I'll look after things."

Louise gave her a grateful smile. "Thank you, dear."

Basil, who helped Alice replace the linens and books in the trunk before he accompanied her downstairs, also noticed. "Your sister didn't look well at all, Alice."

"Louise suffers from headaches every now and then. I think the dust and the musty smells up there might have brought one on." She went to check the answering machine, which Louise had switched off, and saw the message light blinking. *She must not have noticed it.* "Excuse me for a minute, Basil." She pressed the button to play the recorded message.

"Miss Howard, you said if we ever needed help we could call you." The girl's voice was low and sounded frightened. "I know you're not there, or you're busy, but I really need to

talk to you. Please call me back when you hear this. Please."
The message ended.

Basil looked as concerned as she felt. "That sounds like
a child. Do you recognize the voice?"

"Yes, it's Lisa Masur, a member of my girls group at
church." Alice retrieved her phone and address book from
under the desk. "Lord, what could have happened?"

"Is Lisa a petite little girl with brown ponytails and
braces?" he asked.

She stared at him. "Yes. How did you know?"

He didn't answer, but went to the front door and opened
it. Lisa Masur came hurrying in.

"I just got your message." Alice came from behind the
desk and hurried to the child, who flung herself in Alice's
arms. "Lisa! What's wrong, honey?"

The girl was trembling and in tears. "I'm sorry,
Miss Howard, I know I should have asked first if I could
come over, but I couldn't wait. I had to talk to you right now."

Outside it began to rain hard, and lightning flashed.

"That's all right." Alice smoothed a hand over the top of
the little girl's head and glanced at Basil, who nodded and
quietly retreated upstairs. "Let's go into the parlor. We can
talk privately there."

She settled Lisa on the sofa with a box of tissues before
she closed the parlor door. Then she went and sat beside her.
"Do your parents know you're here?"

Lisa shook her head. "My dad is at work, and my mom
is out shopping with my cousin. I stayed home so I could talk
to you without anyone listening, but then I was afraid they
would come back before you called."

Alice knew the Masurs from church. Lisa's parents were
a pleasant, active couple who adored their only daughter.
"Tell me what's wrong."

"It's Darla." The girl balled up a tissue in her hand. "Ever
since she came to stay with us she's been *so mean*."

Just another squabble between two girls. Most of Alice's fears abruptly melted away. "How is she being mean to you?"

"Lots of ways but there's this one thing that's really, really bad." The girl looked up at her. "Miss Howard, you said in group once that God wants us to tell the truth."

"Yes. That's one of God's commandments, too." Alice said.

Lisa looked down at her sneakers. "What if you knew about something that you should tell, but if you tell you'll get into super trouble for something else? It's not lying if you don't say anything, right?"

Alice shook her head. "Hiding the truth by keeping silent is just as bad as lying, I'm afraid. As Christians, God expects us to be honest people. Being honest means speaking the truth and living in truth. The Bible says, 'God is spirit, and his worshipers must worship in spirit and in truth.'" She took a tissue from the box and wiped the fresh tears that spilled down Lisa's cheeks.

"I want to be a good Christian, Miss Howard. Honest, I do," the girl said, her voice plaintive. "But she said she'd get me in big trouble if I said anything about what she did."

This sounded more serious now. "Lisa, why don't you start by telling me the truth. I can't help you if I don't know what you're talking about." When the child ducked her head, she added, "I promise that whatever you tell me will stay just between you and me."

"Okay." Lisa gulped. "Last week my mom left me and Darla while she went to run some errands. Darla wanted to play with some of my mom's makeup. I told her I'm not allowed to, but Darla said it would be okay and we could wash it off before she came home."

Alice nodded. "Go on."

"When my dad went to Paris, he brought back a really nice bottle of perfume for my mom. It's her favorite, and she keeps it on her vanity table." Her bottom lip trembled. "I didn't mean to knock it over, but . . . I did, and I didn't notice right away, and then I smelled it but by then . . . all the perfume had spilled out and got soaked into the carpet."

"And you didn't tell your mother that you spilled it," Alice guessed.

"Darla said that we could blame it on Sheba, my cat. She brought Sheba in my mom's room and closed the door, and then we washed off the makeup and we didn't say anything. When Mom came home and found Sheba and the empty bottle, she cried."

Alice tried to untangle the story in her mind. "So Darla said that if you tell your mother that she put Sheba in the room, she'll tell her that it was you who spilled the perfume?"

The child nodded her head and rubbed her nose with the back of her hand. "Darla did something else, something *really* bad, and I found out about it. But she says if I tell on her she'll say I spilled the perfume bottle *and* that I put Sheba in the room."

Alice had thought Darla stubborn, but not vicious. It disturbed her to think that the child was manipulative enough to use her cousin's guilt as means to protect herself. "What did Darla do that she doesn't want you to tell anyone?"

What Lisa told her next completely flabbergasted Alice. "She made Sissy Matthews quit playing the piano."

∞

Jane decided to hold on to the letters Fred had found in the old desk until she got home. They were too great a surprise not to share with her sisters. In addition, she was hoping that Alice could decipher the handwriting, which appeared to her own gaze as clusters of fancy swirls rather than words.

"Here, Jane." Fred gave her a piece of plastic wrap and a clean cloth to wrap around them and keep them from getting wet. "Were you able to make out the name and address?"

"Not much of it, and it's starting to make my eyes dance.

Didn't anyone block print back in those days?" She showed him the first envelope. "What do you think that is—an *M* maybe?"

"Hard to tell." He peered at it and scratched his head. "That last part there could be 'Berry'—any M. Berrys in your family?"

"Only my mother, that I know of, and these letters are too old to be hers." She wrapped up the letters and slipped them into her oversized purse, and then took out the compact umbrella she carried. "I'll show them to my sisters and let you know what they say. Thanks for finding them, and for everything, Fred."

She left Town Hall and met Fred's wife just outside. "Hi, Vera. I was just coming over to see you."

"Fred mentioned that you'd be here this afternoon, so I thought I'd stop in on my way home from shopping." Vera seemed excited. "Can you come over to our house for a few minutes? I have something to show you."

Jane agreed, and drove Vera back to her house. Along the way, she told Fred's wife about Basil Kirchwey and how he had had them all fooled into thinking he was the Innside Reporter. "He's up in the attic right now with Alice and Louise, trying to find out who that sketchbook belongs to. It was wrapped up in that old quilt that you rescued. Speaking of which, why on earth did you?"

Vera glanced sideways. "You don't know what it is, then?"

"I didn't get the chance to see it yet." She pulled up to the front of the Humberts' home. "But from what Louise said, it's a really old, dirty, torn-up quilt."

"That's just on the outside. There's another quilt on the inside," Vera told her.

"It's two quilts in one?" She frowned. "No wonder it was so heavy."

"It's what we call a hidden quilt. I also believe from the

pattern of the patchwork that the one on the inside may be a funeral or mourning quilt." At Jane's shocked look, she added dryly, "That doesn't mean it wrapped a body."

"Thank goodness." She followed Vera into the house. "If I told Louise and Alice that it had, they'd never set foot in our attic again."

"I knew there was something unusual about it from the moment I spotted it at Town Hall," Vera told her as she folded her umbrella and left it to dry in a stand by the front door. "I could see that it was old, but the thickness was all wrong. Vintage quilts are very thin, since the cotton batting used in them becomes compressed over the years. Yours, in contrast, looked more like a comforter. Then I saw that the corner of the top quilt was torn, and that the patchwork of another quilt showed through the tear."

Jane was bewildered. "Why would someone hide a quilt inside a quilt?"

"The quilt was not really hidden so much as it was recycled," Vera explained. "Fabric was often hard to come by in years past, so thrifty women would take worn quilts and sew new tops and backings on them. The old quilt then served as the batting for the new."

"Oh, I get it now. Sort of like reupholstering." It was making her curious about what was underneath the ugly old wool. "Can you tell what the inside quilt looks like?"

"I only saw a bit of one square," Vera said. "What I'd like to do, with your permission, is remove the top so we can see the inner quilt properly. The outer coverings are badly deteriorated and of no value. They weren't quilted to the inner piece, either, and because they're only tied in a few places, I can take it apart with a few snips of the scissors."

Jane saw no reason why she shouldn't. "Sure, I want to know what's inside." She looked out the window at the rain, which was now coming down very hard. "Might as well— looks like I might be staying here awhile."

"Wonderful." Vera smiled. "Let me get it."

She returned a moment later with the quilt and nodded toward her front room. "Let's spread it out on my living-room floor so we can get a better look at it."

Jane moved some chairs out of the way and helped Vera lay out the quilt on the hardwood floor. Fred's wife showed her how the outer layers had been tied to the inner quilt with loops of twine, which she snipped and carefully tugged out. Since the outer binding, which sandwiched and covered all the edges, was ragged, and in some places almost gone, all Vera had to do was snip it away here and there to remove it. After she peeled away the top covering, she stood up and moved back.

Lightning flashed outside, very close, but Jane hardly noticed.

The quilt that Vera had revealed was a faded brown, with blocks of green, blue and black appliqué work. Many of the patches were threadbare, but all were intact, thanks to the dense, tiny lines of stitching that covered every inch. It was beautifully made, but so somber that it made Jane feel sad just to look at it.

"I was wrong. This isn't a funeral quilt, it's a mourning quilt," Vera said, sounding much more subdued than before. "It's also very, very old. Jane, if you and your sisters don't want it, you might consider selling it or donating it to a museum."

"How old do you think it is?"

Vera sat beside it and studied the pattern. "At least one hundred and fifty years, maybe more. It's quite a rare pattern. I've only seen one like this in a book on quilt history. That one had the same type of appliqué work and was embroidered with all the names of the men in the maker's family who were killed during the Civil War."

Jane suppressed a shudder. "But why would someone make such a gruesome thing? I thought quilts were supposed to be made for happy occasions like weddings and babies and stuff."

"They were, for the most part," Vera said. "I think the difference is that life was very hard for women in the 1800s. They were lucky to live to the age of thirty or forty in those days."

"That's really depressing."

Vera nodded. "Aside from the wars, women themselves often died in childbirth, and if they survived they usually lost at least one baby to childhood disease. They had to face a lot more death than we do."

"I still can't imagine why someone would want to make a quilt for a death." Jane gently traced the edge of one appliquéd curve with her fingertip. "It seems so . . . depressing."

"Women made quilts for times of grief, just as they did for births and weddings. They made special laying-out quilts for the wake, and draping quilts to place over the coffin," Vera told her. "When the pioneers died on their journeys to the West, their women would often wrap the body in a quilt before it was buried, as a substitute for a coffin."

Jane gave the quilt a dubious look. "What do you think ours was used for?"

"It was probably made as a memorial for the deceased— hence the name, mourning quilt—and given as a gift to the surviving family. There are thirty individual appliquéd blocks, and while none of them is signed, from the variations in the stitching I'd say each was made by a different hand."

Her eyes widened. "Thirty different women worked on it?"

"That would be the right number of women if it was made by a large quilters group. You can tell the purpose from some of the symbols used in the blocks, too." Vera opened one fold to show Jane a square. "See these acorns, laurel leaves and roses? Those are the traditional symbols for immortality, eternity, and the brevity of human life. The women who made your quilt used bits of navy blue home-spun, which might have come from the men's Union Army uniforms. They would cut patches and appliqués from the clothes that belonged to their lost loved one."

"I guess working together to make the quilt was a way to deal with their loss." Jane gave Vera a sad smile. "Thank you for rescuing it for us."

"Please just don't let it be tossed aside again. I know your mother would have wanted her family heirloom to be looked after."

"My mother?"

"Didn't you see the name and dedication embroidered in the very center block?" Vera pointed to it.

Jane had to bend close to make out the tiny words: *In memory of your dearest one, his final battle has been won.* Beneath that was stitched *For Emily Berry.*

∽

After an hour, the lightning and thunder faded away as the rainstorm moved on. Like the sun, people in town cautiously emerged after the battering of wind and rain.

Louise had never seen Jane look more excited as when she arrived back at the inn with the quilt and the letters that Fred had discovered in their mother's desk. She sent Alice to get Basil so he could hear what she had learned from Vera Humbert.

If only I had her energy, Louise thought, watching her youngest sister's animated face as she related the tale of the mourning quilt. Ever since Carol Matthews had called, she had felt so defeated. *And I wish I had her way with people. Jane would never alienate a child.*

"So it's definitely possible that the Emily in the sketchbook is the same Emily Berry whose name is embroidered on the quilt, and therefore, our ancestress," Jane finally said.

"That would explain why she looks so much like Mother." Alice looked at the quilt and the bundle of letters. "But that still doesn't tell us who the sketchbook belonged to."

"May I look at the letters you found, Jane?" Basil asked.

"They're really old." Jane took them from her purse and handed them to him. "I can hardly read the writing on the envelopes. I was going to ask Alice if she could. She's used to reading doctor's notes."

As Basil cautiously loosened the ribbon, Louise noticed for the first time how very precise he was with his hands. The man seemed terribly clumsy at times, but at other times he had the fine motor control of a talented artist or a skilled musician. She wondered if he had ever tried to paint or play.

"These look genuine, in which case they're very old," Basil said as he sorted through the letters. "The earliest one dates back to 1859." He looked at Louise. "May I open them?"

"Please."

He carefully opened the envelope, which turned out to be the outside of the letter itself, folded and sealed. The golden paper appeared to be quite heavy. His gaze moved over the opening paragraph. "This is a letter of sympathy."

"Would you mind reading it out loud, Basil?" Alice asked.

"'August 19, 1863. My Dear Emily,'" he read, "'with great sorrow and consternation did my wife and I receive the news of your brother's premature death at Gettysburg. We write to offer you our sincerest condolences and to inquire as to how we can be of service to you in this time of need. My wife has particular concerns about your being alone at this time, and you have but to say the word and she will be happy to travel to Acorn Hill and provide whatever assistance that she may.'" He paused and skimmed down the rest of the page. "He goes on to express his sense of loss, and mentions pleasant memories of her brother and visiting their farm, and he expresses wishes for her husband's safe return. Toward the end he repeats his offer to send his wife or to provide any help she might need. It's signed 'Your friend, Peter Hamilton.'"

"Poor thing, no wonder she looked so sad in that portrait." Jane sighed.

"Here's another one in a different hand." Basil opened another letter that appeared to be made of slightly flimsier paper. "It's dated April 14, 1859, to 'Emmie' from 'Rob.'"

Basil went on to read the letter, which described the rather ordinary life of a common foot soldier in a Union Army camp. However, the facts were liberally peppered with affectionate, almost teasing phrases that clearly showed the writer and the recipient were very close.

"'I must gather wood for the cook fire now and then Fred and I have guard duty. It is only at moments like these that I miss your cooking, which you will be gratified to know is vastly superior to Fred's. As for my own cooking, the camp surgeon has declared my biscuits durable enough to serve as substitutes for cannon balls, although he believes they would be more effective if fed to the enemy.'" Basil looked up and grinned as the sisters chuckled over that. "He signs it 'Your Faithful Servant and Brother, Rob.'"

"Emily's brother!" Alice seemed moved.

He turned over the letter, which had a small notation on the back. "It was sent by Robert Charters, 5th Infantry, Cumberland Landing, Virginia."

"Obviously Emily married into the Berry family," Louise said. "Her maiden name was Charters."

Alice glanced at the wall clock and rose. "I hate to run at a time like this, but I promised I'd meet with a couple of my ANGELs before our regular meeting."

After Alice left, Basil studied the handwriting for another moment. "It could be that your sketchbook belonged to Robert Charters."

Louise went and retrieved the sketchbook, but she soon determined that the handwriting did not match.

"Rats!" Jane looked glum. "If Robert Charters wasn't the artist, who was?"

"Maybe it belonged to Emily." Louise looked at the letters. "Are there any there that she wrote?"

Basil searched through them. "No, they're all addressed to her, and most are from her brother."

The door to the kitchen swung open. "Ethel, they're all here in the kitchen." Lester Langston came in, and held the door until the sisters' aunt sailed through. She was carrying two brown paper bags and was looking very pleased with herself.

Jane got up to help her. "Did you bring me a present?"

"Why, are you still six?" her aunt demanded.

"I can be." She looked in the top of one bag, which was quite heavy, but only saw wads of newspaper. "What's all this?"

"Treasures." Ethel seemed in a very happy mood from the way she beamed at the lawyer. "Thank you again for taking me with you, Lester. I'm completely hooked now." She turned to smile at her nieces. "I have a brand-new hobby— junking."

"Indeed," Louise said, her tone clearly expressing what she thought of the concept.

"It's wonderful. Lester took me to this wonderful row of junk shops over in Potterston. I was telling him how Lloyd likes to collect political memorabilia, and he said the junk shops are a great place to look for campaign badges people wear during elections." She put down her bag and started rummaging through it. "You won't believe what I found."

The eldest Howard sister drew back. "Junk and rusty old badges, I would imagine."

"Treasures." Ethel produced three items, one after the other, and placed them on the table. "Now, guess what these are."

"Well, they're not campaign badges." Jane examined the lot. "My guess is, an old hair brush, a Christmas tree decoration, and an ugly brick with holes in it."

Her aunt gave her a slightly exasperated look. "This is a camel-hair hat brush, a coat cane, and a scouring brick." When no one said anything, she threw up her hands. "They're antiques for your town display."

"Oh. Okay." Jane studied the items again. "They made women scour things with bricks? Wouldn't that be a little rough on the hands? Or is this a gift for Lloyd?"

"No, dear. My grandmother had one, and she would grind a bit of dust from the brick and use it with water and soap to clean everyday utensils."

"Gotcha."

"I understand the hat brush," Louise said, and held up the coat cane, "but what was this used for?"

"That's how they did dry cleaning a hundred and fifty years ago," Lester chimed in. "You would hang your jacket or coat on a clothes horse and beat it with that cane to get the dust and dirt out before you brushed it." He grinned. "I think back in those days, lawyers might also have used them to get money out of their clients."

"I have other things, too," Ethel told them. "Mostly some odd dishes, but also three old *Life* magazines, some postcards and a bobbin lace tablecloth too. No campaign badges, but I'm going back for another search with Lester later this week."

Louise looked astonished. "And you found all these things in *junk* shops?"

"People often donate or sell off the contents of old houses to the folks at the junk shops, which are run by different charity organizations," Lester told her. "The folks at the shops are all volunteers, and they sometimes leave things in the original boxes for the customers to sort through."

"That's where you find the real treasures." Ethel looked out through the window at the garden. "Is someone outside?"

Jane went to look out the side door. "I don't see anyone."

"I could have sworn I saw someone pass by that window." Her aunt shrugged. "Come, Jane, help me unpack these dishes."

As they sorted through Ethel's remaining treasures, Lester took an interest in the old letters on the table. Louise explained the mystery of the sketchbook and how Jane had found the letters in their mother's old desk.

"I still wish we could find a sample of Emily's handwriting," Louise said. "I know it's unlikely that the sketchbook belonged to her, but I would like to know for sure."

"You should check to see if she has a marriage license," Lester suggested. "Pennsylvania began to record marriages back in 1852, and some justices of the peace required both husband and wife to sign the license."

"Where would we look for something like that?"

"The records are usually kept at the county courthouse and maintained on microfiche by the clerk of the court. But as it happens, I've learned from my work here that until the turn of the century, the justice of the peace for this particular region lived right here in Acorn Hill." The lawyer smiled at her. "His dockets and ledgers may still be on file at Town Hall."

Chapter Sixteen

After Lisa told Alice what Darla had done to Sissy Matthews, Alice tried to talk the girl into going to her parents and telling them everything.

"This isn't something you can keep to yourself, Lisa. You know that."

The girl nodded. "I just . . . I just can't, Miss Howard. I know I'm supposed to, but I can't. I've never done anything like that. Plus I knew what Darla was doing and didn't tell anyone. My mom will hate me for that."

Try as she might, Alice had not been able to persuade her to change her mind. Lisa had been too frightened of the consequences. Since she had promised to keep what the girl had told her confidential, Alice felt she might have better luck confronting the source of the problem.

"Is your cousin coming with you to our ANGELs group tonight?" she had asked Lisa.

"Yes, ma'am."

"Ask your mother to drop you off at church a little early, and I'll talk to Darla before the meeting."

"But you promised that you wouldn't tell anyone," the child had protested.

That she had, and Alice suddenly realized that she

herself couldn't speak of this to anyone, either—including Darla—or she would be breaking her word to Lisa. By trying to help the child, she had, in essence, trapped herself in the very same situation she was trying to resolve.

As she walked to the church, Alice tried in vain to think of how she could help both girls. Her father had often referred to situations in youth ministry similar to this as "tests of faith" and believed strongly in using counseling and guidance through Scripture to motivate children to find their own resolutions.

She glanced up at the sky. "Somehow I don't think telling Darla that 'the truth will set you free' is going to work, do You, Lord?"

Alice continued to mull it over as she set up the assembly room at church. Somehow she had to reach Darla, who was at the center of it all. If the older girl would only come clean about it, Lisa would surely follow.

She opened her Bible to find and bookmark a passage in Matthew for that night's discussion, when her gaze fell upon the verses that told of Jesus' healing a blind, mute man who was possessed by demons. Jesus' own words, printed in red, seemed to jump from the page.

Alice closed her eyes for a moment. *Thank You, Lord. I know what to do for Darla now.*

"Lisa said we had to come early." Darla walked in and looked around the room as if expecting to see the other girls. "What for?"

"Hello, Darla. I wanted to get your opinion on something. Come in and sit down." Alice saw Lisa lingering in the doorway, and smiled at her. "You too, Lisa."

Once the girls were seated, Alice brought the Bible over to Lisa and placed it in front of her. "I'm working on a lesson plan, and I want to make sure I explain these verses clearly. Lisa, would you read Matthew 12:35–37 aloud, please? Darla, please listen."

In a slightly wavering voice Lisa read, "'The good man brings good things out of the good stored up in him, and the evil man brings evil things out of the evil stored up in him. But I tell you that men will have to give account on the Day of Judgment for every careless word they have spoken. For by your words you will be acquitted, and by your words you will be condemned.'" She looked up with her eyes round and fearful.

"Thank you, Lisa." Alice turned to Darla. "Those are Jesus' words to the Pharisees, who accused him of using evil power to cure a sick man. Do you understand what they mean?"

Darla shrugged. "It means that bad people are bad inside, and good people are good, and everyone should watch what they say."

She's much more intuitive than I thought. Good for you, Darla. "Jesus believed that what we keep hidden in our hearts comes out in every word we speak," Alice told her. "So that no matter how clever we think we are, and how much we watch what we say, the truth always comes out in the end."

"Not always," the girl argued. "I know plenty of kids who lie and get away with it." She shot a smirk at Lisa, who looked ready to sink into the floor.

"That might seem to be the case, but is it really true?" Alice met Darla's defiant gaze. "Someone who lies or conceals something that they have done wrong, and is clever about it, may not get caught. But because there are no consequences, they won't hesitate to do it again. That's the nature of sin. If they still don't get caught, they go on to commit bigger sins, because they got away with the little ones."

"So?"

"Remember that this person would never be able to tell the truth, would never show what's really inside his or her heart, and would always be afraid someone might find out about the bad things in the past." Alice met her defiant gaze.

"Even if this clever person never gets caught, would that be a good life?"

Darla's expression changed to one of uncertainty. "I don't know." Her face became flushed.

"I think sins are like little weights on your heart," Alice said. "The more sin you conceal and carry inside, the heavier they get. The only way to get rid of them is to repent and make amends." She smiled. "Well, thank you, girls. You've helped me a great deal with my lesson plan." She walked back to her desk.

"Miss Howard?" When she turned, Darla asked, "What if you never stop and . . . and make amends, like you said? What happens?"

"If you can't be close to God, then you can't be close to anyone else," Alice said.

The two girls were very quiet during the ANGELs meeting, and several times Alice caught Darla watching her with that same, uncertain look in her eyes. Lisa, on the other hand, fidgeted and seemed ready to bolt out of her chair at any moment.

Alice felt as if she had planted the seeds, and now she had to give them time to sprout. She also decided that the next time she would think through a situation before she made a promise of confidentiality.

When the meeting was over and Lisa's mother arrived to pick up the two girls, Alice simply thanked them again for coming in early. Darla went with Lisa's mother to the car, but Lisa ran back a few minutes later.

"I need to ask you something." The child looked miserable. "You're really not going to tell my mom about me or Darla, are you? We have to do it ourselves. That's what you were trying to tell us with the Bible verse from Matthew."

Alice nodded.

The child swallowed hard. "I'm going to tell my mom what I did as soon as we get home, but I'm not going to say anything about Darla. She'll have to admit what she did on her own, like I'm doing." Lisa sighed. "That's the right way to do it, isn't it? You're not going to say anything either, are you?"

Oh, how she wished she could. But if she was to teach this lesson to Darla, she had to maintain her silence. "No, I won't say anything. I think what you're doing is very brave, Lisa." Alice gave her a hug before the girl smiled and ran back out to the waiting car.

Darla looked out through the car window at Alice, and then turned away.

"I think it's working, Lord," she murmured as she watched the Masurs drive away. "Only please see what you can do to inspire that child to find honesty, and soon."

∞

Over the next week the Howard sisters divided their time between running the inn and finishing the display at Town Hall. Contributions from other local merchants added many delightful touches, and with Fred's help, the sisters found ways to arrange them all artfully.

There was only one problem.

"Lloyd Tynan," Jane announced one morning after breakfast, while she was washing dishes and her sisters were folding the brochures they had had printed for the inn, "needs to go on vacation . . . to an exotic place . . . far, far away from Town Hall, and our Visitors Center, and *me*."

Alice, who was finishing her juice from breakfast, nearly choked. "Heavens, Jane. It's not that bad."

Her younger sister frowned. "Look me in the eye and tell me that the mayor isn't driving you crazy."

"He's . . ." she ducked her head. "Okay, he's become a bit of an obstacle."

"I suspect that every marketing strategy has its challenges," Louise said, suppressing a smile.

"Oh, I can deal with a challenge, Louise," Jane assured her, shaking a dishtowel in her direction. "Bring on the challenges. After what we've dealt with this week, they'd be a vacation for Alice and me."

Alice glanced at her uneasily. "I guess this wouldn't be the best time to mention that Florence has called a church board meeting about Pastor Thompson and those books."

"That does it." Jane finished stacking the last dish, then looked around the sparkling clean kitchen. "I need to weed something." She stalked out through the side door into the garden.

Louise looked at Alice. "What is the mayor doing to get her into such a tizzy? And what on earth is Florence up to now?"

Alice took her empty glass to the sink. "Lloyd has some definite ideas about how he wants the displays to look. He's asked us to make changes."

"How is that a problem?"

She glanced over her shoulder. "He's been asking us to make the changes pretty much hourly."

"Ah," Louise grimaced, "I can see where that would drive Jane to weeding. Why is the mayor interfering so much?"

"It's not that he interferes, exactly." Alice finished rinsing out her glass and returned to the table. "It's more like he tries to supervise things."

"Well, that can be helpful."

"Not when he tries to supervise things like how Fred hammers nails into the wall, and the way Jane dusts." She stacked her folded brochures and placed them in the upright clear holder. "I've never seem him so critical, and he's always . . . hovering, sort of."

"I know Lloyd wants to make sure the Visitors Center will look good." Louise finished folding her own stack and added them to Alice's. "But I know what you mean. Some people want to help so much that they end up in the way. And then there's Florence."

"Yes, there's Florence. June called me about her. It seems that Florence wants to sell the M. E. Roberts books and use the money for the church and our missions." Alice put down the brochure she was folding wrong. "She also wants Pastor Thompson reprimanded for lending them to the project without consulting the church board first."

"Oh, good Lord!" Louise set down the brochure she was folding. "She can't be serious."

"You know Florence, and there's also something going on between Lloyd and Aunt Ethel," she said. "He asks me about her every time I see him, but the questions are so odd. It's as if he suspects she's doing something that she shouldn't."

Louise shook her head. "All he has to do is call her, and she would tell him that herself. Aunt Ethel is not the type to keep secrets."

"That's another thing. Have you noticed how distant they've been with each other lately? I can count on one hand the number of times I've seen them together in the past few days." Alice looked worried. "After seeing each other so steadily for so long, I'm beginning to think, well, that they're ready to break up or something."

"If they were, I think Ethel would be much more upset. She cares very deeply for Lloyd. I doubt she would still be going out trying to find a birthday present for him, either. I am sure that whatever it is, they'll work it out." Louise looked up as Jane came back in from the garden. "Did you run out of weeds?"

"We will *never* run out of weeds, Louise." Jane washed her hands at the sink. "Fred's waiting for me out front. I forgot he was coming by to pick me up. I'll be back around lunchtime, if I'm not charged with multiple counts of felony assault and battery, that is."

"Patience, little sister," Louise advised her.

"That or plane tickets to Fiji for the mayor and a Florence-sized gag." She took the brochures from Alice and gave her sisters a wry smile before she left.

"Well, I'd better get going, too." Alice pulled a sweater over her white nurse's uniform. "By the way, has Sissy Matthews been over for lessons this week?"

"No." Louise had not told her sisters about the situation with Sissy yet. "She has decided to stop for a while."

"I was hoping . . ." Alice paused for a moment before she asked, "When is the recital at the school?"

"Next week. Sissy dropped out of that, too." Her sister's expression was odd, as if Alice was struggling with something. "Why do you ask?"

"I was hoping . . . to hear her perform." Alice gave her a direct look. "You should talk to Sissy, Louise. Find out why she's given up her lessons and won't perform in the recital."

"I've tried."

"Try again," was all Alice said before she left.

Louise took the remaining brochures back to the reception area and stored them. She felt guilty that she had not done more to help with the project, but the approaching piano recital seemed to hang over her head like a dark, depressing cloud.

She had not been exactly truthful about trying to talk to Sissy. Louise had picked up the phone several times to call Carol Matthews, only to hang it up without dialing the number. She told herself it was to spare Sissy any more discomfort, but in her heart she knew it was also to keep from hearing that she, Louise, was indeed to blame for the child's decision to give up music.

Louise had always attempted to teach her students to the best of her ability, and she had long ago accepted the fact that not every child was suited to learning the piano. She often recommended that parents not force her more reluctant students to continue taking music lessons.

Yet losing a child as talented as Sissy Matthews hurt her on so many levels that she did not know what to think or do. She felt completely responsible for Sissy's loss of confidence, but she couldn't think of what she had done to bring it about.

Louise thought about discussing the problem with Rev. Thompson, but the truth was that the only person who could answer her questions was the one person she was afraid to ask: Sissy herself.

Try again.

Alice's suggestion rang in her ears until at last she decided to call Carol Matthews and ask to see Sissy one more time.

"I am not going to try to pressure her into continuing her lessons," she told the girl's mother. "I would simply like her to tell me why she decided to stop so abruptly."

"I hope you can get her to do that because she flat-out refuses to tell me or Tim." Carol sighed. "I'll bring her over after school, but I'll have to drop her off and come back for her. I have to run some errands in town and Charles has soccer practice."

Louise decided to keep things as informal as possible and to serve some refreshments in the parlor. Just before Sissy was to arrive, she went to the kitchen to prepare a tray. By then, her youngest sister had returned from town. "Jane, do you have some cookies to spare?"

"Of course." Jane brought over her cookie jar and examined the small pitcher and glasses that Louise had prepared. "Macadamia white chocolate chips should go great with that raspberry cooler. Am I invited to share in this snack?"

"Not this time." She arranged the nutty cookies on a plate. "I'm having a private conference with one of my students."

"Then you'll have to sit up and have a midnight feast with me later." Jane studied her face. "You don't look very happy. What kind of conference is this?"

"The kind that you cannot put off." Louise smiled and picked up the tray. "Thanks for the cookies."

"You're welcome. Yell if you need more," Jane called after her.

Louise nudged the parlor door open with her shoulder, but stopped when she heard the sound of a lovely little melody being played. She put on a firm smile and walked in. "Hello, Sissy, I—" she halted when she saw Gwen Murphy sitting in front of the piano. "Oh."

Gwen took her hand away from the keys and gave her a distinctly challenging look. "Aren't guests allowed to touch the piano?"

"Of course they are." She put the tray down on the coffee table. "I just wasn't aware that you played."

"I do, a little." She pulled the piano lid down to cover the keys. "It seemed like a waste to go through all those lessons without learning something."

"We can all learn a great deal from music."

"Yes, I can see where someone like you would believe that." She regarded Louise. "You don't like me very much, do you?"

Louise considered denying it, but since Gwen was being so forthright, she saw no reason why she could not do the same. "No, I can't say that I do."

The other woman smirked. "That's a surprise. I thought for sure you'd say something like 'Heavens no, whatever gave you that idea?'"

I'm just full of surprises. "I am glad to hear that I am not so predictable."

"You are in some ways. Like the way you're always so polite, even to someone you'd love to kick out of your inn." She walked over and helped herself to a cookie. "Do you mind? Jane's goodies are fabulous."

Louise folded her hands. "Please, go right ahead."

"See what I mean? You brought these in for yourself, but

you would never say that to me." She took a bite and wandered back to the window. "I'd rather be honest and disliked for it than hide behind a bunch of phony manners."

Once again Gwen's remarks were provocative. It was as if she was trying to pick a fight with Louise. "I don't think you know me well enough to decide when I'm being genuine, and when I'm not. As for the cookies, I brought them for one of my students, who will be here shortly."

Gwen did not turn around. "So I should get out now?"

Louise silently counted to ten. "It is a private conference, but if you would prefer to use this room I will meet with Sissy somewhere else."

"Sissy. That would be the kid who ran out of here crying the other day." Gwen did not turn around. "What's the matter, Teach, didn't she play well enough to suit your standards?"

"Sissy plays beautifully, and she has exceeded any expectation I might have had." Louise recalled Gwen mentioning her unpleasant experience with her music teacher, and wondered if she was being used as a stand-in to absorb the resentment the artist still felt. "Why are you so eager to judge me, Ms. Murphy?"

"I saw the way you looked at me when you walked in. You don't want me putting my grubby hands on your precious piano."

"My piano is an expensive instrument, so yes, I do care what happens to it. But when I heard you playing, I thought you were Sissy."

"Well, now you won't have to wait any longer. Her mother just dropped her off," Gwen said, staring out the window. "She's walking up to the porch." She took another cookie. "She looks like a nice kid."

"She is," Louise said.

"Then give her a break, why don't you?" With that, Gwen sauntered out.

Chapter 🕯 Seventeen

Louise closed her eyes and thought of one prayer that had always seen her through the worst of times. *God grant me the serenity to accept the things I cannot change; courage to change the things I can; and wisdom to know the difference. Living one day at a time; enjoying one moment at a time; accepting hardships as the pathway to peace; taking, as He did, this sinful world as it is, not as I would have it; trusting that He will make all things right if I surrender to His will; that I may be reasonably happy in this life and supremely happy with Him forever in the next. Amen.*

"Mrs. Smith?"

Louise opened her eyes and smiled at Sissy. "I appreciate your coming, dear. Please, come and sit down. I have some cold drinks and cookies for us."

"I'm really not hungry, thank you, and my mom said she'd be back in a few minutes." Sissy looked everywhere but at Louise. "I can't stay long."

"I understand." Now came the terribly hard part. "I simply wanted to tell you how sorry I am that your lessons with me did not work out. You are a very talented musician, Sissy, and a gift like yours should be nurtured. Whatever I did to upset you, I hope in time you will forgive me for it."

The girl swallowed and stared at her shoes. "It's not your fault, Mrs. Smith," she said, her voice low. "Please don't think that and please don't be mad. It's me. I just can't play."

"I know it feels like that now, but in time you may not feel the same way." Louise wanted to gather the little girl up in her arms, but settled for patting the back of her hand. "If there is any way you could give music another chance, try to take lessons with another teacher, as your mother suggested. That would make me feel much better."

"I loved my lessons with you." Big tears welled up in Sissy's eyes as she lifted her face and met Louise's gaze. "They were wonderful. You're the greatest music teacher in the world, Mrs. Smith."

Louise blinked rapidly a few times to prevent her own tears from spilling over. "If you mean that—really mean that —would you please tell me what is wrong? What happened? Why do you want to stop playing the piano?"

"I do want to play. I miss it so much, and I think about it all the time. Oh . . ." She bit her lip and looked at the window. "I want to have friends, too, but she said I never will if I keep playing."

"Who said that to you?"

"Darla Masur." Suddenly the confession seemed to tumble out of Sissy. "She told everyone at school that only stupid geeks play the piano, and all the girls think she's so cool that they started making fun of me just like she did. Then Charlie and his friends started doing the same thing because they think Darla is cool, too. Now none of my friends will even talk to me."

Louise remembered Darla Masur quite vividly. She had come for music lessons, too, but while she had already learned to read music from her last teacher, the child had been uninterested in practicing her scales. After three unproductive sessions, Louise had suggested to Darla's mother that she wait on music lessons for a few years until Darla was a bit more mature. Unfortunately Mrs. Masur lost her temper with her daughter, who proceeded to put on quite an act.

"Mrs. Smith is a terrible teacher," the girl had claimed. "She makes the lessons too hard and goes through everything too fast. I don't understand anything she tells me."

Luckily Darla's father had also been there, and was evidently very familiar with his daughter's penchant for exaggeration. He had apologized to Louise and made Darla do the same.

"Is this all that Darla has done, Sissy?"

The girl nodded. "I went to talk to my brother about her, and I overheard him talking to his friends. They were planning to hide behind the curtains during the school recital and make rude noises while I play. Just to impress Darla."

Louise felt her own throat hurt as she gathered the sobbing child in her arms. "Oh, Sissy, you should have told me this." Children were often thoughtless and unkind toward each other, but this was far too deliberate. Knowing how Charles and Darla had hurt Sissy's confidence made Louise wish she could demand that their parents ground them until they could make a proper apology. "Have you told your mother or father about this?"

"No. I didn't want to be a tattletale." Sissy's tears slowed, and she accepted Louise's handkerchief for her nose. "Charles looks up to Darla. Plus he hates that I can do things that he can't. Usually I just ignore him, but my music is special. It's really important. But I never thought other kids would make fun of me because of it." Her shoulders hunched. "I thought if I just quit, they'd stop being so mean to me."

"Hi, Sissy." Gwen unexpectedly came in and sat down next to the youngster. "Has quitting made you feel better? Does it make you happy to do what other kids want you to do?"

The woman had obviously been eavesdropping. Louise felt a moment of outrage, but she was able to squelch it. She would deal with Gwen Murphy later.

"No," Sissy admitted. "I've never felt so awful in my life."

Gwen put an arm around the girl's shoulders. "Then you have to stand up to bullies, honey, or you will never be happy. Believe me, I know what I'm talking about." The look she gave Louise was angry and challenging, as if she were daring her to disagree with her.

"Ms. Murphy is right, Sissy." Louise felt an inner tension she had not known she was carrying around slowly ease. *Of course, Gwen was bullied by her music teacher, so she thinks all music teachers are bullies.* It was as if a light clicked on and she was seeing the other woman clearly for the first time. "If you let other people push you around and tell you what to do, then they will never stop doing it."

"Really?" The girl looked from Louise to Gwen.

Gwen gave her a slow, solemn nod. "You have to deal with this, Sissy."

"But how can I? Charles has all his friends on his side, and you know how boys are." She made a face. "All of my friends think Darla is so cool, and they do whatever she tells them to." She rubbed at her eyes. "I don't have anyone on my side."

"You have your mom and dad, and Mrs. Smith and me." The artist smiled. "And to tell you a little secret, that's like having your own personal SWAT team."

"Indeed." Louise's squared her shoulders. "I think we should put our heads together and come up with a plan."

"I already have one," Gwen said. She looked at Sissy. "Charles and Darla are the ones who started this nonsense, and everyone is following along with them—is that right?" Sissy nodded. "Okay, so here's what we need to do."

�❦

"My, you two have been busy," Vera Humbert said when she stopped in at Town Hall one afternoon to give her husband a message.

"I've been trying to convince Fred to give up the hardware

store and come and work with me at the inn." Jane gave him a teasing look. "He says he wouldn't be happy unless he's surrounded by tools and nuts and bolts."

"That I believe," Vera said dryly. She spotted the display of restaurantware June Carter had set up on the dark, bird's-eye maple pie safe donated by the Good Apple Bakery. Pies and cake, made of ceramic clay but modeled to look like real food, were stacked on the shelves, and several faux slices decorated the plates. "How clever."

Jane told her how the Coffee Shop's owner had come up with the idea of combining her display with Clarissa Cottrell's.

"I love this pie safe. Clarissa's parents actually used it to cool the pies they baked for their customers. See these?" Jane pointed to the decorative circular pattern of holes in one of the pie safe's twelve panels. "These serve for ventilation, letting air in while keeping household pets, mice and sticky little fingers out."

"You're making me want to go over to the Holzmanns' shop and spend too much money again." Vera looked over at the large quilt frame her husband was securing to the wall. "Oh, I see you've got the frame ready. My quilters guild was delighted to hear that we could display some of our vintage patchwork quilts. They might tempt some of the locals to try one of the sewing classes we've been holding over at Sylvia's shop."

Jane picked up a large box and opened it. "I'm hoping we can feature a different quilt every other month. Did you see what your friend Germaine sent over?" She took out a soft, old blue quilt with dinner plate-sized circular blocks. "This will be the first one we display."

"A Dresden plate quilt. I think this was made back in the thirties." Vera touched the sunflower-shaped appliqué work. "These candy-colored fabrics were so popular back then."

Jane checked the label on the edge of the quilt. "Dresden Plate, unknown maker, 1932. You're right on the money."

"It's my passion." Vera carefully replaced the quilt. "Have you thought about displaying your family's mourning quilt?"

Jane nodded. "We plan to put it up in May so that it will be displayed during Memorial Day weekend. That seems an appropriate time."

Vera gazed around. "This whole project is starting to look like a window in time, isn't it?"

"It will," Jane said, looking with pride at what they had accomplished, "as soon as I can get the mayor to quit fiddling around with things."

As if on cue, Mayor Tynan came out of his office and greeted Jane and Vera. "I haven't found those records you're looking for, Jane. But the old dockets were left in a bit of a muddle." He frowned at the empty quilt rack that Fred was hanging. "Shouldn't that be a little more to the left?"

"Fred and I measured the wall and marked it to hang in the center." Jane saw Rev. Thompson come in carrying a stack of books. He was accompanied by Florence Simpson, who, it seemed from the sound of her raised voice, was having a small tantrum. "Excuse me for a moment, Vera, Mayor."

Rev. Thompson smiled in Jane's direction before he stopped and turned to Florence. "Mrs. Simpson, you can call the church board meeting and make whatever recommendations you like. But before you do, you should listen to what I have to tell Jane."

"All you have to do is give me those books, and none of this will be necessary," Florence told him.

He looked down at her for a moment, and Jane thought she saw a glint of sympathy in his eyes. "That's not my decision anymore."

Unwilling to let Florence harass the pastor a moment longer, Jane went over to them. "Good afternoon, Pastor, Florence."

"You can't have these books, and he can't give them to you," Florence said angrily. "They are worth ten thousand dollars, and as such they are a church asset. Only the church board can decide what to do with them."

"They don't belong to the church," Rev. Thompson said quietly. "They belonged to Daniel Howard."

Florence made a sputtering sound. "That's absolute poppycock. You found them in the church book closet."

"More recently I also found Pastor Howard's personal library list." He carefully placed the set of books on a table and extracted a folded paper from his jacket pocket. To Jane he said, "Like most ministers, your father often brought his own books to the church for use in meetings like Bible study groups. He would also lend them out to other group leaders for their use. To keep them from getting mixed up with the church's property, he kept track of them with this list." He handed the paper to Jane. "There are about thirty books in the library that belong to you, including these."

Jane studied the list for a moment before she looked up into Florence's astonished face. "I guess that means they're *my* books."

The heavyset woman flushed. "Have Alice bring that document to the next church board meeting, so the board members can decide if it's authentic." Despite the threatening words, her tone was already edging toward defeat. She gave Jane a perfunctory smile. "Until then, I suggest you lock those books in a safe place. You wouldn't want anyone to steal them."

Rev. Thompson stood by Jane's side and watched Florence depart in high dudgeon. "There goes what may be the greatest challenge to my ministry."

"I thought that was me."

He smiled at her. "Not even close, my friend."

Jane decided to secure the books for the time being, and opened the locking display case that Fred had set up against the center of the wall.

"Patsy Ley wrote up some cards with information about the Little Shepherdess series." The pastor removed them from where they were tucked in the front of one book. "She also mentioned that autographed editions are extremely rare, and that there are only a handful of them in existence. You and your sisters really should consider having them insured."

"Basil was telling us that the author never had any book signings." Jane trailed her fingertips over one embossed cover. "If my sisters and I decide to keep the books at home, maybe I'll display the old sketchbook in their place."

"May I see it before you do?" Rev. Thompson asked. "I've heard so much about it."

"Sure." She handed him the sketchbook, then decided to move one of the Shepherdess books to the back of the case. The title caught her eye. "*The Little Shepherdess and the Lost Lamb. Hmm*, that sounds familiar, but I don't remember reading that one."

"Jane." Rev. Thompson, who was skimming through the sketchbook's pages, stopped and turned to her. "Look at this."

The artist had drawn an old scraggly tree atop a hill. At the base of the tree was the curled-up form of a young, sleeping lamb. Beneath the sketch was written "the lost lamb."

"What an odd coincidence." Jane looked at the cover on the book, which showed an illustration very similar to the artist's sketch. She glanced up at Rev. Thompson. "Or is it?"

"I don't believe it is." He flipped to the next page. "What's the title of the next book?"

"*The Little Shepherdess and the Old Red Barn.*"

He turned some pages and stopped. "Here's a sketch of an old barn."

Jane read more of the titles as the pastor looked through the pages. For each title Rev. Thompson was able to find a corresponding sketch.

"*The Lost Lamb, The Crooked Path, The Old Willow Tree, The Stone Well,* even *The Lop-eared Puppy*—they're all here." Jane felt dizzy. "How is it that we ended up with a sketchbook filled with pictures that are the same as titles of famous books?"

"I think this is the evidence your Mr. Kirchwey was looking for," the pastor said. "I can't believe that he didn't make the connection between the sketches and the titles."

"He never really did more than glance at a couple of sketches," Jane explained. "Just think how close he was to this discovery."

"Well, this book could prove that M. E. Roberts actually did visit the area," Rev. Thompson said. "Quite frequently, I imagine, if he named all his books after landmarks and animals he saw here."

"I can't believe it. All of the Little Shepherdess books were named after things right here in Acorn Hill?"

"It would seem so. And that's not all, Jane." He tapped the cover of the sketchbook. "There is a strong possibility that your mystery artist may have been M. E. Roberts himself."

⚭

At Jane's request, Rev. Thompson agreed to meet with her and her sisters at Grace Chapel Inn that evening to discuss the ownership of the books, their future and the possible connection to Basil Kirchwey's quest for evidence.

Jane was thrilled telling Louise and Alice that the M. E. Roberts books had belonged to their father, and therefore now belonged to them. Before the pastor arrived, she described the scene with Florence Simpson at Town Hall.

"After he showed her that list, you could have heard a pin drop," Jane said. "Of course," she giggled, "I used the time to watch Florence's ego deflate."

"I don't think I've ever touched a book worth almost a thousand dollars." Alice regarded the neat stack in the center of the dining room table dubiously. "I don't know that I want to."

Louise was the practical one. "First, we photograph the books and have them added to our home-owner's insurance. Second, we decide on a safe place to keep them. Third, we get the rest of Father's books from the church."

"Good idea," Jane agreed. "That way, we won't have any more wrestling matches over ownership with Florence." She sat back in her chair and studied the books. "I remember reading the same books when I was a kid, but I think Father bought them new for me, didn't he?"

"He got you some for Christmas and some for your birthday one year," Alice recalled. "If you're wondering why he didn't give you these, I think you should remember some of the things you used to do to books when you were a child."

"What are you talking about?" Jane scowled at her. "I read books. Lots of books."

"You *read* books?" Alice made a strangled sound. "Please, child. You wrote in the margins. You drew your own illustrations. You painted and glued new covers on them. You crossed out and rewrote the endings you didn't like. The ones you said were boring books became rafts and pup tents for your dolls."

"Do you remember the time when she glued all the pages of one book together and then tried to cut out the middle so that she could hide trinkets in it?" Louise asked Alice.

"Okay, okay." Jane ducked her head. "So I was a little rough with them."

"A *little*?" Her oldest sister chuckled. "You wreaked havoc on every book you ever received before the age of twelve. We could not let you borrow books from friends or leave you alone in Father's study for a minute. We will not even talk about the ladies at the library. Those poor women had to patrol the children's section every time you visited."

"Do they still have her picture tacked on the wall by the check-out counter?" Alice asked Louise.

"I believe there's a permanent plaque now."

Jane felt relieved when she heard the front door open. "Okay, quit picking on me. The pastor's here now."

Chapter Eighteen

Louise and Jane greeted Rev. Thompson, while Alice went upstairs to ask Basil to join them. Jane took a moment to prepare some refreshments for them as Rev. Thompson showed Daniel's personal book list to her sisters and told Basil about the strange correlations between the sketches in the sisters' sketchbook and the titles of the Little Shepherdess books.

When Jane carried in a tray of hot cider and Scottish shortbread to the dining room, Basil and Rev. Thompson were in deep discussion over the evidence.

"Signed first editions and an unsigned sketchbook don't conclusively prove that Roberts ever visited Acorn Hill," Basil said. "It's possible that whoever made the sketches read the Little Shepherdess books first." He accepted a cup of hot cider from Jane and thanked her before he added, "The best we might be able to do is to match a real landmark here in Acorn Hill with a sketch from the book and a Roberts title. That's going to be difficult, because we still don't know how old the sketchbook is, or if any of the structures in the drawings still exist."

"What about the drawings of the three boys: Killian, August and Manfred?" Alice asked. "How old would you say they were when the artist sketched them?"

"They looked to be fairly young," Rev. Thompson said. "Probably about ten to twelve years old."

"That's what I think, too," Alice said. "According to the birth dates on their headstones, that would mean that the sketches were drawn sometime during the early 1850s."

"More than ten years before the first Little Shepherdess book was published." Basil tugged at his bow tie. "That proves that the artist couldn't have read the books first."

"Do you know where M. E. Roberts was born?" Rev. Thompson asked suddenly.

The other man shook his head. "There are no records of his birth or death. The only reason his publishers knew that he had passed away in 1907 was because his attorney notified them."

Alice took in a quick breath. "My, he really was secretive."

"Is it possible that Roberts could have been born right here in Acorn Hill? Because if he was," the pastor said, "he could be one of the boys that the artist drew. One who wasn't killed during the Battle of Gettysburg, but survived and returned home. You'd simply have to find a man who passed away on the same day in 1907."

Alice nodded. "And if he was wounded during the war— disfigured in some way—that might explain why he never wanted to be seen."

"I don't have the exact date Roberts died, only the year." Basil frowned. "I have to fly back to New York tomorrow. Let me see if I can find out anything from the publisher while I'm in the city."

"I didn't realize you were leaving tomorrow," Alice said. "Has it already been two weeks?"

"I'm afraid so. I had hoped to give my editor something concrete for this article. My deadline is in four weeks." He gave her his crooked smile. "But you know, I think we're on to something big. We might be able to show M. E. Roberts' face to the world."

After Basil excused himself to go up to his room to make some notes, Rev. Thompson discussed the problem of what to do with the precious books themselves.

"I think Louise's suggestions are very practical. Also, selling these books would help boost your finances, and you should consider that as well. May I?" At Louise's nod, Rev. Thompson picked up one of volumes. "These books are valuable in another sense too. Whoever owned them before your mother and father knew M. E. Roberts, and was able to convince him to sign them, which, from what Basil says, was a near-impossible feat. That says something about your past, your roots. Through these books, you're connected to days long ago, and to the people who lived them."

"Like a window in time," Jane said, "or a portrait of the past."

He replaced the book and touched the scrolled signet ring he wore. "I wear my grandfather's ring as a reminder of a man I revered, someone who helped me become the man I am today. The ring is an antique, and the gold is valuable, but the memories are priceless."

∞

The next morning Jane went into town to keep an appointment with Carlene Moss, who wrote, photographed, edited and printed the stories in the *Acorn Nutshell*. Carlene interviewed her about the work that had gone into creating the community Visitors Center and then asked if she could take some photos to go with the story. As the display was in its final stages, Jane felt confident that they would be ready for Carlene that afternoon and invited her to stop by after lunch.

"What about these rumors I've been hearing about you and your sisters coming into some valuable books?" Carlene asked before Jane left the *Nutshell's* offices.

Considering Basil's research was involved, Jane did not want to comment. "What about them?"

The editor gave her a shrewd look. "Someone told me Florence Simpson's nose is so far out of joint over it that she can smell from the back of her head now."

"When have you known Florence's nose not to be in that position?" Jane asked, making Carlene laugh.

She went over to Town Hall to make sure everything was ready for photographing and saw Fred sitting outside, obviously waiting for her. Her heart sank when she saw the look on his face.

"Let me guess," she said. "The mayor wants something else changed."

"I haven't changed anything yet, since I thought you might want to have a word with him." He opened the door for her.

Lloyd was walking around the different displays but stopped as soon as he saw Jane enter. "Jane, I'm glad you're here. I told Fred to move this pie safe a little more to the left. I think you should rearrange those dishes, too. They look a bit jumbled the way they are now."

"Fred and I will take care of everything." She put an arm around his shoulders. "You should go and do mayor stuff."

"I can spare a few minutes to supervise."

Jane took a deep breath and turned so that she was facing him. "Lloyd, you're a wonderful mayor, a terrific man, and one of my dearest friends. And if you spend one more day supervising me, I'm going to go home bald and talking to myself."

"I thought I was helping." Instead of taking it as a joke as he normally would, he backed away and gave her a wounded look. "I guess I'm not needed."

Jane reached out to him. "Lloyd . . . wait, I'm sorry. I didn't mean . . ." Her hand dropped as he turned and walked swiftly back to his office. *Way to go, Jane.*

Chapter Nineteen

At church on Sunday, Alice opened her hymnal and stood to sing "No Tears in Heaven" with the rest of the congregation, when she realized something was wrong. She could not quite put her finger on what it was until she looked to her right and saw Jane sharing her hymnal with Aunt Ethel and mouthing the words.

Jane looked fine. Her dress was the color of fall leaves, and, next to Aunt Ethel's more subdued lavender twin set, seemed bright and exotic. She even acted fine as she lip-synched the song. Then Alice saw that Aunt Ethel's eyes were red-rimmed and slightly puffy. Twice she lifted a lace-edged handkerchief and dabbed at her eyes and nose. Alice couldn't imagine why, until her eyes went back to the hymnal her aunt was sharing with Jane. Aunt Ethel always shared her hymnal with Lloyd Tynan.

Alice leaned forward a little, and saw the empty space beside her aunt. Then she let her gaze drift slowly around the church until she saw the mayor sitting with Florence and Ronald Simpson on the other side of the church.

What is he doing over there? Lloyd always sat with her aunt. *Could things between them really be this bad?* She had to do something about this before the rift between her aunt and the mayor became irreparable.

Louise gave her a discreet nudge. "Alice. *Alice.*"

She soon realized why Louise was nudging her. The hymn was over and almost everyone else in the church was already seated. Quickly Alice sat down and looked back at Lloyd Tynan. From where he was sitting he could turn his head and see them, but he kept his gaze focused on Rev. Thompson.

Alice sighed, and as she turned her head to do the same, she caught someone watching her. Darla Masur, who was sitting with Lisa and her parents two rows ahead of the mayor, was staring at her. As soon as Alice's gaze met hers, the girl frowned and looked away.

Alice instinctively knew the girl had not admitted to her aunt and uncle what she had done . . . just as Alice had said nothing to Louise or the Masurs about Darla's efforts to ostracize Sissy. She was keeping the promise she had made to Lisa, but at what cost? She had told the girl that keeping silent was as great a sin as lying, and here she was doing it herself. There was no more time to wait for Darla to do the right thing, either; the school recital was in two days.

Alice prayed for guidance and for the answers to solve both problems. She felt a little better after services were over, but she still was not sure what to do about either situation.

I only know that I can't carry this burden by myself any longer. As they left church, Alice glanced at her older sister's calm expression. *I have to tell Louise.*

Jane went off to talk to Sylvia Songer and June Carter, so Alice decided to take the opportunity to seek her older sister's counsel. "Would you mind if we take a little walk, Louise? I need to speak with you about something."

"Certainly." Louise followed her to the little path their father had made in the process of walking back and forth between their home and Grace Chapel for so many years.

As they walked together, Alice tried to think of how to tell her sister about Darla and Sissy. She was not even sure

anymore if her original decision to encourage Darla to confess to, and repent for, what she had done to Sissy had been
the right one. She should have confided in Louise. She
should have confided in *someone*.

"Alice." Her older sister stopped and rested one hand on
her shoulder. "Whatever you have to tell me can't be that bad."

"You have no idea." She flinched as a yellow-brown leaf
floated down from a nearby tree, and then she caught it in
her hand. "Louise, I made a promise that in good conscience
I don't think I can keep any longer."

"I think I might already know what it is." Louise glanced
back to make sure they were out of earshot of the others leaving the church. "Does this promise involve Sissy Matthews
and Darla Masur?"

"Yes." She felt like bursting into tears and suspected that
before their discussion was over, she might. She tried to
concentrate on the leaf instead. "If I tell you what I've been
holding in confidence, I'll be breaking that confidence. I just
don't know what else to do."

"I suspected that you and I had somehow ended up on
opposite sides in this situation with Darla. Unfortunately, I
have made promises that I have to keep too." Louise put an
arm around her. "Pastor Thompson is coming over for
dinner tonight. I can't think of anyone better to confide in,
especially for help with tough, last-minute decisions." She
kissed Alice's cheek. "As for you and me, I think that we
should talk about this after the recital. All right?"

Over dinner that evening, Rev. Thompson and the sisters
discussed the Visitors Center, M. E. Roberts' work and
a number of other interesting topics. Jane's baked lasagna,
the sauce for which had been made from more of her fabulous tomatoes, was delicious. But while the conversation was
lively, Alice could not do justice to it or to her dinner.

Louise volunteered to help Jane with clearing and
kitchen cleanup, which left Alice alone with the pastor.

In some ways Alice dreaded telling Rev. Thompson more

than she had Louise, particularly as she was in a position where she was expected to provide stable spiritual guidance for the children she worked with in her youth ministry. Still, she felt sure that he would not condemn her for her uncertainty. "Pastor, do you have to leave now, or may I discuss something privately with you?"

"I'm certainly not under any deadline." He looked over and saw Gwen Murphy pass by the door. "Why don't we take a walk out in the garden while it's still light?"

The fall weather had abbreviated some of Jane's lush flowerbeds, but some roses were blooming, and the trees seemed to be on fire. *Summer is over,* Alice thought as she felt the coolness of the evening breeze. It was the season of harvests and gatherings now, one of her favorite times of year, and yet she wished she could roll back time so that she could see her aunt and the mayor happy again, and have a second chance to help Darla.

"I thought your Aunt Ethel would be joining us tonight," Rev. Thompson said as he sat with her on the wrought-iron bench under one of the oak trees. "Is she feeling well? She looked a bit under the weather this morning at church."

"She's a little tired, I think." Alice caught a falling leaf just as she had during her talk with Louise. "She's one of the reasons I wanted to talk to you."

Rev. Thompson listened as Alice told him about what had been happening between Ethel and Lloyd, and how powerless she felt watching them splitting apart.

"How long has this been going on?" he asked after she finished.

"For a couple of weeks now." Alice traced a finger over the veins in the leaf. "Pastor, I know they're both adults, and it's none of my business. It's just that they've been so happy together. Then there's my other problem."

She briefly described the situation with Darla Masur, and how she had tried to intervene and provide guidance for her.

"I had hoped that when she saw Lisa admit to what she

had done, it would give Darla the courage to do the same." Alice looked down at her hands. "Yet I'm sure she hasn't. The recital is the day after tomorrow, and I think Sissy is going to play. It could be that Darla and the other children will try to disrupt the recital, so I feel that I can't keep silent about this any longer."

Rev. Thompson caught another leaf and looked at it for a moment. "Alice, what do you think that you personally can do to help in these two situations?"

"I could speak with my aunt and the mayor, somehow convince them to talk to each other. I could tell Louise and Sissy's mother about what Darla has done to ostracize the poor child. People I care about are suffering—I need to *do* something." She hunched her shoulders. "But I also know that I'd be interfering in my aunt's life, and breaking a promise I made in good faith."

"There's nothing wrong with wanting your aunt and Mayor Tynan to find happiness together, or for trying to help Darla find repentance for her sins. But we can't always protect the people we love, or make choices for those who have lost their way." Rev. Thompson showed her the leaf in his hand, which had turned a beautiful palette of red and gold colors. "It's like trying to make this leaf turn green again."

"But God wants us to be happy, and to make others happy."

"He does. Remember that God also knows the nature of His children, and despite our sins and our weaknesses, He wants to have a relationship with us. He wants to bless us and see us well and happy. He sent us His Son to die for our sins, and to bring us into His light." Rev. Thompson met her sad gaze. "He does all this, and yet when His children refuse His grace, He accepts it. He shows unlimited compassion and understanding, no matter what we do. And when we find our way back to the light, He forgives us. Wouldn't it be an amazing world if we could do that for each other?"

"So I should accept the choices people make," she said slowly, "instead of running around trying to 'fix' everything?"

"You can try to help when it's possible. You can offer love and guidance, and share your faith. But you can't fix everything, and you can't live people's lives for them. Often in situations like those you've described, I think you have to turn matters over to God."

Those were the words she had been reaching for, so desperately, since this morning.

"I have the same failing, you know," Pastor Thompson admitted. "I see a problem, and my first inclination is to try to solve it. But sometimes the greatest service we can do for others is to let them know that we care, but that we will also allow them to find their own path."

"I think I can do that," Alice said quietly.

"Instead of trying to solve your aunt's and Darla's problems for them, I would let them know how much you care. Offer to share your strength with them, listen to them, and pray for them." He took her hand in his. "Your love and faith may be what makes all the difference in what they choose to do."

∽

Things were unusually quiet at the inn on Monday. Basil was gone, Lester was spending the day with one of his clients, and Gwen was immersed in her art. Consequently, there was no one to create any work. When the hospital called to see if Alice could come in to work an extra shift on a short-staffed ward, Louise suggested that she go in.

"Jane will be back shortly, and I have everything else under control." She brought out one of the heavy research books that Basil had recommended that they get from the library and let it thump on the desk. "And plenty of light reading to keep me amused."

With things quiet and Alice gone, Louise had time to

make a few calls. She had discussed her plan on how to handle the school recital with Sissy and Gwen, but they all agreed that it would not work if too many people knew about it.

"I am only going to tell your parents and Darla's father," Louise had told Sissy. "The parents especially need to know what we intend to do, in the event they have any objections. I don't think they will, however. You're not the first person Darla has tried to bully."

Sissy had been shocked at that, and dumbfounded when she learned that Louise was another person Darla had tried to bully. Still, she had been very reluctant about her parents' learning of her brother's involvement.

"We try never to tattle on each other. I know some kids do, but . . ." She lifted her shoulders. "Charlie's my brother."

"I admire your loyalty," Louise told her, "but if Charles was bullying someone else, or trying to hurt that person, would you keep quiet about it?"

Sissy shook her head, and then she said, "I know how I can tell my parents without it being tattling."

Later, after Louise had relayed Sissy's idea to Gwen, the artist uttered an appreciative laugh. "Now that's what I call a smart kid, and some real poetic justice."

Louise made her calls to Carol Matthews and Ronald Masur, and then decided to make herself a pot of tea. On her way to the kitchen, she saw Gwen coming downstairs. "Gwen, do you have a moment? I have some updates."

"Sure." The artist followed her into the kitchen. "Did you talk to the parents?"

"Yes, and everyone has agreed to follow our lead. Charles and Darla will not know anything until it happens." She put on the teakettle, and then glanced at the younger woman. "Will you still be able to attend?"

"If Sissy is still willing to go through with it, I'll be there." She leaned against the counter. "How are you feeling about this?"

"Me? Fine." She made a dismissive gesture. "I have the

easy part. All I have to do is talk into the microphone and tap Charles on the shoulder."

"I know." Gwen leveled a shrewd look at her. "I also know how much you care about that little girl. Look at how you're going along with this scheme of mine. Not what I'd call your cup of tea."

"I like all kinds of tea, but we are taking a bit of a risk, and it does worry me." She poured a steaming cup for herself and then offered one to Gwen. "Now I am working on ridding myself of the anger I feel toward these children. They made Sissy suffer for no reason. I would still like to give both of them a piece of my mind."

"But?"

"But you are right," she said simply. "Sissy has to stand up to this girl and to her brother. If she does not, they will make her life miserable." She sat down at the table and added a spoonful of sugar to her cup. "It is not an easy thing to do, though."

"No, it's not."

Louise wondered if it would be wise to ask, and then found herself asking anyway. "Did you ever stand up to your music teacher?"

"Yes, I did." Gwen set down her cup. "One day I made so many mistakes that I thought my music teacher's head would explode. She yelled at me and jabbed me with her pointer so many times it left marks all over the insides of my wrists."

"Horrible woman! Did you tell your parents?"

"I finally shouted for my mother when she jabbed me so hard that I started bleeding. When Mom came in, I showed her my wrists." Her expression turned stony. "My teacher told my mother that I had made the marks myself by deliberately banging my hands on the piano."

Louise had been afraid it had been something like that. "Did your mother believe her?"

"Not when she saw the blood . . . and the expression on my face. The first thing she did was snatch that pointer away from my teacher and break it in half, and then she ordered her out of our house. Mom made sure that other mothers learned about my experience. The music teacher never taught another student in our town and ended up working as a grocery store clerk."

Louise let out a long breath. "Thank heavens."

"Standing up to her changed everything for me. It made me feel strong and safe. I was never afraid like that again." Gwen's grin widened. "For her part, my mother never made me play the piano, or doubted my word, again."

"You fought back fairly and you won." She felt oddly proud of the younger woman. "That is very inspirational."

"Oh, I'm not the only one still fighting the good fight," Gwen told her. "Look at how you went the extra mile for Sissy. I just wish . . ." she gave her a wry look. "I wish I had had you as a music teacher."

Louise felt genuinely touched. "Why, thank you, Gwen. I think I would have enjoyed having you as a student."

"Probably not." The artist grinned. "But you never would have been bored."

⚭

Alice had just finished her shift at the hospital and was walking out to the parking lot when she spotted her aunt sitting in the front lobby by the gift shop. Ethel had a shopping bag beside her, but she didn't look happy. She looked upset.

"Aunt Ethel?" Alice called out and quickened her step. "What are you doing here?"

"Alice, I hope you don't mind. I got a ride here because I have to speak to you right away." She looked around at the curious eyes watching them. "Is there some place we can sit and have a private conversation?"

"Come with me."

Alice led her aunt to an empty staff lounge on the first floor and sat down with her on a sofa. When her aunt set down her bag, it fell over, and a bright swatch of red fabric spilled out. As Ethel bent over to right the bag, Alice asked, "Did you come over to do some clothes shopping?"

"No, this is some material Vera Humbert special ordered, to make a cover for the base of Fred's model." Ethel stuffed the fabric back in the bag. "Alice, I'm so stirred up I could just scream."

"Well, don't do that." She nodded toward the door. "You'll scare the patients in ER, and someone might come running in here with a crash cart." She rested her hand on top of her aunt's. "What's made you angry?"

"Lloyd Tynan." She rose and began pacing back and forth. "Do you know what he did? He went to Potterston today."

"I think he's allowed to do that, Aunt."

"He was checking up on me. I caught a glimpse of him going into one of the junk shops Lester showed me. I went and looked through the window, and saw him talking to the clerk. He didn't browse or buy anything." She threw up her hands. "It's as if he thinks I'm not to be trusted."

"I'm sure that Lloyd trusts you, Aunt." Alice shifted uneasily. "There could be a dozen reasons why he went to that particular shop."

"Is that what you think?" Ethel planted her hands on her hips. "And what would those reasons be?"

She had no idea, of course. Then she remembered Rev. Thompson's advice: *"Sometimes the greatest service we can do for others is to let them know that we care but allow them to find their own path."* "I can't say, Aunt. I am very sorry that you're upset with Lloyd, though."

"I'm well past upset." She lifted her chin. "I don't want to see him anymore."

Alice's heart twisted, and again it was terribly tempting to plead with her aunt to reconsider. "You have to do what you think is best, of course. Just remember that I love you and I'm here for you if you need me."

"Oh, Alice." Suddenly Ethel looked defeated. "I may be an old woman, but I don't think I'm a foolish one. I value my independence. One of the reasons I've gotten along so well with Lloyd is because he respected that. Or I thought he did." She rubbed her brow. "He's been constantly hovering around me for weeks, always wanting to know where I'm going or what I'm doing, as if I'm some doddering old fool who can't be trusted out of his sight."

Alice put an arm around her. "You are not doddering, old or foolish."

"We were so happy together. You know, I couldn't care more for that man unless I married him and moved him into the carriage house." Ethel's expression darkened. "I'm not ready for that, and whatever he thinks, I will not be forced into it or treated like this."

"Are you going to talk to Lloyd?" she could not help asking.

"No." Ethel snatched up her shopping bag. "I don't want anything to do with Lloyd Tynan, and I'm not going to see him ever again."

"She can't break up with Lloyd like this," Louise said after she heard the news from Alice that night. "There's no reason to. It seems like utter nonsense."

"She sounded very serious to me. And hurt," Alice added. She glanced toward the kitchen. "I should tell Jane about this."

"You can talk to Jane later." Louise thought for a moment. "Why on earth would he be checking up on her like that? It makes no sense."

"He has been acting very strange lately." Alice looked up and smiled as Lester Langston came downstairs. "Good evening, Lester."

"I was hoping to catch one of you ladies before I went out," Lester said, and brought a large, rather heavy envelope to the desk. "Would you mind giving this to your aunt for me? She said she'd stop by the inn tonight, but I have to leave now for a business dinner with a client."

"We'd be happy to." Alice placed the envelope on the reception desk. "You might want to take a coat with you, Lester, it's getting a little chilly outside."

"Oh, this is nothing. You know when it's really cold outside? When you see a lawyer with his hands in his *own* pockets." He chuckled as he departed.

"That man knows more lawyer jokes than anyone I've ever met," Alice said.

"An occupational hazard, I would imagine." Louise glanced at the envelope. "What sort of lawyer is Mr. Langston again?"

"He's mentioned overseeing trusts and investments for some of his clients a few times," Alice said, "although he's never been very specific. Why?"

"Mr. Langston is leaving these documents for Aunt Ethel, and you know Uncle Bob left a trust to take care of her living expenses." Louise picked up the envelope and turned it over in her hands. "I wonder if he is giving her some sort of legal advice."

"That would be Aunt Ethel's business, not ours." But Alice looked at the envelope, too.

Before Louise could say anything else, their aunt came through the front door. She was slightly out of breath. "I could not get that man off the phone." She looked around. "Did I miss Lester? I was supposed to meet him here half an hour ago."

"He just left," Louise said. "Who was keeping you on the phone?"

"Lloyd, who else?" Ethel made an exasperated sound. "You'd think a mayor would know a little something about tact, wouldn't you? But not Lloyd. I thought he was calling to apologize, and our conversation was very nice, at first. Then, just as I was getting ready to forgive him for being so nosy and to tell him about the birthday party I'm still going to give him—just out of the goodness of my heart—he starts up with that twenty questions business again."

Alice frowned. "What sort of questions has he been asking that would upset you like this?"

"He wanted to know where I was all day, and where Lester took me in Potterston. Of course, I couldn't tell him that I was out looking for his birthday gift. When I told him I was only shopping, he asked me if I could afford to, and was I being careful about my finances. As if I can't be trusted with my own money."

"Perhaps Lloyd is only concerned about you, Aunt," Louise said. "I wish you wouldn't be so judgmental."

"Judgmental? Me?" Ethel looked indignant. "Louise Howard Smith, it does not take a judge to figure out what that man wants. He thinks I can't make decisions for myself anymore, and he seems to want to make them for me. Next thing you know he'll want to have me declared incompetent and move me into some sort of nursing home."

"That's nonsense," Louise said firmly. "For one thing, we would never allow it."

"I should hope not."

"Aunt Ethel, I'm sure the mayor doesn't think that way," Alice said, then bit her lip as if she had said too much.

Ethel blinked rapidly for a moment. "Well, whatever he's thinking, he's upset me again, and I don't want to talk about it."

"Before I forget, I have something to give you." Louise held out the envelope. "Mr. Langston left this for you."

"Oh, good." Ethel took the envelope and then squinted at Louise. "Why are you looking at me like that?"

Louise gave her an encouraging smile. "Alice and I were just wondering what sort of documents you would need from a lawyer."

"You were, were you?" Ethel's flushed cheeks turned a brighter shade of red. "I suppose Lloyd has said something to you, and now you girls think that I can't handle my affairs, either."

Alice frowned. "Aunt, we haven't spoken to the mayor at all."

"I find that hard to believe, considering that Lloyd was just on the phone asking me the same question." Ethel drew herself up to her full height. "What I talk to Lester about is my business, and I am entitled to some privacy, even from my family."

"Of course you are." Louise looked offended. "We are just concerned, that is all."

"Why? Because you think I'm a silly old woman who can't be trusted to handle her own affairs, too?" Ethel snapped, and before her nieces could reply, she ripped open the envelope. "Here, since you have to know."

Ethel tipped over the envelope and shook out a rectangular length of cardboard with rows of small clear pockets. In each pocket was a colorful political campaign badge from the past.

"Lester knew someone who could mount these, and he kindly offered to pick them up for me," their aunt told them. "It's Lloyd's birthday gift. Are you satisfied now?" Before either of her nieces could reply, she added, "Never mind. I'm going home. Good night."

∞

Alice went to see Darla on the afternoon before the school recital.

"Miss Howard, how kind of you to stop by." Lisa's mother welcomed her in. "Lisa is upstairs in her room." Her expression turned apologetic. "I'm afraid I had to ground her for lying to me about something."

"That's hard for a parent to do, isn't it?" Alice gave her a sympathetic smile.

"Usually it is, but you know something strange? At the time, she seemed almost happy about it. Kids." She chuckled a little. "So what brings you here today? Would you like to visit my little prisoner upstairs?"

"No, actually I was hoping to speak with your niece Darla," Alice said. "It's about a lesson that we've been discussing at the ANGELs meetings. I'd like to see if she has any new ideas."

Lisa's mother called her niece in from the family room. "Miss Howard stopped by specially to talk to you, sweetheart," she said as the child joined them.

Darla nodded. "Hello, Miss Howard." She would not meet Alice's gaze.

"I'm going to be vacuuming in here so it will be a little noisy," Mrs. Masur said. "Why don't you two go out on the deck?"

Darla led Alice out to the deck at the back of the house. As soon as the door closed, she scowled. "I know why you're here. You came here to tell my aunt about Sissy."

"No, I came to see you."

"I know Lisa told you about it." The child evidently did not believe her. "That's why you made her read that dumb Bible verse and made me talk about it. You wanted to make me feel bad. Well, it didn't work." She went over and flopped down on one of the lawn chairs. "So just go and tell her. I haven't done anything wrong."

"Haven't you?" Alice sat in the opposite chair. "Darla, I'm not going to tell your aunt what your cousin told me. I can't, because I promised her that I wouldn't."

"Oh, I get it." The girl made a scoffing sound. "You want me to do it myself, like Lisa. So I can be a good Christian and everything."

"I'd like that very much, but that's your decision, not mine." She leaned forward. "I came to see how you're feeling, and to let you know that I care."

"You care about me and how I feel." Darla snorted. "Yeah, right."

"It may be hard to believe, but I do."

The girl erupted into anger. "My mom sent me here because she doesn't care about me. Neither does my dad. They're too busy with selling the house and getting new jobs. Lisa won't talk to me anymore, and her parents are only nice to me because I made them think I'm all sweetie-sweetie like Lisa. The only friends I have are the girls at school, and that's just because they're afraid of me."

There was so much unhappiness behind the angry words that Alice's heart twisted. *She must feel so lonely and abandoned.* "Is that why you think that no one cares about you?"

"No one does."

"God does." Alice smiled at her. "So do I."

"Whatever!" She glared back at her, as incensed and rebellious as ever. "I'm going to that recital tonight, and if Sissy Matthews gets onstage, she'll be sorry. You can't stop me with your dumb Bible verses."

"No, I can't. You know right from wrong, and it's your choice." She took in a steadying breath. "I will keep you in my prayers. If you need someone to talk to, Lisa has my phone number." She got up from the chair. "Take care, Darla."

The girl blinked. "That's all you're going to do?"

"Is there something else you need me to do?"

"No."

"Then that's it." Alice looked up and saw Lisa looking down at them from her bedroom window. She gave her a little wave. "I guess I'll see you tonight at the recital."

⌒⌒

Louise took the stage and looked out into the audience filling the school auditorium. She could see Darla Masur and her friends sitting just behind their parents in the third row. Judging by the sounds coming from behind the curtain, Charles and his friends had already hidden themselves.

The initial stage of the adults' plan was working perfectly.

"Good evening, ladies and gentlemen, and thank you for coming to our school recital. We have a wonderful evening of music and surprises planned for you."

While everyone applauded, Louise let her smile drift to the third row, where the girls were whispering to each other, and where Darla Masur stared back at her with a challenging smirk.

When the auditorium was quiet again, Louise said, "Before we begin, I would like to invite our special surprise performers to come up to the stage. Is Miss Darla Masur here?"

That was Gwen's cue. She and Pastor Thompson slipped onto the right side of the stage, while Carol and Tim Matthews entered through the left.

"Darla? Are you here?" Louise looked around before letting her gaze fall on the Masur girl, who looked utterly confused. "Oh, there you are. Would you come up to the stage, please?"

The girl stood, then bent over and said something to her parents. Darla's mother looked ready to explode at her. Louise knew that her husband had informed her of Darla's behavior just before the recital, but Mr. Masur put his hand over his wife's and spoke tersely to his daughter. As her friends watched with round eyes, Darla Masur sullenly marched up to the stage.

Now for stage two. "Would you please give our first special performer a round of applause?" Louise asked the audience, who responded appropriately.

Darla glared at Louise and under the sound of clapping hands said, "I don't play the piano, remember?"

"Yes, dear, I know. You are not here to play." She waved toward the bench seat in front of the grand. "Sit down."

The girl's lips tightened before she went and plopped down on the bench seat.

Gwen escorted Charles Matthews out onto stage. As soon as Charles and Darla saw each other, their faces flushed.

"I'm gonna get Sissy for telling," Charles muttered under his breath as he passed the girl and went to the empty chair Louise had set up. He looked bewildered, however, when Gwen placed a steel triangle and beater in his hands.

Louise waited until she saw Gwen and Charles's parents remove the other boys from behind the stage, and then nodded to the auditorium manager. "I believe we are ready to begin."

The auditorium lights dimmed, and a spotlight focused on Darla and the piano.

"As some of you may know," Louise said to the audience, "performing in front of an audience is one of the greatest challenges a musician faces. Especially when it is a first performance. It takes a special courage to share one's gift with others." She noticed that Darla kept her head down and squirmed a little. "Tonight our first performer will be giving her debut public performance, but she will not have to do so alone. Her brother Charles will be providing accompaniment, and her good friend Darla Masur will assist her with the sheet music. Ladies and gentlemen, please welcome Miss Cecilia Matthews."

The curtains drew back, and Sissy walked out and performed a flawless curtsey before sitting beside Darla on the piano bench.

As the applause died, Louise felt the overpowering urge to stand beside Sissy and make sure Darla did nothing to ruin her performance. But if she did, the plan would never work. Yesterday, she had given Sissy a verse from Proverbs 3:5–6 (NIV): "Trust in the Lord with all your heart and lean not on your own understanding; in all your ways acknowledge him, and he will make your paths straight." Now she had to let Sissy do this, and she had to let God watch over her.

Louise heard Sissy say to Darla, softly but firmly, "Please turn the page when I reach the second-to-last line."

"I don't have to," Darla whispered back, but she did not sound quite so brave now. She looked at the audience before she added, "What are you going to do if I don't?"

Sissy gave her a long, unsmiling look. "I'll stop playing and make everyone wait until you do."

Louise went to stand behind Charles, and bent over to say in an equally low voice, "When I tap your shoulder with my finger, I want you to strike the triangle once."

"Why?" Charles whispered back.

"Because you are playing accompaniment." As a second spotlight focused on Charles, she patted his shoulder. "Also, your father has authorized me to inform you that if you do not, you will be grounded until New Year's Day instead of Thanksgiving."

Charles turned his head to see his father watching him from the wings, and then swallowed hard.

Over at the piano, Sissy took in a deep breath before she placed her hands on the keyboard and began to play.

Louise smiled as she heard the opening notes of an adaptation she herself had written for Mozart's *Concerto in A Major*. She had left the final choice of what to play up to Sissy, but she had hoped she would select this piece for her debut performance. The original was one of Mozart's most beguilingly lyrical compositions, which Louise had adapted for her more advanced students. It was perfectly suited to Sissy's light touch.

As the music rippled through the air, Louise tapped Charles's shoulder at the appropriate moments, and the *ting* of the triangle blended exquisitely with the rhythm of the piece.

She kept an eye on Darla, too. She had expected the girl to show off a little for her friends, or perhaps encourage them to make catcalls, but being in the spotlight seemed to have the opposite effect. The girl seemed completely intimidated.

Good, Louise thought. *Then you know how you have made Sissy feel.*

As Sissy neared the end of her first sheet of music, Darla lifted her hand, hesitated, and then finally turned the page.

Between glances at Darla and heavy sighs, Charles struck the triangle dutifully. Yet as his sister's music cascaded from the piano, he gradually turned his attention to Sissy and the movements of her hands. He had never stayed after his lessons to hear his sister play, and consequently had little idea of how much Sissy loved music.

Please, Lord, do not let this drive a bigger wedge between them, Louise prayed. *Let the boy see the beauty and promise in her talent, instead of becoming more jealous of it.*

Sissy's long hours of practice and nimble-fingered dexterity allowed her to play her way expertly through the first movement. She made two small mistakes, which she ignored, and continued playing.

Louise nodded with approval both times. Eliot had always said that was the mark of a true musician—not freezing up or throwing a tantrum over an error, but forging on until the piece was finished.

Of all the adagios Mozart had written for the piano, Louise had always thought the *Concerto in A Major* was one of the most magical. A small shiver ran down her spine as she imagined Sissy as an adult, playing the original score with full orchestral accompaniment.

That might be possible now, she thought, *because she didn't give up on music, and I didn't give up on her.*

Sissy played to a dazzling finish, then rested her hands in her lap and looked out at the audience, who were sitting in silence. Louise had a terrible moment when she thought that one of Charles's or Darla's friends might boo, but a heartbeat later the entire audience—including all the children present—were on their feet and applauding noisily.

Sissy leaned over to murmur something to Darla, who gave her a stunned look, then rose from the bench and walked to the center of the stage. Darla followed and stood beside her.

Louise took the triangle and beater from Charles. "Go up there with your sister."

"What for?"

Stage three. "You'll see."

Charles reluctantly went to stand beside Sissy, who smiled at him before she took his hand and Darla's in hers. She said something to them, and then the three children bowed together, which drew even louder applause from the audience.

Even better, not a single boo or catcall was uttered.

Gwen came over to stand beside Louise. "I'd say that was a complete and resounding success, wouldn't you?"

"I believe it was," Louise agreed. She turned and took the artist's hands in hers. "Thank you, Gwen."

As the front curtain closed, Sissy left Charles and Darla to come to Louise. "I made two mistakes in the second movement," she said, her cheeks flushed and her eyes bright, "but I think that's all."

"My dear, you played like the angels dance." She leaned over to press a kiss against her brow. "I have never been prouder of any student than I am of you tonight."

"Thanks, Mrs. Smith." Her smile dimmed a little as she glanced back at Charles and Darla. "Are they going to get into an awful lot of trouble? I mean, they didn't do anything."

"They were wrong to treat you as they did, Sissy. They will have to face the consequences for the choices that they made, but that is really up to their parents to decide." She looked up as the other two children approached them. "At least now I think they know how they made you feel."

"Yeah, I think they do." Sissy went over to Darla and Louise heard her say, "Thanks for turning the pages for me."

Darla glared at her. "I didn't turn that first one when I was supposed to." She pressed her hands against her hips. "Why didn't you stop playing like you said you would?"

"I didn't want to embarrass you." Sissy shrugged. "Plus I already knew the music by heart."

"Huh?" The side of Darla's mouth formed a reluctant curl. "Pretty good trick."

After the recital, Pastor Thompson came onstage to shake Louise's hand. "That was exceptionally brilliant, Mrs. Smith."

"I have to agree, Pastor." They looked over at Sissy, Darla and Charles.

"So how long did it take you to learn all that stuff?" Darla asked.

"Like a whole year." Sissy rolled her eyes. "But it's not so hard if you practice every day."

Mr. and Mrs. Masur appeared and congratulated Louise and her student before escorting Darla offstage. Out of the corner of her eye, she saw Alice walk up to the Masurs and introduce herself.

My dear sweet sister, who always tries to see the good in people. Do not give up on Darla, for if anyone can reach her, you can.

Sissy watched them go before she glanced at her brother. "Still think I'm stupid?"

"No." He thrust his hands into his trouser pockets and shuffled his feet. "But it's not fair. You play the piano like that, and you get straight *A*'s, and every team you're on in sports wins." He scowled. "I can't beat you at anything."

"That's not true," Sissy told her brother. "You can skateboard and I can't. You always catch bigger fish and more fireflies than me. I've never beat you at Monopoly, not even once." She thought hard. "Oh, and you can spit cherry pits and grape seeds like twenty times farther than I can."

"Yeah, I guess so." His dark expression cleared for a moment, until he saw their parents climb up on stage. "But did you have to *tell?*"

"Charlie, I just told Mom and Dad that I thought you might try to make me mess up tonight. That's all. If you hadn't done anything, you wouldn't be in trouble now." She lowered her voice and poked her finger into his chest. "But if you *ever* try to do something like that to me again, I will tell on you for the *rest* of your *life*."

"Yikes, okay!"

Carol Matthews came over and gave Louise a grateful hug. "What can I say? You're amazing."

She smiled at Sissy. "Your daughter is a good influence on me."

Chapter Twenty

"W hy are you two so glum?" Jane asked as they were tidying up the dining room after breakfast. "The Visitors Center has been going well, and after Sissy's stellar performance last night, Louise, you should be floating around on a cloud of happiness."

"I am quite pleased about her debut." Louise placed a bowl in the dishwasher.

"Well, something must be wrong. You two look like you just lost your best friend . . . but I'm still here." Jane finished spreading out a clean tablecloth over the top of the big table. "Look, I know it wasn't my quiche. Even my ex-husband loved my quiche."

Alice went to look outside the dining room door, and then closed it. "It's Aunt Ethel."

"Did she complain about my quiche?" Jane stopped smiling when she saw Alice's brown eyes fill with anxiety. "Hey, I'm sorry, I'll stop joking. What's wrong with our auntie?"

"She is not speaking to Mayor Tynan," Louise said.

"I noticed they weren't at the recital last night." Jane looked from Louise to Alice. "Uh-oh. This is not a temporary not-speaking, I take it."

Alice shook her head. "She told us that she's *never* going to speak to or see Lloyd Tynan again."

"Huh?" Jane gawked at Alice. "That's crazy. Why on earth is she splitting up with Lloyd?"

"Evidently he has been asking her a lot of questions about things she considers very private matters. She, in turn, resents the fact that he does not trust her and feels that he is threatening her independence."

Louise sighed. "I understand how she feels. I certainly would not like someone I care for questioning my decisions. But she is overreacting. I know because I do it occasionally myself."

"She's not the only one. I promised Lloyd I wouldn't say anything about this to Aunt Ethel, but I didn't promise to keep it from you two." Jane told them what Lloyd had said to her about Lester Langston. "He's worried to death about her. I tried to reassure him, but he's convinced Lester Langston is going to take advantage of her in some way."

"We think that Lester might be giving Ethel some kind of financial advice," Louise said. "He is an estate lawyer, and they have been spending a lot of time together."

"Lloyd must believe that Lester is going to swindle Aunt Ethel," Alice added. "That is why he has been asking so many questions about her and following her around. Ethel only sees him spying on her and decides he does not trust her."

Louise nodded. "That makes sense."

"Neither of them will talk to the other." Alice sighed. "We'll have to be really supportive of her as she goes through this."

"No, Alice. We have to *do* something to stop it and do it now," Jane snapped. "We have to find a way to keep them from doing this. They've been so happy together. If only they'd listen to their instincts and trust one another."

"C. S. Lewis wrote, 'Telling us to obey instinct is like telling us to obey people. People say different things: so do instincts,'" Louise said.

Jane's long ponytail swung as she shook her head. "But if

they knew each other's reasons for being upset, I'm sure that they'd forgive each other."

Alice felt the same way. When she and her sisters had become angry with one another, Daniel Howard would always remind them not to speak unkindly to each other when they were upset. Thinking of her father's advice, Alice quoted aloud from Ephesians 4:29 (NIV): "Do not let any unwholesome talk come out of your mouths, but only what is helpful for building others up according to their needs, that it may benefit those who listen."

"It may benefit those who listen," Louise repeated thoughtfully; then she hesitated. "Wait! Jane, Lloyd has an intercom on his phone, doesn't he? He uses it to speak with his secretary."

"Yes. He was just saying the other day how much his secretary loves it. It keeps her from having to make twenty trips a day to his office." Understanding dawned on Jane's face. "I think I see where you're going with this, Louise. It just might work. We could call Ethel and ask her to help with the display at Town Hall."

"After last night, she is probably not going to want to talk to me," Louise said. "It would be better if you called her."

"Lloyd's secretary goes to lunch at noon," Jane said.

Louise nodded. "Then that is when you will ask Aunt Ethel to meet you at Town Hall. Alice, would you mind staying here to keep an eye on things?"

"Not at all, I'd be happy to."

Once her sisters had gone off to put their plan into action, Alice turned her thoughts to Darla, who like Lisa had been grounded, but for a much longer period. *She could probably use a phone call from a friend right now*, Alice thought. She went into the reception area and dialed the Masurs' number, crossing her fingers.

Lisa's aunt was surprised to hear from her but had no objections to letting her speak with Darla. "She's been a bit down in the dumps since her parents left this morning," she told Alice. "Hold on just one sec."

The next voice she heard was Darla's. "Hello, Miss Howard."

"Hi, Darla. How are you feeling?"

"Okay I guess." She sighed. "My mom and dad had to leave."

"Will they be back soon?"

"They think they found a new house for us in this place where we're moving. Somewhere in Kentucky." She sniffed. "Why are you calling?"

"I thought you might need someone to talk to."

"That's all I can do. That and read books. I'm grounded like until Christmas," she said, her old sulky tone returning for a moment. Then, more tentatively, she added, "My mom said Sissy Matthews told Mrs. Smith about me. That's why they did everything at the recital." There was a long moment of silence, then she asked, "Why didn't you tell anybody?"

"I had faith in you, Darla. I prayed you would do the right thing." As she would from now on.

The girl took in a quick breath. "But I didn't do the right thing. Aren't you mad? Don't you want to yell at me?"

"No. I'm sorry you were grounded, but I hope you'll make a better choice next time. And I still have faith in you." Alice smiled as she imagined the expression on Darla's face. "So, do you think you'd like to read some books about Kentucky?"

∞

At first her aunt refused to go to Town Hall, but Jane was able to talk her around to the idea with a bit of cajoling.

"You haven't seen how much we've accomplished," Jane said over the phone. "Besides, we can have lunch together over at the Coffee Shop. I bet June has all the latest gossip."

"I haven't been to town in a few days," Ethel admitted,

her dull tone acquiring a spark of interest. "I suppose it would do me good to get out of the house."

"Plus you get a free lunch," Jane reminded her.

"Oh, very well. It's not as if I have done anything to be ashamed of, right?"

"Of course not. I'll meet you at noon, then." Jane hung up the phone and looked at her sisters. "Louise, you will have to get there before us and keep Lloyd in his office."

"I will take care of Lloyd," Louise said. "I need to talk to him about these justice of the peace records anyway."

Gwen Murphy came downstairs to check out, and caught Louise on her way out. "All good vacations must come to an end." She held out her hand to Louise. "I'm very glad to have met you, Mrs. Smith. You've changed my mind about a lot of things."

"I only wish I knew how to thank you for what you did for Sissy." Forgoing the handshake, Louise caught the younger woman in a gentle hug, and whispered, "Keep fighting the good fight, my dear."

The artist gave her a wide smile. "I will, Louise. I will."

A short time later, Louise arrived at Town Hall, just as the mayor's secretary was preparing to go to lunch. "Hello, Mrs. Smith. May I help you?"

"Yes, would you let Mayor Tynan know I'm here? I need to speak with him about some archived information." She watched as the young woman used the intercom to do so.

Lloyd came out of his office, and Louise was shocked to see how drawn and tired he looked. "Did you need something, Louise?"

"Yes, I wanted to speak to you about those justice of the peace records that we are trying to find."

He frowned. "I haven't had time to find them, I . . . I've been a little busy."

"I have some new names that we would also like to check. I am afraid that I did not write them down," she looked around as if searching for a pen and paper.

He waved toward his door. "Come back to my office and have a seat. I'll make a list."

As Louise gave him the names of three soldiers killed in battle at the same time that Robert Charters had been, she noticed that the mayor's normally tidy desk was quite cluttered. "You do appear to be swamped with work today."

"I always have time for you, Louise." He took the list and rose. "Let me go and check the files. I'll be right back."

When the mayor had left, Louise checked her watch. Jane and Ethel would be arriving in five minutes, so she would have to work fast. She went around the desk and pressed the intercom button on his phone. *Now, to get him to talk to me about Ethel without his noticing that the intercom is on,* she thought as she quickly returned to her chair.

Lloyd returned with a pair of files. "I think the death certificates will be in here."

"Let me look through one while you sort through the other." Louise took one of the files and began examining the contents. When her watch read a few minutes after noon, she said, "We missed you and Ethel at the recital last night."

"I intended to be there, but things, well . . ." he sighed. "Things just didn't work out."

"Lester Langston has been seeing a great deal of my aunt in the last couple of weeks," she continued, keeping her tone casual. "I was wondering if that had something to do with it."

"Lester Langston is only interested in your aunt for her trust money," Lloyd snapped. "That's why he's been cozying up to her. You should throw that scheming con artist out into the street."

"He will be checking out tomorrow," she informed him, "so I doubt that will be necessary."

Lloyd gave her a fearful look. "Ethel isn't going to keep on seeing him, is she? I've been trying to find out if she's planning to, but I've had no luck."

Louise was confused. "Why would you wonder about that?"

"Because she's fallen for that smooth-talking devil, and now he's trying to take her away from me." The sound of a feminine shriek came from the lobby, startling them both. Louise pointed to a red light on his intercom, and Lloyd looked at it, appalled. "Good Lord, was that on the entire time we were talking?"

"Yes, it was. I turned it on." Louise turned her head at the sound of rapidly approaching footsteps and took a deep breath. "This would be Jane and Aunt Ethel, I think."

"Ethel's here?"

She gave him a weak smile. "Aunt Ethel is the reason I turned on the intercom."

Her aunt was the first one through the door. "Lloyd Tynan, did I hear you correctly? You think I've been dating another man behind your back?"

"Well, haven't you?" Lloyd threw open his hands. "You've been going off with him in the morning and not coming home until late at night for weeks now. Every time I see him around you, he's telling you how good you look and smiling at you. I suppose his fancy suits and those silly jokes have turned your head, but don't do this, Ethel. You're too good for him, and he'll just end up breaking your heart."

Ethel's mouth opened and closed a few times, but no sound came out. Louise knew exactly how she felt.

"Okay, time out." Jane came in behind Ethel and gently guided her aunt to a chair. "Everyone sit, take a deep breath, and calm down."

"I'm calm," Lloyd said, sitting down and looking righteous. "All I want is the best for her, and he's not it."

"No, he is not," Louise said. "Seeing as Mr. Langston is already married to another woman."

Lloyd's jaw dropped. "He's married?"

She nodded. "Very happily married, from what I understand. He and his wife have five grown children and many more grandchildren. His wife usually travels with him, but she could not accompany him on this trip because she is helping one of their daughters move into a new home."

"I see." The mayor looked ashamed. "I didn't know that."

Ethel finally found her voice. "This is why you've been pestering me with questions and acting so suspicious? Because you were jealous of Lester˙ Langston and you thought I was smitten with him?"

"I did it because I care about you." He tried to smile. "I can't help wanting to look out for my girl."

Her eyes brimmed, and she reached across the desk to take his hand with hers. "Oh, Lloyd."

Jane silently gestured to her sister, and the two of them slipped out of the mayor's office. Louise gently closed the door behind her.

For a moment they stood out in the hall and stared at each other.

"That was . . . an unexpected twist." Jane grimaced.

"Lloyd and Aunt Ethel were not the only ones jumping to conclusions," Louise said ruefully. She glanced at the door. "Do you think they will work things out now?"

"I hope so. I don't think we can use the intercom trick again." Jane walked with her to the lobby, then heard laughter and saw Lloyd's secretary staring at her phone with a puzzled look.

"Hello, Ms. Howard, Mrs. Smith," the young woman greeted them, and then frowned as more laughter came over her intercom. "Do you know if the mayor, um, needs anything?"

"Not right now. He is in a private meeting." Louise reached over and turned off the intercom. "I would hold his calls for a bit, too, if you could."

"Sure." Still looking confused, the secretary went back to her typing.

As they walked out of Town Hall, Louise released a sigh. "I feel so much better, now that this is over. So must Aunt Ethel."

"Let's see, how would I feel in Aunt Ethel's place?" Jane pretended to think. "Well, for one thing, that man wouldn't have to cook for himself for a solid month. Maybe two."

Louise laughed and linked her arm with her sister's. "I think you and I have at least earned lunch."

∽

Alice was relieved when her sisters returned with the good news about the mayor and their aunt. "To think we suspected he was looking out for her financial future, and the whole time he was just worried sick about losing her to another man."

"I am glad that this is out in the open." Louise ran a hand over her short silver hair. "Keeping things from each other never helps a relationship. Although perhaps next time we should try something other than the intercom method of mediation."

"Oh, I don't know. We could use an intercom here at the inn." Jane had a gleam in her eye. "Think of how much more efficient we'd be."

Louise's lips twitched. "And how many conversations you could listen in on."

Alice went behind the desk to file an invoice, and then frowned at the odd way the blotter looked, as if something was stuck underneath it. She lifted one edge and found an unmarked envelope. "Did either of you leave this here?"

"Not me," Jane said. "I stay away from paperwork."

"While I file mine right away." Louise took the envelope and examined it. "There is no address and it has not been sealed."

"That, I believe, is the universal sign for 'open me,'" Jane said.

Louise opened the flap and took out three neatly typed pages and a handwritten note, which she read aloud. "'Dear Alice, Jane, and Louise, I hope when you read the enclosed that you will be pleased and not too angry with me. This was a terrific working vacation for me. Thanks for a wonderful stay, and don't change a thing. Warm regards, Gwen. PS—If I was especially hard on you, *Teach*, it was only because I felt that you were up to the challenge.'" She looked at the top of the first typed page and uttered a startled laugh. "Oh no."

"Oh no, what?" Jane looked over her shoulder. "'There's No Place Like Home? Think Again. A Review of Grace Chapel Inn by the Innside Reporter.'"

"Gwen Murphy was the Innside Reporter?" Alice clapped one hand over her mouth. "I can't believe it! She was sizing us up all this time, and we never knew."

Jane shook her head. "Oh, this is too good. We thought Basil was . . . and it was really Gwen." She burst out laughing.

Louise read the review Gwen had written, which was glowing and filled with praise. "'The staff is more like family . . . wonderful food, the finest I've ever had, hands-down . . . honest and caring . . . the heart of Acorn Hill . . .'" Slowly she put down the article. "I don't believe it."

"What is it?" Alice asked.

"She calls Grace Chapel Inn the finest inn at which she has ever stayed. And after I told her that I . . . Oh, Lord, I think I need to sit down."

"So do I." Alice had a strange look on her face. "Do you know that she nearly caught me looking through Basil's notebook that day?"

"While I came really close to scolding her for being so mean to you, Louise." Jane held her side. "Could we have made a worse impression if we'd tried?"

"She had us totally fooled." Louise closed her eyes briefly before laughter bubbled up from inside her. "I should have known."

A thumping sound from outside on the porch made Jane turn around. "If that's Gwen, may I yell at her?"

"No, you may not." Louise gave her a stern look. "Not until after I do, anyway."

Alice went to open the door and nearly collided with Basil Kirchwey, who was coming in.

"Alice!" He put down his suitcase and seized one of her hands in his. At the same time, the wind came rushing in from behind him, and sent his hat flying. "Blast it!" He grabbed for the bowler.

Alice reached up and caught it neatly. "This hat seems determined to get away from you, Basil. Maybe you should invest in a nice, friendly fedora."

"It was my father's," he said with a grin. "He was an editor for the *Baltimore Sun* and wore it to work every day. But he had a much bigger head, I think."

That explained his affection for the hat. Like Rev. Thompson's ring, it connected him to a man he had obviously respected and loved.

"Come inside." She closed the door and escorted him over to the desk. "How was your trip?"

"The flight was delayed and terribly crowded, my editor was in a bad mood, and there was some sort of salespeople's convention at my hotel, so I hardly got any sleep." He set down his case. "But it was worth it for what I found out about M. E. Roberts from his publisher."

"And what was that?" Louise asked.

"They still have copies of his manuscripts as they were originally submitted," Basil said. "They allowed me to examine them and make photocopies of the actual pages." He looked around. "Is your sketchbook here?"

"No, we have it at Town Hall in our historic display," Jane said. "Why?"

"Roberts wrote his manuscripts in longhand," he told her. "I'll need to compare the pages to the sketchbook to be sure, but I think I've seen that handwriting before. I believe it is the same handwriting that's in the sketchbook."

Everyone stayed up talking about M. E. Roberts and the discovery Basil had made in New York, and did not get to bed until quite late. Jane could hardly wait until the next day, when they could go and look for the records that Basil now felt sure existed.

"Whoever Roberts was, he died on January 27, 1907," he had told them. "If we check the records of those who passed away on that date, we might find a match."

The next morning after breakfast, they all decided to ride together into town.

"I called ahead to Town Hall, and Aunt Ethel and Mayor Tynan are going to wait for us," Jane said as she came out to the car. "I'm so excited."

"We should not be counting our chickens just yet," Louise advised her. "The note you found is wonderful, but we still do not know who M. E. Roberts was, and he may not have been a resident of Acorn Hill when he passed away."

"But, Louise, the sketchbook was in our house. M. E. Roberts had to know someone in our family." Jane put on her seat belt. "He could have slept at our house. You know, like a president. We could use that on our Web site and in our marketing material."

Her oldest sister gave her a direct look. "We are not renaming any of the guest rooms."

"Spoilsport."

"If the handwriting does match," Basil told Alice as they drove to town, "then the sketchbook is a find of immense historical importance. Several universities teach courses about Roberts' work, but no one has ever had enough material to write his biography."

"You could write one," she said, surprising him. "You have so much knowledge about that time period, and Louise said you're very well-known in literary circles."

"I'm known for writing articles that challenge the status quo. But a book-length biography about Roberts. . ." He moved his shoulders uneasily. "He had such a tremendous influence on me when I was a boy."

"You read the Little Shepherdess books?"

He nodded. "Growing up and being unable to see colors the way everyone else does, I always had a little trouble imagining things. But from the first time I read one of M. E. Roberts' books, I could see the world the way everyone else does. Green was how cool grass felt on your face. The blue of the sky was what you felt when you dipped your foot in a little stream. He gave me the chance to see all the colors of the rainbow, Alice, in every book he wrote."

"Wouldn't writing a biography be a little like writing a bunch of articles about his life, except in a certain order and all tied together?" Alice suggested.

He smiled at her. "I guess it would be."

As promised, Lloyd and Ethel were waiting for them at Town Hall. They both looked much more relaxed and happier than the sisters had seen them in weeks.

"See?" Jane murmured to Louise. "I told you if we stuck them in a room together they'd make up. We should incarcerate people more often. It works great."

Louise eyed her. "You will not be happy until you are listed on the FBI's Ten Most Wanted list, will you?"

Jane winked. "They'll never catch me."

Alice took Basil to retrieve the sketchbook from where it was displayed, and Jane and Louise went to the filing room with the mayor to see the documents that he had unearthed.

"I found the Charters boy's death certificate, but no marriage license. There was one for an Emily Charters who was married in 1859 to Benjamin Berry, the only child of Ethan Berry." He handed Louise both documents.

"Maybe Benjamin was M. E. Roberts," Jane said. "That would explain why the sketchbook was in our attic."

"His handwriting does not match." Louise showed her the marriage license, signed by Benjamin Berry, whose slanted writing looked nothing like the writing in the sketchbook. "But this is proof that Emily was our mother's great-grandmother."

"I'm sorry I couldn't be of more help," the mayor said.

Louise smiled at him. "You have added another branch to the Berry family, Lloyd. I would call that fairly remarkable."

The two sisters went out to where Alice and Basil were excitedly comparing his copied manuscript pages to the sketchbook.

"It's a match. These sketches were drawn by M. E. Roberts himself." As he turned to show them, his elbow jogged Louise's hand and the documents they both held went flying. "Sorry."

After nearly bumping heads with him, Louise bent and picked up the papers. That was when she saw that the signature on Robert Charters' death certificate was identical to the handwriting on the manuscript pages.

Slowly she straightened, placed both documents side-by-side on her mother's desk and had another long look.

"What is it, Louise?" Alice asked.

She blinked once, then rubbed her eyes and checked a third time. "I know who M. E. Roberts was."

"You do?" Basil gawked at her.

"The person who signed this death certificate as next of kin to the deceased has the same handwriting that is in the sketchbook and on your manuscript." She moved to one side, and looked at her sisters. "M. E. Roberts was Emily Berry."

"A woman?" Basil looked stunned, and then shook his head. "No, there has to be a mistake. M. E. Roberts was a man."

"How can you be sure of that?" Jane said at once. "You said there were no photographs of him, no one ever met or spoke to him, and his attorney handled all the details with his publisher."

"It just seems so outrageous," Alice said. "A woman didn't go around pretending to be a man in those days."

"But don't you see? She didn't pretend to be a man," Jane insisted. "She lived here in Acorn Hill as Emily Berry. She just *wrote* under a man's name. The sketch in the book was a self-portrait."

"But why would she do such a thing?"

"Actually there were a number of women authors in the nineteenth century who regularly wrote under male pseudonyms," Basil said. "The Brontë sisters published an anthology under the names Acton, Ellis and Currer Bell, and Mary Ann Evans wrote under the name George Eliot. But the practice was more prevalent among Victorian women writers in England than here in America."

"She must have had her reasons," Louise said. "Perhaps she used a pen name so that she would not embarrass her husband or her family. Ordinarily, women in those days were not the household wage earners."

"We may never know why she concealed her identity, but I think I know why she chose the particular name," Alice said. "Roberts, for her brother Robert of course, but M. E. because of his pet name for her. Remember? He called her that in his letter. Dear *Emmie*."

"That's the final link in the chain of evidence," Basil said. "Robert's letter to her. If you ladies will allow me to photocopy it, along with the death certificate she signed, I can prove Emily Berry was the author of the Little Shepherdess books."

"You will write another of your articles, I suppose." For a moment Louise looked mildly upset.

"No, this time I think I'm writing a book," he said, smiling at Alice. "I'd like to write Emily Berry's biography."

"While we get to add a whole new chapter to our family history," Alice said.

"You know what this means," Lloyd said. "Once word about this gets out, we'll have more visitors to Acorn Hill than ever."

"That means adjusting our marketing strategy and broadening our communications base," Jane told him. "You know, Mayor, we should do lunch and discuss it sometime."

Ethel rolled her eyes. "Here we go again."

Crepes Benedict
MAKES EIGHT TO TEN CREPES

∞

CREPES

∞

2 eggs
1 cup milk
2 tablespoons melted butter, margarine
   or vegetable oil
1 cup all-purpose flour
Dash of salt
Cooking spray

Whisk together eggs, milk and oil in a small bowl. Gradually whisk in dry ingredients, and transfer batter to small pitcher in order to pour. Spray a small frying pan with a tiny amount of cooking spray (not necessary for nonstick pans), and pour enough batter to cover the bottom of the pan (about a half cup for an eight-inch pan). Cook crepe over medium heat until set, turn or flip over to cook the other side. You can keep crepes warm on a covered, heat-proof plate in a two hundred-degree oven.

FILLING

6 eggs
½ cup diced cooked ham
1 tablespoon chopped chives
Dash of tarragon, rosemary and
    cayenne pepper (optional)

Place all ingredients in a small mixing bowl and whisk together. Pour into a large frying pan and scramble together until eggs are thoroughly cooked. Fill crepes with scrambled egg mixture, and roll.

HOLLANDAISE SAUCE

Prepare package mix of Hollandaise sauce (available at most grocery stores) according to package directions. After filling the crepes, mix up about a cup of sauce and drizzle over the crepes.

# About the Author

Rebecca Kelly wrote her first book at age thirteen and hasn't stopped writing since. When she's not writing or being a mom, Rebecca volunteers weekly at an animal shelter, creates comfort quilts that are distributed to children hospitalized for cancer treatment, and teaches creative writing to local public school students. Rebecca was recently honored by the United States Air Force for her efforts over the last six years in sending books and other reading materials every month to American soldiers serving in Iraq.